Liquor

Liquor

a novel

POPPY Z. BRITE

THREE RIVERS PRESS
NEW YORK

Published by Three Rivers Press, New York, New York.
Member of the Crown Publishing Group,
a division of Random House, Inc.
www.crownpublishing.com

THREE RIVERS PRESS and the Tugboat design are registered
trademarks of Random House, Inc.

Printed in the United States of America

Design by Fearn Cutler de Vicq

Library of Congress Cataloging-in-Publication Data
Brite, Poppy Z.
Liquor : a novel / Poppy Z. Brite.—1st ed.
1. New Orleans (La.)—Fiction. 2. Male friendship—Fiction.
3. Restaurants—Fiction. 4. Unemployed—Fiction. 5. Cookery—
Fiction. 6. Cooks—Fiction. I. Title.

PS3551.R4967 L57 2004
813'.54—dc22
2003017508

ISBN 1-4000-5007-3

10 9 8 7 6 5 4 3 2

First Edition

For John Kennedy Toole,
who got it right the first time

acknowledgments

I'm trying to wean myself off these acknowledgment lists since I invariably omit some vital person who gets his feelings hurt, but in the case of *Liquor,* too many people gave generously of their time, knowledge, stories, support, and food for me not to offer some small thanks. These people include Kirin Anderson, Angel & Candy, St. Paul Bell, Anthony Bourdain, Connie Brite, Cwm Brite, Bob & Anita Brite, Ramsey & Jenny Campbell, Casamento's, Andrei Codrescu, Dennis Cooper, Deep Toque, O'Neil De Noux, Stephen & Casey Ellison, Shayne Fenton, David Ferguson, Neil Gaiman, Laura Guccione, Anne Guérand, Hansen's Sno-Bliz, John Harris, Eman Loubier, David & Sid Luna, Louis Maistros, Gerard Maras, Thom Maras, Ti Martin, Marion Mazauric, Mary Ann Naples, J.K. Potter, Bill Schafer, Cynthia Sciortino, Jamie Shannon, Ira Silverberg, Sidney Snow, Peter Straub, Samuel Tewelde, Carrie Thornton, Kevin Unsell, and Peter & Janis Vazquez. Apologies to the vital person or people I've forgotten—please blame my aging, sievelike brain rather than any lack of gratitude.

An extra portion of thanks to Christopher DeBarr, the master chef without whom none of this would have been possible.

"How you like them ersters, Mr. President?"

—New Orleans Mayor Robert Maestri to Franklin D.
Roosevelt during a meal at Antoine's

Liquor

It was the kind of October day for which residents of New Orleans endure the summers, sparkling blue-gold with just a touch of crispness, and two old friends were sitting on a low branch of an oak tree in Audubon Park drinking liquor. They had started out with tequila shots upon waking up, but harboring a residual grudge against the drink, they soon switched to vodka and orange juice, which they carried to the park in a large thermos.

John Rickey and Gary "G-man" Stubbs had been born and raised in the city's Lower Ninth Ward, but they'd lived Uptown since they were eighteen: "From the 'hood to the ghetto," Rickey had described the move at the time. Their current neighborhood hardly qualified as a ghetto, but the remark revealed a downtown boy's discomfort at living Uptown. In the Ninth Ward, "Uptown" signified rich and snooty.

They were twenty-seven now, but only Rickey had begun to develop the comfortable little paunch common to natives past their midtwenties. The few extra pounds did not diminish his sharp-featured good looks, but he wouldn't have cared much if they had; physical vanity was not among Rickey's numerous sources of anxiety. Six months ago he had bleached his light-brown hair platinum. Now it was half split ends and half dark roots, and though it looked very bad, he hadn't yet gotten around to having the bleachy ends cut off. Since he had neglected to brush it this morning, it formed a two-toned nimbus around his head. Rickey was a young man with a great deal of nervous energy; even when he was half-drunk and trying to relax, he had a hard time sitting still.

G-man had no trouble sitting still. He was a little taller than Rickey, and quite skinny for a New Orleanian. Though he wore his chestnut-colored hair very short, a slight curl still made it unruly most of the time. His mother had been a Bonano, one of the city's vast population of Sicilian-Americans, but this heritage was reflected only in the darkness of his large, myopic eyes. Otherwise he looked like his Irish-blooded father, rangy and fair-skinned, with a long blunt nose and a rather sensitive mouth.

Like many young men in New Orleans, Rickey and G-man made a precarious living in restaurant kitchens. They'd begun in their teens as dishwashers and worked their way up to line cook positions. Now cooking comprised most of their lives; asked to define themselves in a word, they would not have given their family names or (as would many New Orleanians) the name of their high school; they would simply have said, "We're cooks." A few days ago they had been dismissed from their latest kitchen in what they considered a travesty of justice.

Jesse Honeycombe, a country-pop crooner from Florida, had one big radio hit called "Tequilatown" and opened a restaurant on the strength of it. Tequilatown was a French Quarter tourist trap that served indifferently barbecued ribs, elaborate sandwich platters, and margaritas in plastic buckets. Jesse Honeycombe wasn't exactly responsible for the firing, but that didn't matter to Rickey and G-man, who had been cursing Honeycombe's name ever since the incident went down.

Honeycombe had played a show at the Lakefront Arena that night, and fans packed the restaurant afterward in hopes that he would show up. The kitchen was slammed. Rickey was working the hot appetizer station, making loaded nacho platters and spicy chicken quesadillas. G-man, for some reason, was on salads, the most hated position in the kitchen. Everyone from the kitchen runners to the head chef was in the weeds for three solid hours. They fell into a rhythm where they weren't really thinking about the food or how many tickets were lined up; they were just moving their hands and hustling their asses and slamming out orders as fast as they possibly could. When the hellacious rush finally slowed to a trickle, Chef Jerod passed around cold bottles of Abita beer. Drinking on the clock was forbidden at Tequilatown, a restaurant with liquor in its very name, but the crew had rolled so hard tonight that the chef decided to make an exception to the rule. Of course, the manager chose that moment to drop in and see how things were going.

Chef Jerod managed to hang onto his job by the tips of his knife-scarred fingernails, but the manager made him fire almost everyone else, including Rickey and G-man. This would create no crisis; there were half-assed kitchen workers looking for jobs all over town. The hospitality industry provided New Orleans with its major source of revenue, and the city responded by providing an inexhaustible source of fodder for the industry: poor but able-bodied young men who came into the kitchens with very little training and could be easily replaced when they got fired, quit, or died. Most of these young men were black, but there was a sizable minority of white boys. Some, like Rickey and G-man, stayed in the business and became skilled cooks. A place like Tequilatown, though, didn't really need skilled cooks; it made sense to replace them with hapless kids who would work for considerably less money.

Chef Jerod had apologized to everyone as he handed out the severance pay envelopes. Though he was a hardass, he was almost weeping with humiliation. "I swear I'd quit this place myself if they weren't paying me so fucking much," he said. No one really held it against him. They knew that the manager, Brian Danton, was the real asshole. That was almost always how it was, and there was nothing you could do about managers.

So now Rickey and G-man sat in the park passing the thermos, watching the joggers and golfers, occasionally expressing mild amazement at the fact that people would expend that kind of energy when they didn't have to. This was not simple laziness—though they could be lazy with a will—but more a reflection on the sheer physical work of being a halfway-decent cook. Cooks on the line in a busy restaurant spend all their time in motion, preparing the mise-en-place of ingredients they will use throughout their shift, lining up sauté pans on burners and flattops, keeping track of their tickets, burning their hands, reducing their feet to hunks of abused and stinking flesh that feel like nothing more than a couple of raw stumps by the end of a shift. Cooks don't go jogging on their day off.

Rickey and G-man had been friends since their grammar school days. The Lower Ninth Ward was a cross between a country village and a Third World slum, far below the Garden District and the French Quarter and the other parts of the city known to tourists. Most of the houses were old, small, and in disrepair; the streets were prone to sudden flooding; the air smelled of frying sausage and the nearby Industrial Canal. Rickey and G-man had Ninth Ward street smarts and the hoarse, full-throated downtown accent: "Ax ya momma can we have some'a dem cookies she bought?" They had always been vaguely aware of each other, as the few white kids in the public schools were. The first time they really took notice of each other was in fourth grade, during Job Week, when the class was assigned to pair up and put on a skit about one of their parents' occupations. Even at age nine, Rickey and G-man (then still known as Gary) recognized the thoughtless cruelty inherent in this assignment. Many of their classmates had mothers who worked at McDonald's or as hotel maids, and no fathers to speak of. It wasn't that all black people in New Orleans lived this way, but that the black people who could afford it—just like the white people who could afford it—sent their kids to the superior Catholic schools.

Rickey's father was a chiropractor who lived in California, paid minimal child support, and hadn't seen his son in three years. As a result, Rickey had a distorted idea of what chiropractors (and fathers) did. He and Gary stole a box of red hair dye from the K&B drugstore and borrowed a bunch of Play-Doh from one of Gary's young cousins. Two dowels provided the framework for a surprisingly realistic false arm with a plastic bag of dye tucked into the shoulder end. Gary folded his right arm inside his shirt and wore the false arm in a sling.

"A chiropractor is a doctor who performs adjustments on the spine," Rickey told the class before bending Gary backward and "adjusting" him, ripping off the false arm and spraying red hair dye all over the classroom. Gary howled in "pain" and collapsed dramatically on the threadbare school carpet, his legs flailing a bit before hitting the floor with a terrible, final-sounding *thunk*.

That was the first time they were sent to the principal's office together. They had to apologize to their teacher and explain to their classmates that doctor visits were unlikely to result in surprise dismemberments. Gary's mother, who had never known her youngest child to do such a thing before, made him go to confession and tell the priest all about it. (He thought he heard the priest stifle a laugh, but he never told his mother.) Rickey's mother, who had been something of a bon vivant in her youth, found the episode hilarious. She called up the Stubbs family to chide them for overreacting, and the two families ended up friends. To Rickey, an only child, the crowded Stubbs household was pleasantly chaotic; some of Gary's five older sisters and brothers had grown up and moved out by then, but they had kids of their own and there were always children around.

After the false-arm incident, Rickey and Gary got beaten up a lot less, because their classmates now thought they were funny, crazy, or both. More important, they recognized something in each other that had kept them together from then until now, fired and broke, sitting in an oak tree drinking liquor.

Rickey pushed his hair out of his eyes. "It's too damn bright out here," he said. "Can I borrow your extra shades?"

"They're prescription."

G-man had already been wearing glasses in the fourth grade; from his ferocious squint when he removed them, Rickey always figured he'd been one of those little kids who'd needed them since he was three or something. Now he wore dark lenses almost all the time, even in the kitchen when chefs would let him get away with it. "I don't care," said Rickey. "Just give 'em here."

G-man stretched out his long legs, reached into his pants pocket, and pulled out a slightly squashed pair of gold-rimmed, pimp-daddy-style dark glasses. He passed them to Rickey, who put them on, surveyed the park through what appeared to be several inches of murky water, and said, "Goddamn, your eyes are fucked up."

G-man had heard this before and let it pass without comment.

"This orange juice is warm," Rickey complained. "I wish I had a daiquiri."

"You want to walk over to the zoo? I think they got daiquiris in the Beer Garden."

"No, dude, it's like seven dollars to get in the zoo. You know where I wish I was, G? I wish I was in *Tequilatown*."

"Scratchin my balls and watchin the sun go down," G-man sang, riffing on Jesse Honeycombe's big hit.

"Pickin sea salt outta my ass crack . . ."

They went on in this vein for several minutes, an extension of the dialogue they'd been having since the incident. Though they were trying to console themselves, the thing always ended up making them mad all over again. This time, Rickey went off first. "Fuck that place!" An old lady walking a Chihuahua near their tree gave him a sharp look, but he took no notice. "Fuck Jesse Honeycombe, fuck Brian Danton, and fuck Jerod Biggs too. Fuck 'em all."

"Rickey . . ."

"What? We're the victims of injustice. It sucks."

"This doesn't suck," G-man pointed out. "It's a beautiful day, and right now the poor bastards they hired are prepping dinner and getting ready to take it in the ass all night, and we're sitting here drinking. Tell me how that sucks."

"I'll tell you next week, when our rent's due."

"You're a real cheerer-upper, you know that?"

"Well, damn, G. We got about two hundred dollars in the bank. Favreau's not gonna give us another extension." Favreau was the landlord who rented them a shotgun cottage on the river end of Marengo Street. They were fortunate that he was a patient man; nonetheless, the mention of his name depressed them further.

The October shine had gone off the day. They rocked glumly back and forth on the tree limb. Rickey drained the last of the vodka and orange juice. "Tequilatown's a shithole. But did you ever notice how much money it's making?"

"About a hundred grand a week, I'd say."

"And the food is garbage. All Honeycombe has is a name. You know, G, we could run a better restaurant than Tequilatown."

"Uh huh."

"We could," said Rickey. "We're *good* cooks." He knew this was so. Right after they graduated from high school—almost ten years ago now—Rickey had even spent several months in Hyde Park, New York, at the fabled CIA, the Culinary Institute of America, hardcore training ground for chefs all over the country. He did well there until a run-in with another student resulted in his return to New Orleans, which was not an entirely unhappy thing: living up north was expensive and cold, and he was lost without G-man.

"Course we're good cooks," said G-man. "But it takes more than that. Like money."

"We might could raise some money if we had a good idea."

"Lots of people get ideas. Remember Lamar King's Bordello?" This had been a failed concept by another washed-up rock star, his claim to fame being that he had once shared a stage with Bob Dylan. He and his backers had bought a huge, decrepit building in the French Quarter, spent millions of dollars bringing it up to code and decorating it to look like a whorehouse, or what they imagined such a place to look like: lots of red velvet swags, stained glass, a grand piano. The menu had boasted items like "Pretty Baby Prime Rib" and "Aphrodisiac Oysters." The place closed its doors within a month. Rickey and G-man had passed several afternoons in various bars debating why a rock star would want to open a restaurant anyway. Rickey posited that chefs were actually cooler than rock stars, and Lamar King knew it. G-man thought King might have been around the amps too long.

Rickey was lost in thought. He held the empty thermos in his hand, staring into its shiny depths. A faint distorted reflection of his own eye winked up at him, blue and bloodshot. *Lots of people get ideas,* G-man had said, but how many of those ideas were good ones? More to the point, how many of those ideas were suitable for New Orleans? Plenty of would-be restaurateurs came from out of town, opened a place, watched it fail, and left cursing the city's moribund economy, punishing summers, fossilized tastes, or all of the above. Rickey was used to all that. Surely he could come up with an idea for a restaurant that would be uniquely suited to his lifelong home. He tilted the thermos and watched one last drop spill out, and that was when it came to him.

"You know what the Bordello's main problem was?" he asked G-man.

"It sucked."

"Yeah, but what sucked most about it? *It didn't deliver what it promised.* It wasn't a bordello, and nobody ever thought for one minute that it was gonna be a bordello. And that, my friend, was its downfall. We could open a successful restaurant if we *promised* a sin we could *deliver on.*"

"Like what?"

Rickey held up the thermos and waggled it in front of his face. He had the distinctly ridiculous expression of a drunk trying to be very serious, but there was also a spark in his eye that caught G-man's attention. It was the same spark he'd first seen in Rickey's eye back in the fourth grade, when Rickey described the idea for the bleeding false arm.

"*Liquor,*" Rickey said.

"Liquor? Dude, I know you're upset about getting fired, but c'mon. Every place in the city serves liquor."

"But no place has a menu *entirely based on it.*"

"You're really losing me."

"New Orleans loves booze. We love drinking it, we love the *idea* of drinking it, we love being *encouraged* to drink it. You think all those drive-thru daiquiri stands in Metairie are just serving tourists? Tourists don't go to the suburbs. Locals are drinking most of those daiquiris, and they could get 'em anywhere, but they love getting 'em at the drive-thrus because it makes them feel like they're doing something *naughty.* We could open a place that does the same thing on a *much bigger scale.*"

"A whole menu based on liquor."

"Picture it, G. A nice dining room—looks like, say, a cross between Commander's Palace and Gertie Greer's Steakhouse. Big bar in the front, mirrors, three hundred bottles—every kind of liquor and liqueur, every brand you could name. But that's just the beginning. The real draw is that we use liquor in all the food. Oysters poached in whiskey. Tequila barbecue sauce. Bourbon-glazed duck. Even goddamn bananas Foster. And that's just the obvious shit. There's not a recipe in the world that we couldn't find a way to stick a little liquor in it."

"You think that'd even be legal?"

"It's New Orleans. If you got enough money, anything's legal."

Rickey gave G-man his biggest smile. All his life, people had remarked on Rickey's smile—its warmth, the way it lit up his intense blue eyes, its power to beguile a person who had no intention of being beguiled. "Gawgeous!" G-man's own mother had pronounced it once, when she'd been trying to punish them for some infraction and Rickey had turned its full force on her.

Though G-man knew its charms well, he had long believed himself impervious to its manipulations. Now, for the first time in as many years as he could remember, he wondered.

°   °   °

Mostly sober and far less cocksure now, Rickey couldn't sleep. He'd swallowed some Excedrin PM, an old habit from his CIA days, but he couldn't stop thinking about his idea. He still thought it was a brilliant concept for a New Orleans restaurant. He just didn't see how he could pull it off. He was great at starting things, but not always so good at finishing them.

Rickey's parents hadn't sent him to cooking school out of any belief that he was destined to be a great chef. Mainly they had wanted to get him out of New Orleans and—more to the point—away from G-man. Rickey's mother had concocted the plan with G-man's parents, then convinced her ex-husband to pay for it. Apparently it was OK for a couple of boys to spend all their time together at age nine, but not OK at seventeen. Rickey still cringed at the memory of how easily he'd been manipulated, and their actual time apart had been so terrible that neither liked to recall it.

Even so, he sometimes wished he had been able to finish the two-year curriculum instead of getting kicked out after four and a half months. He could have learned a lot about cooking. As it was, he and G-man moved into a crappy little apartment on Prytania Street. Though the apartment was a dump, Uptown seemed luxurious, with its giant oaks and its proximity to the St. Charles streetcar line. G-man already had a decent job at a seafood place downtown. Rickey got hired as a PM salad guy at Reilly's, a restaurant in one of the formerly grand old hotels that still haunted Canal Street like maiden aunts not quite far enough gone to send to the old folks' home. A few months later, G-man quit the seafood place and came to Reilly's too. Soon they were both working on the hot line. Despite the name, Reilly's claimed to serve classic French cuisine, which apparently meant small dry cuts of meat or fish mired in stiffening yellow sauce. It was seldom pretty, and sometimes it was actively disgusting, but it was where they learned the skill of volume: making and putting out vast amounts of food.

They'd been at Reilly's for a couple of years when a cook from the old seafood joint, now a sous chef at the Peychaud Grill, offered G-man a dollar more an hour to be his sauté guy. The Peychaud was smaller than Reilly's and more hard-core. Once G-man had nailed down his position, he lobbied for Rickey when another line job opened up. That was their first experience being part of a crew that was tight in every sense of the word: smooth in the kitchen, close-knit, and more alcohol-drenched than any group of people Rickey had known before or since. New Orleans kids learned to drink young; Rickey and G-man had been able to hold their liquor since their early teens. The Peychaud crew, though, put them to shame at first. They came in at three, prepped up for dinner service, cooked their asses off for four hours, broke down the kitchen, and dragged themselves to the bar, where Dionysian challenges were made and met. There was a pot-smoking area behind the ice machine, a long series of razor scratches on the bar where somebody had scraped up lines of cocaine, entire cases of nitrous oxide chargers that never got turned into whipped cream. Once there was a bottle of ether in the reach-in. It was kind of a dangerous place, but it was also fun. Rickey and G-man partook of everything available. They were intoxicated not just with liquor and drugs but with their status as part of a culinary pirate crew, slashing and burning and taking no prisoners.

They stayed at the Peychaud Grill for nearly five years, but never rose higher than sauté because there was no turnover among the kitchen staff. The Peychaud was a prestigious place to work, and once you had a job there, you hung onto it. Still, those were pretty good years all in all: they were making enough money to move from the crappy apartment to a little shotgun house on a shade-dappled block of Marengo Street, and they were cooking some great food. Chef Paco Valdeon was a prodigious cokehead who'd learned to cook in France. Though he was usually incoherent by two in the morning, he could answer any food question and discourse on any food subject as long as he remained conscious. Some people considered him a thug, but he was a culinary genius.

Toward the end of this time, though, G-man calculated that they had worked an average of ten hours a day, six days a week, 312 days a year. And they'd spent most of the rest of the time partying. They had no time to see their families who lived just a few miles away, much less to think about hazy concepts like "vacation" or "health insurance." Not yet twenty-five, they felt like broken old men. But they couldn't quit. They'd come up at the Peychaud and imprinted unhealthily on it; it was their gang, their abusive surrogate parent, their hell away from home.

Rickey sometimes wondered what would have become of them if the Peychaud crew hadn't imploded one night in a marathon of apocalyptic drunkenness. No one remembered much of this night, but by the end of it, two cars were totaled, the sous chef and the bartender were in Charity Hospital, the chef was in jail, and the grill guy's wife was filing for divorce. The owner decided to close the place and they found themselves jobless. Rickey guessed this kind of thing was known as a "wake-up call."

They had spent the past couple of years jumping from restaurant to restaurant, taking whatever job paid best, working together when they could but never getting all that tight with any kitchen crew. Sometimes they had a few drinks after service; mostly they just went home. Life wasn't bad. In a lot of ways it was better than the constant soul-grinding revelry of the Peychaud Grill. But Rickey had put off being disappointed with himself after he left school because he was so glad to be back home with G-man, living the life they had wanted to live since they were sixteen. Then the Peychaud years kept him from thinking too hard about anything. Now that he wasn't drunk all the time and he and G-man were as comfortable as an old married couple, he sometimes felt that he had given up too easily. Given up what, he wasn't sure. He'd never really burned with ambition to be a head chef; most of them worked harder than anybody else and didn't make all that much more money.

And yet . . . once upon a time he had been truly curious about cooking. He'd wanted to know everything about it, to be the best cook possible. That was why his folks had been able to bribe him with the CIA. Even now he hadn't completely lost that curiosity: he read *Gourmet* and *Bon Appétit,* watched the Food Network, had a big cookbook collection. And he took pride in being a roller. He knew faster cooks and better cooks, but few who were faster *and* better.

Still something gnawed at him. Something always had, really; it was not in his nature to be content. Usually G-man was content enough for the both of them. But right now their situation was bad, and their bitch session in the park had excited the gnawing thing. Liquor: his thoughts seized on that idea and would not leave it alone. A restaurant based on liquor, but not too gimmicky. A really good menu, so people would keep coming back after the novelty wore off. Rickey had spent nearly half his life observing the New Orleans restaurant scene, and he felt certain that the place would be a hit.

But what difference did it make? You needed money to start a restaurant. If you didn't have money, you needed collateral. If you didn't have collateral, you needed rich friends who could invest. And if you didn't have any of that, you at least needed a credit card. Rickey and G-man had exactly none of the above.

He lay in bed thinking about this until the sky began to brighten, but none of it mattered in the least, because he was broke and he had to start looking for a new job tomorrow.

They both did. Probably they wouldn't be able to work together for a while. Rickey smoothed his pillow, closed his eyes, and tried to resign himself to a spell of crappiness. As he did so, G-man rolled over in his sleep and threw an arm across Rickey's chest, and Rickey fell asleep thinking that maybe things weren't *that* bad.

chapter 2

It was a rare luxury in the kitchen, knowing there was always one person watching your back, one other cook whose habits and motions you knew as well as your own. It was a luxury Rickey didn't have any more, and it was making him crazy.

Weeks behind on the rent, they'd had to get separate jobs. G-man had an easy-ass no-brainer of a gig making bar snacks at a watering hole on Tchoupitoulas, within walking distance of the house. Rickey had snagged a position as saucier at Escargot's, a Tourist Creole restaurant in the Hotel Bienvenu that went through staff almost as quickly as the manager went through cocaine. After Reilly's he had sworn he would never work in another hotel restaurant, and he hadn't until now.

Being a saucier was hot, heavy work. He handled the bulk prep for the whole kitchen, made stocks, sauces, and demi-glaces with enormous veal bones in stainless steel vats, and worked all the banquets and private parties, making for frequent eighteen-hour days. His one bright spot was cooking the staff meals, which were no challenge but upon which everyone complimented him: apparently the last guy had been a real scrub, slinging ground chuck and week-old vegetables into a pot with rice or dead pasta every day.

Rickey caught the streetcar to the French Quarter at 6 a.m. G-man worked bar hours, four in the afternoon till four in the morning. Not only were they not working together, they hardly ever saw each other when they *weren't* working. The house was filthy; they hadn't cooked at home in weeks; Rickey ate his own staff meals, G-man grabbed sandwiches at the bar, and they both ate a lot of cold cereal. Fortunately a twenty-four-hour corner grocery up the street stocked milk, beer, and liquor, which was all they needed.

Rickey arrived at Escargot's one day, the sour early-morning smell of the Quarter assaulting his nostrils, his bloodshot eyes hidden behind a pair of G-man's shades. "Kevin ain't here yet," said the porter by way of greeting.

"Aw, shit."

Kevin, the production guy, was supposed to arrive before Rickey and get the morning prep rolling. If he flaked, Rickey was automatically in the weeds. He stowed the sunglasses in his knife bag, tied a bandanna around his head, and turned on the oven, cursing under his breath the whole time.

As he hauled fifty-pound sacks of bones out of the freezer and smashed them on the floor to break them up, he began to sing. "Massa got me workin . . . workin in this kitchen . . . Ole kitchen sucks so bad . . ."

Terrance, the 280-pound dishwasher, joined in from the other side of the kitchen. He'd grown up in the Lower

Ninth Ward, and though they had not known each other back in the neighborhood, he and Rickey had soon become friends at Escargot's.

"What's the good word, Terrance?"

"Ain't none that I know of. I been saying bad words since I got here."

Rickey scanned his produce, deciding on a soup du jour. The cauliflower looked good, so he cooked it down in butter and dumped it into a Lexan container with several pints of cream. He looked for the puree wand on its usual shelf, but couldn't find it. "You seen my wand?" he asked the sous chef, who was making notes about the day's specials.

"Nope. Maybe Kevin's using it."

"Kevin flaked on me again."

"He gets here, you gonna send him home?"

"Don't know. I guess it depends on how far behind I get."

"You gonna tell Mike?"

"I'm not telling Mike shit," said Rickey. Mike was the manager. He seldom arrived before 10:30, and no one ever told him shit.

Rickey looked for the wand in the pantry area, the sinks, even the refrigerator. It was a large, expensive tool and he couldn't imagine how it might have gotten lost, but eventually he gave up and dug out the food processor. He pureed the soup in small, tedious batches, all the while invoking dire curses upon Kevin.

As he was whirling the last batch, Terrance called, "Hey, Rickey, what's that smell?"

Rickey sniffed the air and realized that it was acrid. The

odor was like a concentrated version of certain miasmas that used to settle over the Lower Ninth Ward in his childhood, when a lot of chemical processing was still done out there: something cooking that shouldn't be.

At his station, the sous chef began to cough. "Rickey," he called, "you burning something?" Rickey checked the stove burners, found nothing wrong. Remembering that he had lit the oven, he got a sick feeling in the pit of his stomach. He snatched open the oven door. Foul smoke billowed out. There was his puree wand, its plastic handle partially melted onto the top rack.

"Who the *fuck* left this in here?" he yelled, knowing it was futile, that one of the PM guys must have done it during cleanup and there was nobody he could take it out on now. He grabbed the wand with a pair of tongs, ran over to Terrance's sinks, and dropped it in. It lay on the wet stainless steel like a Dali sculpture, totally useless. The porter passed through the kitchen and wondered aloud, "Who farted?"

It was 8:30 now. Rickey went to the bar and fixed himself a screwdriver. Orange juice, he figured; it was good for breakfast.

The wand incident set the tone for the rest of the day. He didn't mind everybody in the kitchen making jokes about his limp wand, but the loss of the tool itself slowed him up considerably. Kevin was never heard from, which meant Mike would fire him, which meant Rickey would have to fill in for him until they hired a new production guy.

Just to make things symmetrical, one of the banquet crew flaked out as well—his wife called to say he was in jail, which might or might not be true. Mike pissed and moaned

about it for a few minutes, then told Rickey to ask the pur-
chasing manager to stay and help. Rickey was almost sick
enough of the job to say "Why don't you ask him yourself?"
but he thought about the rent and forbore. Instead he
headed for the purchaser's cubbyhole of an office, dreading
the trapped and hateful look he knew the man would give
him.

°   °   °

While Rickey and the banquet crew were clearing up the
remains of steam-table jambalaya, rubber shrimp Creole,
and gumbo boiled to a pot-crust by a Sterno flame, G-man
was sitting in the Apostle Bar eating a quesadilla and reading a copy of *Big Easy* magazine somebody had left in the
men's room. *Big Easy*'s restaurant reviews weren't long on
culinary daring, he noted. In a feature on the Ethnic Hide-
aways of the West Bank, the writer recommended a certain
Chinese place "only if you're in the know about what to
order," then went on to tout the egg rolls and lemon chicken.

The Apostle Bar was a moderately successful watering
hole owned by Anthony Bonvillano Jr., with whom Rickey
and G-man had once worked at a St. Charles Avenue restaurant built from leftover parts of the Eiffel Tower. Like
Rickey and G-man, Anthony had been in one kitchen or
another since his teens, but he'd always wanted to own a bar.
When Big Anthony died, he left his son enough to open a little place, stipulating only the maintenance of his annual St.
Joseph's Day altar. St. Joseph had once saved Sicily from
famine, and local Italians—most of whose families hailed
from Sicily—often built altars in their homes and businesses

for his feast day. Every March, Anthony brought out his father's tall plaster statues and placed them on a three-tiered altar near the video poker machine. Bonvillano sisters and cousins sent over an array of food to heap at the statues' feet. The family took out a classified ad saying what days the altar would be open so the public could visit. Visitors usually contributed a few dollars and took home a small bag filled with Italian seed cookies, a piece of bread, a prayer card, and a lucky fava bean, which symbolized St. Joseph's aid since it had thrived in Sicily when other crops failed. No one ever seemed to question whether Big Anthony had really intended for the altar to be in the bar, and no one was offended by its being there. St. Joseph was also the patron saint of workers, and everyone knew that workers needed a drink now and then.

Anthony was just coming in now. The sight of his cook sitting at the bar caused him no visible distress. That was one good thing about working for an ex-line cook: he understood that when there was nothing to do, there was no point in staying on the line. "G-man, where y'at," he said.

"Anthony B," G-man replied.

"Much business tonight?"

"Not yet. Let 'em drink a little more and they'll start ordering."

"Maybe you ought to put out some snacks, huh?"

"Anthony, I told you before—you put out snacks, this crowd will eat 'em and not order anything. You want to sell more food, you gotta let me cook a little bit better stuff, bring in a different crowd."

Anthony's ruddy forehead creased. Innovation worried

him. "Well, I don't know," he said, and told the bartender to give them each an Abita beer. They had had this conversation many times since G-man started the job.

Back in the kitchen, G-man made a gallon of blue cheese dressing for the chicken wings. They'd been using packaged dressing mix when he got here. Now Anthony let him make a creamy, tangy fresh version as long as the cheese didn't cost too much. He was scooping some onto a ruffled potato chip when Rickey staggered in.

Anyone outside the restaurant business might have mistaken Rickey for a strangely dressed bum. His hair was rank with sweat, his white jacket and houndstooth check pants greasy. In his eyes was a weary thousand-yard stare. He was a walking miasma of food smells, any one of which might have been appetizing; together they were disgusting. His workboots were crusted horrors. He leaned against the reach-in cooler, let his knees bend slightly, and closed his eyes.

"Hey, sweetheart," said G-man. Every time he saw Rickey fresh from work, he experienced three conflicting emotions: pity, relief that he himself wasn't working in some big thankless kitchen, and guilt at feeling relief when Rickey was suffering.

"Dude," said Rickey faintly. He had a beer in his hand but did not raise it to his lips, as if even that essential act were too strenuous. G-man took him by the shoulder, steered him out to the bar, and sat with him at a table.

"Worse than usual?"

"Kevin didn't show up."

"Aw, shit."

"Neither did Tyrone."

"Jesus."

Rickey leaned across the t
G-man's arm. A small unbanda
finger was leaking bloody lym
impulse to slide his arm away.

"You gotta get me out of this," Rickey sai
don't know how much more I can take. Every morning
Mike comes drag-assing in with his nostrils powdered up,
and he says, 'Hup hup! Busy day, crew! Busy day!' *Every
fucking morning,* G, and all of us standing there with knives
in our hands."

"Dude—"

"I fantasize about watching Terrance just pick him up
by the head and *squeeeeeeeze.*"

"Dude!"

"I'm going sideways, G. I'm gonna lay down on the
streetcar line and let it run me over."

"Hey Laura," G-man called to the bartender, "you got
the paper back there somewhere?"

"I think so. You want it?"

"Yeah, bring us the want ads and a couple of Wild
Turkeys on the rocks, would you please?"

Laura brought the items to the table. She was a petite,
pretty woman with dark Sicilian eyes and straight hair that
hung to the small of her back, and she listened to a lot of
rude bullshit from male customers, but never twice from the
same one.

"Let's see what we got here. Drink your drink," G-man
told Rickey, folding the newspaper to the classified ads.

new steakhouse opening up. Says they need a grill

Is it Porterhouse Charlie's?"

"Yeah."

"I heard they were drug-testing."

"OK, fuck 'em . . . Hey, Commander's is looking for a saucier."

"I applied for that already, remember? Didn't get it."

"What about Lenny Duveteaux's Sundae Dinner? 'Hiring all positions.' That's the voice of desperation there."

"Yeah, and you know why?" Rickey sat up straighter in his chair. The Wild Turkey seemed to have revived him. "Sundae Dinner is another damn gimmick joint. They make everything into a 'sundae.' You order a steak, they cut it in half lengthwise and plate it with three scoops of mashed potatoes so it looks like a banana split. I heard they got a foie gras mousse appetizer, two scoops in a parfait dish with port sauce, some crème fraîche, *and a damn maraschino cherry on top.*"

G-man laughed.

"Exactly. It's a *stupid* gimmick. Lenny can get away with it for a little while because he's a celebrity chef, but it's gonna go belly-up eventually because it's a stupid idea. Our gimmick would be *awesome.*"

"Are you still going on about that thing?"

"You know what, G? You'll be sorry you said that someday, because *that thing* is gonna make us rich."

"What's gonna make you rich?" said Anthony, who had just come over to the table.

"Aw, Rickey's got this idea for a restaurant—*OW!*"

G-man shot Rickey a wounded look as he leaned down to rub the spot on his shin where Rickey had just kicked him. "What, I can't even tell Anthony B? He's got money. You seriously want to do this, we're gonna need investors."

"I ain't got much money, G-man. What you telling him that for?"

"You never wrote me a paycheck that bounced. That means you got more money than some people we've worked for."

"Well, I ain't got enough to invest in nothing."

"You wouldn't have to invest," Rickey said. A fanatical gleam was dawning in his eyes. "You'd just have to let me come work here with G. You wouldn't have to pay me much. And I bet you'd start making a profit off the food."

"Make a profit off the food? That ain't gonna happen at the Apostle Bar. We make all our money off liquor."

"You still would," said Rickey, and explained the idea.

Anthony rubbed the thinning hair on top of his head. "I don't know, y'all. I like running a bar. I never thought about getting back into the restaurant business."

"You wouldn't have to. We'd handle everything. You'd do the same stuff you always do, but you'd have more business."

"You really think people care what they eat in a bar?"

"Look at the wings," said G-man. "You know we're moving them since you started letting me make that fresh dressing."

"Them wings are good," Anthony admitted.

"They'd be even better with some tequila in them," said Rickey.

Anthony gave Rickey a long, searching look, then turned to G-man. "You know, you been doing just fine on your own. You don't *need* no smart-mouth buddy coming in and fixing up all your recipes with liquor. What I mean to say is, you sure you want this maniac in your kitchen?"

"To be perfectly honest, Anthony," said G-man, "I don't know how I got by so long without this maniac in my kitchen."

chapter 3

Rickey gave two weeks' notice at Escargot's. During his time off, he went to work with G-man and they started tossing recipes around.

They were in the Apostle's kitchen late one night, a week before Rickey finished serving out his notice, doing prep work and talking trash. G-man was telling a story about his aunt Charmaine. "She was a total hippie. One day she was watching us kids, and right in front of us, she says to her friend, 'I don't think I'm gonna smoke pot no more.'

"'You're not?' says her friend.

"'Nuh-uh,' says my aunt Charmaine. 'From now on I'm gonna smoke hash!' And that night my little cousin Raymond, he was just four, he says to our grammaw, 'Hey, Maw-maw, guess what! Charmaine ain't gonna smoke no more pot—she's only gonna smoke hash!'"

Rickey laughed. "Whatever happened to her?"

"She got old, got straight."

"Just like most people, I guess."

"Rickey, don't you get scared that could happen to *us* if this Liquor thing works out?"

"Nah," said Rickey dismissively. "Nobody in this business is really normal. Even if they quit doing drugs and have kids and stuff, they stay twisted somehow."

"I guess mostly. But a lot of the owners seem pretty normal to me."

"G, listen to me. We wouldn't just be owners. We'd be chef-owners. *Chef-owners are never normal.*"

"You sure?"

"I got two words for you. Willy Gerhardt."

"Yeah, I guess you got a point."

Willy Gerhardt was a German expatriate who had exploded onto the New Orleans restaurant scene about five years ago. Wildly talented, he debuted as head chef of the Polonius Room at the d'Hemecourt Hotel and soon earned five red beans, the *Times-Picayune* food critic's equivalent of stars. When he got deservedly famous for that, he decided to open his own restaurant downtown. With its slick-surfaced decor and Willy's signature jasmine-grilled lobster, Gerhardt's soon became the hottest spot in town. Willy decided to open a second restaurant and a gourmet deli. He bought a little scooter that he used to ride between the places. He gave strange interviews in which he spoke of a mystical pyramid of stones he kept in his house. These stones were the balancing factor of his life, Willy said, and if they ever toppled, so would he.

It was always said that a jealous rival—or maybe just a drunken friend—broke into Willy's house and tipped the stones over. No one knew the truth. At any rate, Willy's restaurants all closed simultaneously, and New Orleans never heard from Willy Gerhardt again. Kitchen gossip claimed that he was in Angola Prison, in rehab, in Vegas, cooking for a millionaire on a South Seas yacht, dead of a heroin overdose.

"But we don't want to end up like that," G-man said.

"I could live with the yacht option."

"I never did believe that one."

Rickey put down his knife and looked over at G-man, who was dicing celery as if he'd be content to do it all his life. Maybe he would, Rickey thought; maybe G-man just didn't want any risks in his life. The thought made him feel mean, but now that he was so stoked about his restaurant idea, G-man's placidity sometimes got on Rickey's nerves.

"G, aren't you sick of being broke? Aren't you sick of busting your ass to make money for people like Jesse Honeycombe?"

"Sure, but what else can we do? We're just a couple of slobs on the line."

"We're not either," said Rickey. "We're gonna be running this kitchen soon, and someday we'll be running a kitchen bigger and better than this one."

"You really think so, huh?"

"No, I don't *think* so. I *know* so. I got a genius idea and I'm gonna find a way to make it happen. We can do this, you hear me? Liquor is gonna make us free."

° ° °

Rickey went in singing on his last morning at Escargot's, the Monday after Christmas. He wasn't singing "Massa Got Me Workin" any more; today it was "When the Saints Go Marching In." Ever since the year Rickey went to cooking school and had to stay in New York for the holidays, he and G-man had hated Christmas, but they'd had a pretty good one this year thanks to G-man's father. Elmer Stubbs's best friend from high school now worked in the Saints ticket office, and Elmer had snagged them an unsnaggable pair of tickets to the December 30 game against the despised St. Louis Rams. Normally Saints tickets weren't hard to come by, but this was a playoff game, the team's first in seven years. It also turned out to be their first-ever playoff victory. With less than two minutes to play, the Rams receiver fumbled a punt and the Saints pounced on it. Euphoric fans spilled out of the Superdome and swarmed down Poydras Street hollering, dancing, guzzling drinks, even crying as golden fireworks blossomed in the winter sky. People stuck in the parking garage leaned on their horns or set off their car alarms, not out of spite but just to add to the celebratory din. Some fans had suffered with this team for thirty-four seasons, so Rickey couldn't blame them for getting emotional. He was a little hungover himself, but the game had left him in a good mood.

He made a big pot of rice and took out some chicken to thaw. Later he would fry it up and serve it with greens for a special staff meal. Everyone who ate the staff meals had been loudly lamenting his departure, recalling the dreadful concoctions of the last saucier and speculating on those of the next one. The new saucier was a young guy from Texas who seemed OK, if clueless about the evil ways of Mike. He'd learn.

At lunch, the dessert ladies grabbed the best pieces of chicken and crumbled cornbread into their greens. The oldest one, Mrs. Sondra, said, "Lord, Rickey, I wish you'd teach my grandbaby how to cook. Her fried chicken greasier than Popeye's."

"You got that right," said Terrance, who had briefly dated Mrs. Sondra's grandbaby. Mrs. Sondra glared at him, but could not argue since she had broached the subject herself.

Mike failed to make the day difficult in any of the ways Rickey had expected. In fact, he stayed in his office most of the morning and all afternoon. Rickey was coasting through his last hour when the hostess came on the kitchen intercom and said, "Phone call for the saucier up front."

Well, that was weird. Even if somebody had mistakenly called the front of the house trying to reach him, the hostess could have transferred the call to the kitchen. Rickey washed his hands and walked through the empty dining room to the hostess's station. She covered the receiver with the heel of her hand and said, impressed as hell, "It's Lenny Duveteaux."

Rickey took the phone, trying to look slightly bored, as if celebrity chefs called him every day. "Hey, Lenny," he said.

"Hi, Rickey, how are you?"

Rickey and G-man had never met Lenny Duveteaux, but they knew a lot about him. He was a huge and inescapable force on the local restaurant scene. He'd been sous chef and head chef at a couple of high-end places around town before opening Lenny's, a classically beautiful space in the French Quarter that had become a national dining mecca. Crescent, his place on Magazine Street, was trendier and more local. Lenny was from Maine, but he knew New Orleans food as well as anybody. Fame was the problem. Some chefs could handle it and get on with their cooking. Lenny seemed to have fallen in love with being famous. He had his own line of spice blends; he'd done the Playboy Interview; he appeared regularly on Leno and Letterman; now he had this embarrassing new venture, Sundae Dinner. It was whispered around town that his trademark restaurants had suffered as a result of all these frills. He hired good cooks, but you could only let other cooks run your kitchens for so long before somebody else's vision took over.

"I'm OK," said Rickey. "How you doing, Lenny?"

"Pretty good. Busy. I just got back from Vegas, you know, I might open a place out there—"

Just what you need, Rickey thought.

"—but we'll see. Anyway, you put in an application at Crescent a couple of weeks ago? For a hot apps position?"

"Yeah, but it turns out I'm going somewhere else."

"Right. I heard you're opening your own place?"

Christ, the rumor mill never let up for a second. Rickey had no idea how this information had gotten out, or whether the talk bore any resemblance to his actual idea. "No, I'm not opening a restaurant. I'm just gonna cook at the Apostle Bar with my friend G-man."

"Right," said Lenny again, not sounding as if he believed it. "I wasn't exactly calling about the job. We hired somebody else last week."

"OK." Rickey was really confused now.

"But I know you're a good cook. I've heard good things about you from people I trust."

Rickey wondered which of his acquaintances had

Lenny's ear. He'd begun to build a good little reputation for himself at the Peychaud Grill, but most of his coworkers from those days had left town. "So how come you called?" he said.

"Well, I was checking references on those applications, and yours said it was OK to call your current boss."

"Right." The barest whisper of paranoia was beginning to creep into Rickey's mind. "I told Mike I needed more money and he said he couldn't give it to me. He knew I was looking around. He was fine with it."

"Maybe not."

"Why? What'd he say?"

"I tell you, Rickey, it made me really uncomfortable. I know Mike Mouton. I know he only has that job because his father's on the Downtown Development District board. I know he's a shiftless little weasel who cares more about his nose candy than his employees. You understand what I'm saying?"

"Not really."

Through the receiver he heard Lenny sigh deeply. "Mike said you were screwing up on the job, which I know isn't the case because Chef Roger is a friend of mine and he says you've done just fine. So I asked Mike how come he didn't fire you, and he says, 'I'm going to, soon as I find another white boy who can do the job.'"

"Jesus!"

"Yeah, and that's not the end of it. If it was, I wouldn't be calling you. Look, I really think you ought to hear this conversation for yourself."

"How I'm gonna do that?"

"Well, I tape all the calls that go in and out of my office."

"You *do?*" Rickey was dumbfounded. He'd heard people call Lenny the Nixon of the New Orleans restaurant world, but he hadn't known they meant it literally.

"Yeah, that's between you and me, OK? But I have the tape at home. You free this Sunday?"

"Sure."

"Come on over around three. Bring your friend, what's his name?"

"G-man. Gary Stubbs."

"Yeah, bring him if you like. We'll put some ribs on the barbecue." Lenny gave Rickey directions to a posh neighborhood near Lake Pontchartrain and hung up. Shaking his head in bewilderment, Rickey returned to the kitchen.

Mike caught up with him near the walk-in. "You're staying to work the New Year's Eve banquet tonight, right, Rickey?"

"No, I'm going home in thirty minutes," Rickey told him. "I been here since seven o'clock this morning. I got you all set up for dinner."

Rickey wasn't slacking off because this was his last day. He had already stayed to work two banquets this week, neither of which he'd been scheduled for. Mike was always springing banquets on people. Rickey could have used the overtime pay, but he needed to get home and talk to G-man about Lenny's phone call. "Sorry," he said when Mike asked him a second time. "Like I said, I just can't do it."

"You know, that really disappoints me, but it's typical. You never put in much effort here. I might have known you'd be one of those types who'd lay down on the job once he gave notice."

Rickey looked at Mike's narrow face, the nose twitching like a rat's, the little eyes glittering with Mike's latest dose of cocaine. Asshole bosses were a hazard of kitchen work, just like cuts and burns, but suddenly Rickey didn't feel like dealing with this particular hazard for one more second. *Not worth it,* he told himself, and tried to keep his mouth shut.

"I heard you tell Terrance you went to the football game yesterday," Mike said. "I guess you think that's a good reason to ask off, to go to a football game, when I just worked a seven-day week."

"I didn't *ask off,*" said Rickey, incredulous. "I was *scheduled* off, and you called me on Saturday night to see if I'd work the shift anyway."

"It was an emergency."

"It was another one of your scheduling fuckups."

"*I don't make scheduling fuckups!*" Mike screamed.

Rickey saw that there were little whitish wads of dry spit in the corners of his boss's mouth. He suddenly felt very tired. "Look," he said. "It's none of your business what people do on their days off. Some of us have lives outside of this place."

"Yeah, I heard about your life, or should I say your *lifestyle?*"

"What the fuck is that supposed to mean?" said Rickey. He took a step toward Mike and was gratified to see Mike flinch back a little. Rickey was taller than Mike and broader through the shoulders, and he doubted Mike knew how to fight. "You got something else to say to me?" he prodded.

"*Don't expect a recommendation!*" Mike flung the words at Rickey as if he actually expected them to sting. Rickey started laughing; he couldn't help it.

Rickey's laughter seemed to make Mike so insanely angry that he forgot he'd been scared of Rickey a few seconds ago. He reached out and grabbed Rickey by the front of his white chef jacket. Without thinking, Rickey broke the hold, drove his knee into Mike's crotch, and slammed Mike against the door of the walk-in. Mike's body instinctively tried to double over, but Rickey held him up by jamming his thumbs under Mike's collarbone. "You ever put your hands on an employee again," he said into Mike's face, "you better make sure it's a waiter. And I'd bet ten bucks even a waiter could kick your ass."

Mike started to say something, but Rickey never got to hear it, because at that moment a huge black hand came down on Rickey's shoulder and pulled him away. There was no aggression in the touch, but there didn't have to be: Terrance was so much stronger than either Rickey or Mike that he didn't need to use force to separate them. His muscular arms and his shaven head glistened with grease from the pots he'd been washing. Far from being a violent guy, Terrance was even squeamish about killing cockroaches, but Rickey wasn't sure Mike knew that.

"Whatever he said to you, it ain't worth getting in trouble on your last day," Terrance told Rickey. "Why don't you go on home? We can cover the rest of your shift."

"I didn't say he could go home," Mike protested.

"Mike, are you ever gonna learn when to shut up? Go on, Rickey. I'll meet you in the locker room in a couple minutes."

Rickey had finished changing into his street clothes by the time Terrance came in. "What'd you do to him?" Rickey asked.

"Aw, nothing. Soon as he could catch his breath, he just pushed me off and went running to his office. Figure he's hitting the powder again."

"I can't believe he put his fucking hands on me."

"I can. Mike hired you in a pinch and he never has liked you. Know why you got the job? The only other guy who qualified was black. Blacks can wash dishes at Escargot's, and the grammaws can make desserts, but Mike ain't never putting a nigga on the hot line."

"Jeez," said Rickey, digesting the information. He'd had racist bosses before, but none who actually refused to hire black cooks. No wonder Escargot's kitchen was so under-staffed. "He's gonna be pissed at you. You think you'll get fired?"

"Mike ain't gonna fire me. I try not to abuse it too much, but I got a hundred percent job security here."

"How come?"

"Mike don't care for blacks in the kitchen, that's true. But he don't mind them in his office sometimes."

"Terrance, what the hell are you talking about?"

"Well, it just so happens that my cousin supplies our esteemed kitchen manager with his favorite pick-me-up."

"Your cousin sells coke to Mike?"

"Did I say that?"

"Right here in the restaurant?"

"You certainly are making some wild guesses about what goes on when Mike closes that office door of his. Yes sir, you certainly are conjecturing."

"If I ever get my own restaurant, will you come work for me? You know everything."

"I'll take it under advisement," said Terrance.

° ° °

Anthony had decided to close the Apostle Bar's kitchen tonight so he and Laura could concentrate on serving drinks, the big New Year's Eve moneymaker. G-man was at home trying to watch as much basketball as possible before their cable was disconnected. The bill had gone by the wayside while they caught up on rent, but so far no one at the cable company had noticed. He was watching the Lakers play the Spurs when Rickey came in.

Arriving home from the last day of a job you'd grown to hate, you would usually do a little happy dance, or have a daiquiri in your hand, or at least throw your arms in the air and say, "I'm free!" Rickey did none of these things; he just stood there looking dazed. At first G-man thought he had the bludgeoned look one got after a horrendously busy shift; but no, it wasn't quite that.

"How'd it go?" G-man asked.

"I don't know," said Rickey. He sat on the couch next to G-man and watched the game for a few minutes. On the screen, Tim Duncan stepped deftly around Shaquille O'Neal and sank a bucket off the glass.

"I am so freaked out right now," Rickey said at last.

"Well, what happened?"

Rickey outlined his day: the phone call from Lenny Duveteaux, the dustup with Mike, Terrance's intervention and revelation. "Why's Lenny taking an interest in me?" he finished. "Sure, Mike's a dick—he proved that beyond the shadow of a doubt today—but why would Lenny call me up to tell me about it?"

"Maybe he's headhunting you."

"He had his chance to hire me. I wanted that hot apps job at Crescent. I love making appetizers."

"Maybe he wants you to do more than apps. Maybe he's thinking about you for sous chef or something."

"But *why?* I've never been sous chef anywhere, and Lenny Duveteaux doesn't know anything about me."

"Hate to argue with you, dude, but it looks like he does."

"Who would've told him?"

"Forget it for now, Rickey. You're done with Escargot's. Be happy. We'll go out to Lakeview on Sunday and you can find out who put a bug up Lenny's ass."

"Things are weird lately," said Rickey. "I don't like it when things are weird."

"I guess things are a little weird," G-man admitted. "Hell, the Saints won a playoff game and New Orleans hasn't even frozen over yet. You like that, huh?"

"Yeah, I like that. But—"

"C'mon now, shut up about it or you'll just get yourself worked up. Go grab a beer." G-man glanced at the TV, where Spurs players swarmed around Shaq like climbers on a mountain. "Watch this game with me and I'll rub your feet."

"They probably stink."

"That's OK."

G-man must really want to see this game. Rickey knew he should go shower, but he didn't have the energy yet. G-man was right: he needed to get his mind off all this weirdness and relax for a while. No matter what Lenny wanted with him, he was still starting full-time at the Apostle Bar next week, and they were going to come up with a kick-ass menu. The mystery of Lenny could wait.

Rickey settled back onto the couch, stuck his feet in G-man's lap, and watched Shaq miss two free throws. The beer was cold and tasty. G-man's thumbs on his left instep were almost orgasm-inducing. He began to feel a little better. Maybe later they'd even go out and celebrate. He couldn't remember the last time they'd had New Year's Eve off.

Rickey fell asleep before he finished his beer. G-man made it to the end of the game, then dozed off watching the postgame show. The low deep cough of fireworks in the distance woke them. On TV, the ball in Times Square had dropped an hour ago, and now it was a new year in New Orleans too.

chapter 4

On Sunday morning, Rickey opened his eyes and stared up at the bedroom ceiling. Why did today feel sort of like Christmas and sort of like he had to go to a really tough job interview? He couldn't remember at first. Then he did: today they were going over to Lenny's.

Years ago at culinary school, Rickey had met an older, famous chef who promised to introduce him to Julia Child. It never happened, and ever since then, he'd refused to be impressed by celebrities. You saw them when you worked in kitchens, but Rickey never cared. Lenny Duveteaux was just a transplanted Yankee lucky enough to have a French-sounding name. So why did Rickey have the faintest suggestion of butterflies in his stomach?

G-man was already up, heating milk for coffee in the little kitchen at the back of the house. "I thought I might fix some eggs," he said. "Get a protein rush going for the big-ass meeting."

Rickey sat at the kitchen table drinking coffee, watching G-man crack six eggs into a bowl using only his left hand, slide them over low heat, grate cheddar into the skillet, add some minced scallion tops and a few grinds of pepper. The eggs were fluffy and buttery, the toast crisp but not rock-hard. G-man had always had a nice touch with breakfast.

Not sure how formal this meeting was supposed to be, they attempted to dress up a little. The results were some-what unfortunate. Rickey spent a long time choosing between a long-sleeved purple dress shirt with frayed cuffs and a green-and-yellow Hawaiian shirt with a stain on the hem. In the end, he chose the Hawaiian shirt because it was a warm day and he didn't want to get sweaty. G-man wore a dress shirt made of some blue-gray, faintly iridescent fabric.

"Couple of sharp dudes," G-man said as they regarded themselves in the bathroom mirror.

"Couple of dorks, you mean. I wish we had some decent clothes."

"What are you so nervous about?"

"I'm not sure," Rickey admitted. "It's like we're being summoned. I keep wondering why Lenny would want to see us."

"You don't think it's the tape?"

"I don't think that's the only reason."

"Well, you don't have much longer before you find out."

"That makes me nervous too. I feel like I'm about to lose my innocence."

G-man laughed. "Dude, it's about twelve years too late for that. I ought to know."

"Yeah. But G, I never been involved in anything really sleazy before, and that seems like it could change really fast."

"Damn!" said G-man. "Good thing for Lenny you're not some girl he asked out. You would've already booked the church and hired the priest by now."

○   ○   ○

They had to leave home around one o'clock to be certain of reaching Lakeview by three. The trip required catching a series of buses, at least one of which was likely to be late, break down, or fail to show up altogether. By 2:45 they were walking along a street with exquisitely landscaped yards and houses built in the style of the space age as conceived in the early seventies. One house appeared to have been made of white foam sprayed onto giant balloons. Another was bisected by a flat disc of Plexiglas. Thinking of the effect a hurricane would have on it, Rickey winced.

G-man pulled a city map out of his back pocket and peered nearsightedly at the Lakeview section. It was an old map with the location of every now-defunct K&B drugstore marked in purple. Economically and otherwise, Lakeview was far from the neighborhood where they had grown up, and they were unfamiliar with these streets.

Eventually they found Lenny's house, a pink stucco mansion on a lot that ran right up to the Lake Pontchartrain levee. Two cars were parked in the semicircular driveway, a red Lexus and a black Saturn. The Lexus's vanity plate read GUMBO-1. Rickey smirked at that, wondering if Lenny thought it made him seem local or something, but he kept his mouth shut. Three small steps led up to a set of white wrought iron doors. You didn't see much white-painted ironwork in other parts of New Orleans, but it was a popular look in these lakeside neighborhoods. They climbed the steps and stood on the little porch hunting for the doorbell.

"Try that key thing," suggested G-man.

"What key thing?"

G-man pointed at a brass key protruding from a shiny brass faceplate. Rickey twisted it, and a loud chime sounded inside the house.

"Yeah?" said Lenny's voice from a speaker at the bottom of the faceplate.

"It's us."

"Who's us?"

"John Rickey and Gary Stubbs."

"Yeah, OK, come on in." A buzzing sound came out of the speaker. Nothing else happened. After a minute, Rickey twisted the key again.

"Problem?" said Lenny.

"Uh, we can't get in."

"Push on the door when you hear the buzzer," said Lenny patiently.

"Heavy-duty security," said G-man. "I never seen anything like it."

"They had shit like this in New York," Rickey recalled.

The buzzer sounded again, Rickey pushed the door open, and they stepped into a foyer as large as their living room. On the left was a wet bar, on the right a walk-in closet full of golf gear. "Lenny?" Rickey called.

"In the kitchen," Lenny said from far away. "Come through the great room and follow the little hall."

The "great room" turned out to be a huge central atrium with a ceiling at least twenty feet high. A curving staircase swept up to a gallery edged with more white ironwork;

behind it could be seen the shadowy rooms of the second floor. The carpet was white, as was the sectional leather sofa. A pair of chef's clogs discarded near the sofa and a DVD of *The Good, The Bad, and The Ugly* on the glass coffee table were the only signs of human habitation.

"This must be the little hall," said G-man. It was as wide as their entire shotgun house. They followed it to the kitchen, where they could hear Lenny's voice.

"So I said, 'Well, I just think I ought to be able to buy fish from anybody I want, if it's good fish,'" Lenny was telling a woman seated on a barstool at one of his gorgeous granite countertops. The woman smiled and nodded, obviously trying to look interested. She was a groomed, toned blonde, but her tight black dress and carefully made-up face gave her the appearance of Sunday-morning leftovers.

"I gotta go," she said, eyeing the newcomers.

"OK, honey, you gonna be at the club tomorrow?"

"No, I don't work Mondays. I gotta go shopping."

"Right. I'll call you."

"Nice to meet you," she said to Rickey and G-man as she left, though they had not been introduced.

Lenny stood at the double sink rinsing dishes. He was a stocky man of middling height with a face that was square and honest until he smiled; then it split into a leer that made everyone nervous. He wore a pair of boxer shorts and a wife-beater undershirt from which springy black hair poked in all directions. His eyes were puffy, his upper lip and jaw dark with beard shadow. He was an appalling sight. Rickey and G-man barely noticed. They were too busy looking at his kitchen, which was absolutely beautiful.

In addition to the granite tops, Lenny had a six-by-nine-foot butcher's block with storage space underneath. A smaller block bristled with the handles of heavy carbon-steel knives. There was a six-burner stove, a pair of dishwashers, an enormous reach-in refrigerator, and a wood-burning tandoori oven that shared a hood with a grill out on the patio. The stunning array of appliances included a twenty-five-quart standing Hobart mixer, a big Robot-Coupe food processor, and a 1940s-style silver bar blender.

Perhaps Lenny was aware of the effect his kitchen had on younger, poorer cooks, because he allowed them to drool for a few minutes before he turned away from the sink, wiping his hairy hands on a cotton towel. He draped the towel over his shoulder and came forward to greet them. "Rickey, thanks for coming. G-man, good to meet you."

"Lenny," said G-man faintly. He had just noticed a thirty-piece collection of Le Creuset cookware on a set of shelves near the reach-in, and he was wondering how the shelves kept from collapsing under the weight of the massive pots.

"Wow," said Rickey at last. "Lenny, I'm sorry, our mouths must be hanging open. This is the most beautiful kitchen we ever seen."

"Yeah, it's nice, huh? I love my new stove. I did an endorsement deal with Viking last year—they set me up with that baby. I had an Aga in here before, but I like this one better. Hey, excuse me a minute, let me go put something on."

Lenny left the kitchen. G-man poked Rickey and pointed at the shelf of Le Creuset. Rickey was examining a red Dutch oven when Lenny came back in pulling a golf shirt over his head. He had put on pants and slicked down his thick dark hair with some sort of gel, but he still had an unkempt look, fuzzy around the edges somehow. Rickey wondered how long it took to groom him for television appearances.

Lenny handed them bottles of beer, then took a pan of ribs from the fridge, poured the excess marinade into one of the sinks, and rubbed the meat with a spice blend from a jar with his picture on it. "Come on out in the yard," he said. "We can get these ribs going." He'd been in New Orleans long enough that his nasal Maine accent had begun to soften around the edges, but it sharpened up every now and then— *can* sounded more like *kyan*, and *yard* was very nearly *ya'ad*. To their untraveled ears, he sounded foreign and slightly nerdy. *At least he doesn't say New Or-LEEENZ,* Rickey thought.

They followed Lenny through sliding glass doors to the patio, where he set the pan on a picnic table and began to fire up the grill. A lush expanse of lawn rolled away to the top of the levee. In its center, an egret perched on one leg like a snowy scrap of origami against a green background.

"So I guess you know my history," Lenny said. "I was wondering about yours. How'd you guys come up? What's your training?"

"We've just worked at a bunch of places around town," said Rickey. "We been in the business since we were fifteen. Started out as dishwashers and worked our way up. Most of what I really know about cooking, I learned from Paco Valdeon at the Peychaud Grill."

"I've heard about Paco. Talented guy. Whatever happened to him?"

"Last I heard, he had a place on the beach in Mexico.

Some crappy little shack serving grilled lobster and fish steamed in banana leaves. It sounds great, but I wonder if anybody down there appreciates him."

"I mostly learned to cook from my mom and sisters," said G-man.

"You come from a big family?"

"Youngest of six kids."

"I thought I heard one of you went to CIA."

"That was me," Rickey said. "I didn't graduate, though. I left after a few months."

"How come?"

"Well." What the hell, Rickey decided; he might as well let Lenny know he was a degenerate from the get-go. "I kinda got kicked out for beating up a guy."

"No kidding? What'd you do that for?"

"He was an asshole. He was always giving me a lot of crap, and finally I just punched him out in Skills class."

"Right there in the kitchen, huh?"

"Yeah," said Rickey. "You went to CIA?"

"No, but I've visited the campus. So what kind of crap was this guy giving you? How come you allowed him to piss you off so much?"

No way was he going to tell Lenny the whole story, at least not yet. "He didn't respect New Orleans cooking, for one thing," Rickey said. "He thought we were just some region of the United States. He acted like nobody from here could possibly be any good." And that was true; that had been part of it.

"You get this a lot? People taking a dislike to you for no reason?"

"No. Just that guy, and now Mike."

"That's cool," said Lenny. "Anyway, I suppose you're wondering why you're here. To listen to the tape, sure. But you could have come by the restaurant for that. Right?"

"I guess," said Rickey.

Lenny put the ribs on the grill and turned them with a pair of tongs, letting the flames lick every part of the meat. "So why do you think I asked you out here?"

They glanced at each other. G-man shrugged. "I got no idea," said Rickey.

"Really? No idea at all? Or maybe you sort of have an idea, but you don't want to say so until you see if it's the same idea I have?"

"No. No idea at all."

"OK. You're being honest or you don't quite trust me yet. Either one works for me."

Rickey was starting to lose his patience. "Lenny, are you just jacking us around or what?"

"Easy," G-man murmured.

Lenny was unperturbed. "Yeah, I guess I am jacking you around a little. I like to do that when I'm thinking about working with somebody. To see how much I can get away with."

"Working with somebody?"

"Well, maybe. If you're interested. Like I told you on the phone, I've heard good things about you guys. And I like your restaurant concept."

Rickey stared wildly at G-man, who shook his head, signaling that *he* hadn't been talking to anybody. "What concept?" Rickey said.

"Very good. I could just be fishing, right? I might not know anything at all about this place you're opening. I do, though. Liquor." Lenny smiled at the ribs. "Liquor in every damn dish. I love it. It's perfect for New Orleans."

"Goddamn it!" said Rickey. "Fucking Anthony B!" He couldn't help it. It had to be Anthony; they hadn't told anybody else about the concept. "So did you hear it straight from him, or is it all over town?"

"No, it's not all over town. Anthony and I go way back. He spent a summer up in Maine when we were sixteen—fell in love with my sister. She's married to another guy now, but I kept in touch with Anthony. When I came down here, he introduced me to a lot of people. I don't know if I'd be where I am now without him. He helped me out a lot."

"Yeah, I guess he's still helping people out. Telling them other people's ideas and shit."

"Aw, Rickey, don't be like that. We drink, we tell each other stuff. If I wasn't interested, I never would have called you. I'm not out to steal your idea."

"I guess not," said Rickey. In truth, he didn't know what to think, but there was no point in pissing Lenny off. "You don't need to steal my idea, you got plenty ideas of your own. It's just, well . . ."

"It's just, well, you been working for assholes too long, and you *know* this is a good idea, and you're afraid it might be the best one you ever have. Right? I hear you. I've been there. I wasn't always a rich dickhead with three restaurants. But I don't worry about it. I'm doing all right, huh?"

Lenny actually seemed to expect some kind of reply, so G-man jumped in with, "Yeah, Lenny, you're doing great."

"Pretty great, anyway. I'm not so sure about Sundae Dinner. I think that might have been a dumb idea. Liquor, though, that's brilliant. You guys will make a fortune."

"I don't see how," said Rickey. "All we're doing now is cooking in a bar. We got no money. I got no idea what permits we'd even need. You're taking this way too seriously."

"And you're not taking it seriously *enough,*" Lenny told him. "Don't you see? Your concept is so perfect for this city, I can't believe nobody came up with it yet. You can't afford to fuck around. You need to move on it before a bigger asshole than me hears about it, decides to swipe it from you, and makes all the money that should've been yours. Hell, Anthony B only told me about it because he's worried. He thinks you're going to bring in too much business. He loves his little bar, you know? He doesn't want to turn it into some trendy restaurant. But he wants to see you do well with this, and he knows I can help you."

"But why do you want to?"

"Three main reasons. Anthony thinks you're serious cooks. I respect that. Also, I know people think I'm just cooking for the tourists, but I really love this city. I realized it would be stupid to pour my money into some cash-cow place in Vegas when I could be investing in young chefs right here."

"What's the third reason?"

"Well, it's not as important as the other two." Lenny finished searing the meat and closed the grill top. "But Mike Mouton really doesn't like you, Rickey, and I wouldn't mind spiking that weasel-dick bastard. Somebody sure needs to. Speaking of which, these ribs have awhile to go yet. You want to go in my office and listen to that tape?"

o o o

The tape was worse than Rickey had expected. From the moment it clicked on, when Lenny said "I'm calling about a reference for your saucier" and Mike replied "Where do I even start?" Rickey doubted he would be able to keep his hands off Mike's throat if he ever saw the guy again.

"I'd never have hired him if I'd had a better candidate," Mike said. "You know where his last job was?"

There was a rustle of papers on Lenny's end. "Says here he was sauté cook at Maison Dupuy."

Mike laughed. "Not hardly. That was his second-to-last job. His *last* job was in the kitchen at Tequilatown, and he got fired. He didn't mention it when he applied here either, but somebody told me about it. I got a lot of connections, you know."

"Know what they fired him for?"

"Drinking on the job," Mike said ominously.

"Oh yeah, I think I heard about that. The whole crew was fired, weren't they? Some stupid rule about not even drinking one beer."

Mike hesitated, then said, "Well, but he lied on the application."

"Lied? He omitted a credential. That's not lying. Hell, I've done it myself. Do you have some kind of grudge against this guy?"

"I wouldn't exactly call it a grudge," said Mike. "Rickey's got a bad attitude, is all. My whole crew does, but Rickey's the worst of them. They've all been mouthing off to me more than usual since he got here."

"So he has a bad attitude. What about his kitchen skills?"

"He's nothing special in that department. Typical New Orleans line cook—does the least he can get away with, tries to hide it when he fucks up."

"Does he fuck up a lot?"

"Let's just say we've had a lot of complaints about the food since he started working here."

"Uh huh. How many complaints did you get before he started?"

"Aw, you know the tourist crowd. Somebody's always bitching."

"What does Chef Roger think of Rickey?"

"Fucking Roger, he acts like his whole crew is perfect because it means less work for him. Hell, Lenny, I do most of the work around here myself—I gotta have a little pick-me-up to keep these jerks in line. I don't know if you know Roger, but—"

"He's actually a friend of mine."

"Oh! He's not so bad. Nice guy, you know? Just doesn't ride 'em hard enough in my opinion."

"OK, I'm a little confused, Mike. I'm getting some mixed messages. You keep telling me Rickey's a fuckup, but I'm not hearing where he's actually fucked up."

"Well . . ." Rickey could almost hear the wheels turning in Mike's mind. "He ruined an expensive piece of equipment not too long ago. A puree wand. He left it in the oven overnight, then turned on the oven and melted it."

"That's a fucking lie!" Rickey yelled, springing to his feet. "Somebody on the PM crew left it there, and he god-damn well knows it!"

"Take it easy," said Lenny, who was lounging comfortably behind an enormous desk. "I know Mike Mouton's a liar. Don't worry about it."

Rickey sank back into his chair. On the tape, Lenny was saying, "So, for the record, you think I shouldn't hire Rickey?"

"Absolutely not. I don't mean to bad-mouth the kid— I'm just trying to do you a favor here, Lenny. I'm gonna fire him myself, soon as I find—"

"That's pretty much it," Lenny told Rickey and G-man, turning off the tape recorder. "The rest of it's just Mike setting race relations back a hundred years. I don't feel like hearing that again."

"Jesus," said G-man. They both turned to look at Rickey, who was contorted in the big leather chair, his fingers snarled in his hair so deeply that he might have been trying to rip it out by its unbleached roots.

"You guys ready to eat?" said Lenny.

chapter 5

We make a version of this salad at Crescent," Lenny said. "It's a little too nouvelle-ish for Lenny's. Good, though."

It *was* good, a wilted-arugula deal with big Gulf shrimp, toasted pecans, and a red pepper-bacon dressing. G-man put some more on his plate and watched Rickey gnaw on a pork rib as if it were Mike Mouton's jugular. Rickey hadn't even cringed at the word *nouvelle-ish*; he must be really pissed.

G-man could see why, more or less. Of course Mike's lies were infuriating, but they'd worked for assholes before. Rickey had a good résumé; it wasn't as if he needed Mike's reference. After the things they'd talked about today with Lenny, they might not need anybody's reference. But Rickey said little and smiled less. He sat at the picnic table with his legs crossed and his shoulders hunched, barely touching the salad or the asparagus Lenny had roasted, just gnashing on bones.

G-man couldn't stop eating. He hardly remembered the last time he'd had asparagus, and he was excited by Lenny's interest in Rickey's idea. Sure, they'd made fun of Lenny, but was that any reason not to let him set them up with the restaurant of their dreams? G-man didn't think so.

He was worried, though, about what Rickey thought. He hoped this wasn't going to become an issue of integrity, with Rickey saying stuff like "We don't need his fucking money!" They couldn't afford integrity. With no cash and no prospects of their own, they most certainly *did* need Lenny's fucking money, or somebody's. But Rickey could be stubborn about things like that. G-man liked this quality to a point, since he himself was more easygoing. If Rickey wasn't a bit of a hardass, he supposed, they would be at the world's mercy. Just now, though, he was worried that Rickey might throw away the chance of a lifetime because he was pissed about Mike, or because he thought Lenny was trying to steal his idea, or whatever damn thing had upset him. Though he'd been having a pretty good time, G-man was almost relieved when Rickey pushed his plate away and said, "I think we better go." It was rude as hell, but it was better than saying something he wouldn't be able to take back.

Lenny didn't seem offended. "Sure, you have a lot to think about. Let me know when you get your menu up and running at the Apostle. I'll come by and check it out. We'll talk soon." He gave them his business card, which featured a little cartoon of himself in a toque and kerchief, and walked them to the door.

"Bye, Lenny," said G-man a little sadly. It really was the nicest outing he'd had in a long time.

"*Byyyyye, Lenny,*" Rickey mocked in a high voice as soon as the door closed.

"Aw, fuck you. You wanna tell me what's wrong, I'll be

happy to listen. But don't start with a bunch of crap, because I'm not in the mood for it." G-man turned and started for the bus stop.

"You know what's wrong!" Rickey said, following. "You were there!"

"Rickey, I realize this may come as a shock, but I *don't* always know what's going on inside that little head of yours. Once in a while you just gotta grit your teeth and *tell* me. Is it Mike? Did you really let him get to you that much?"

"Dude—" Rickey flung his arms wide, as if overwhelmed by the enormity of his troubles. "Where do I even start? Am I just nuts, is that why I have to *tell* you what's wrong? Let's see. I got Mike out to stab me in the back. I got a self-proclaimed rich dickhead maybe trying to steal my idea before we even get started. I got your retard boss—"

"Anthony's your boss now too."

"Yeah, great, thanks. I got *our* retard boss telling my business all over town. Is that enough, or should I try to think of some other things that suck?"

"Well, that's just it—you *were* sitting there thinking of things that suck, back at Lenny's. I could see you doing it. What if Lenny really does want to help us? You know of a better way we're gonna get this thing started?"

"I know we need money. I just wasn't planning on getting it from Lenny Duveteaux."

"You see anybody else offering?"

"No, but maybe we could get a bank loan or something."

"Yeah, right—couple of slackers, no house, no car, no credit—they're really gonna be lining up to give us a big wad of cash."

"My mom has her house, she got it in the divorce. Maybe she'd cosign."

"Dude! What the fuck is so bad about Lenny that you'd let your *mom* put up her *house* rather than just take money he can afford to give us?"

"I don't trust him. I don't want to be in debt to him."

"I don't think he wants us to be in debt to him. He wants a piece of Liquor because he thinks it'll make money. He'd make money too. How would we be in debt?"

"We'd just *owe* him," said Rickey. "Don't you see? Debt isn't all about money. He'd have helped us—we'd owe him."

"I don't see what would be so bad about that."

"You want to owe your success to that guy?"

"Look, if we make this thing work, the success will be ours. Your idea—our food—period. We won't *owe* it to anybody. But we gotta get a leg up from somebody, and I wouldn't mind if it was Lenny. I didn't think he was so bad. I kinda liked him."

Rickey did not answer. He just looked helplessly at the sky, as if hoping God would answer for G-man's untenable and inexplicable opinion.

"C'mon, what was so bad about him? He tried to do you a favor."

"What, playing me that tape?"

"Well—yeah."

"You really think that was a *favor*? You're not kidding me? Then maybe we don't even need to be having this conversation, because with that kinda mentality, maybe you'd be happier just working for somebody else all your life."

They boarded the bus without saying another word and

sat silent and scowling across the aisle from each other all the way back to Marengo Street.

°   °   °

G-man lay awake in the dark. A glass of cheap bourbon and ice sat dripping on the floor beside the bed, but he had hardly touched it, figuring that even if he drank himself to sleep he'd just wake up with a headache in a couple of hours. He could hear Rickey in the kitchen, banging sheet pans around, slamming the oven door. When Rickey was upset, he almost always made cheese straws. They were one of the first things he had ever learned to cook, and making them seemed to comfort him.

So, he wondered, how was it that you could know a person well enough to predict what he would cook at a difficult moment, but not to understand why the moment was so difficult? Maybe Rickey was right about him—maybe he *would* be better off always working for somebody else. Maybe he didn't have what it took to run a restaurant. He'd always assumed that if they had their own place, Rickey would be the chef and he'd be the sous chef. That was how their relationship worked. Rickey had always been a little smarter, a little more in charge. But did that mean G-man wasn't chef material? He thought of something his own mother had once pointed out to him: *The trouble with you, Gary, is when your friend Rickey says something, you take it as the gospel truth.*

He wondered whether that really was his trouble. All in all, it seemed that his life with Rickey had been remarkably trouble-free. There had been all sorts of outside trouble, sure, ever since they were teenagers and their families plotted to send Rickey away to culinary school. That had come pretty close to separating them for good, but nothing else ever had.

Though he'd never admit it to Rickey, G-man had actually liked their stint at Reilly's, the stodgy old hotel restaurant, better than their apocalyptic years at the Peychaud Grill. Rickey loved the Peychaud because that was where he had truly become a hardcore cook. He'd always *wanted* to be hardcore, but he hadn't really known how until Chef Paco took his methods apart and said *No,* this *is how you cook.* It was the best kitchen they'd ever worked in, but after-hours life at the Peychaud was exhausting almost beyond endurance, even for a couple of healthy young men who'd learned how to drink and smoke pot before they knew how to drive a car. G-man often found himself thinking nostalgically of Reilly's, where the work was hard but predictable, where the crew was amiable but not close. They'd gone home when their shifts were done; there had been time to talk, have sex, or just lie around together, things hard to come by when they still lived with their parents. At the Peychaud Grill these activities became catch-as-catch-can, all but lost in a haze of bourbon, beer, bud, and blow. G-man was almost glad when the place imploded. Rickey wasn't glad, but G-man could see that he wasn't surprised either; the Peychaud had always had the feel of a juggernaut gathering steam for its own destruction.

Since then, life had been good. Sometimes they were broke, sometimes they were tired, but they had a nice time together. G-man supposed "nice" would never be good enough for Rickey. He had that restless spirit that had lured him off to New York, made him love the Peychaud Grill, and now convinced him he could open his own restaurant on the strength of one crazy-genius idea. Well, hell, maybe he could. If he did, then G-man would be his sous chef. Maybe Rickey wasn't always fair to him, but Rickey made him happy. He wanted Rickey to be happy too, and Rickey would never be happy as long as he was bored. G-man got up, pulled on a pair of pants, and went to the kitchen.

From the looks of it, Rickey intended to make enough cheese straws to supply every wedding reception, confirmation, and bar mitzvah in New Orleans for the next month. He had two sheet pans in the oven and a big plastic-wrapped wad of dough chilling in the fridge, and he was kneading handfuls of grated Cheddar into another batch of dough as G-man came in.

"You really think Anthony's stupid?" said G-man, parking himself at the table.

At first he didn't think Rickey was going to answer. Then Rickey shrugged and said grudgingly, "I don't think he's the sharpest knife in the drawer."

"Maybe that's why he's letting us take over his kitchen."

Rickey laughed. G-man could tell he was trying not to, but they had never been able to stay mad at each other for very long. "I shouldn't have said that shit to you," Rickey admitted. "About working for other people. I don't really believe it. I'm just freaked out."

"I know you are. It's OK."

Rickey set a plate of hot, golden cheese straws on the table. They sat there munching, not saying anything for a while, glad that things were comfortable between them again.

"These are really good," said G-man. "Did you do something different?"

"That's why I made so many. I put a couple tablespoons of cognac in this batch. The ones in the fridge have bourbon, and for the next batch I was gonna try rum."

"Rum?" said G-man doubtfully.

"Sure, why not? I figure it'll make 'em kinda sweet. If they suck, hey, we got plenty more."

"That's true."

"I didn't mean to make so many, but I don't know if I can sleep. I can't stop thinking about Lenny and Mike and Anthony B and all these fuckers . . ."

"Hang on. I got a surprise for you." G-man went into the bedroom, removed a choupique caviar tin from the top dresser drawer, and returned to the kitchen. He opened the tin to reveal a wooden dugout pipe and a single fragrant bud of sinsemilla.

"Sweetheart! You been holding out on me. Where'd you get that?"

"Laura gave it to me on Saturday night. I decided to save it for a time of need."

"This is a time of need, all right. Let's fire it up."

"Sure you wouldn't rather make a few more cheese straws?"

"Blow me."

"Later."

G-man crumbled part of the bud into the bowl, and they sat at the table passing it back and forth, taking deep lungfuls of the sweet, relaxing smoke. Rickey rested an elbow on the table, propped his head on his hand, and closed his eyes, smiling. G-man thought he might be asleep until he said, "You really think we ought to take money from Lenny?"

"I think we ought to consider it."

"You don't think he wants to rip us off?"

"I don't think we have to let him."

"You think—"

"I think we ought to get some sleep and talk about it tomorrow," said G-man, and they did.

°   °   °

Lenny Duveteaux shrugged off a white bathrobe as thick and soft as Chantilly cream, turned on the whirlpool jets, and stepped into his sunken tub. His springy, abundant body hair formed dark whorls on his skin as he lowered himself into the water. He reached for his glass of Chateau d'Yquem—a 1985, not the best year he'd ever had but pretty damn good—and rolled the complex golden wine around in his mouth as he thought about all the money he and these kids were going to make off each other.

They didn't have a clue, not yet. They knew they'd be lucky just to get a restaurant off the ground; even Rickey didn't understand the full potential of his idea. When Lenny first came to New Orleans, he'd been shocked by how much people drank. Three-martini lunches had gone out with the eighties elsewhere. Here, no one raised an eyebrow if you had four. The absorption of large amounts of alcohol was as much a part of the culture as the splashy Catholicism, the three seasons of sweltering heat, the after-school streets alive with young black boys blowing sour notes on rented trumpets. People here loved to drink, and they loved to have fun when they drank; they filled the bars and toasted each other across the tables and nattered about the Saints, politics, what they had eaten for lunch, what they were going to eat for dinner. They were absolutely primed for a restaurant like the one Rickey wanted to start.

When Anthony B first told him about the idea, Lenny was doubtful. He'd dragged Anthony to the Gold Club one night, and while Anthony stared nervously at the acres of tanned, spangled, naked flesh swirling about the place, Lenny sipped cognac and bitched about the moribund state of the New Orleans restaurant scene. He didn't even mean it; he was just pissed because no one had ordered the gorgeous Kumamoto oysters he'd had on special at Crescent that night. "Nobody wants to try anything new," he complained. "You people are perfectly happy eating the same shit you ate in 1840."

"Aw, I'm not so sure of that," Anthony had said. "I know a couple kids who got a real good idea—but no money to do anything about it."

Lenny listened to the idea and immediately recognized its genius. "They're good cooks?" he said. "They're not a couple of shoemakers?"

"What's a shoemaker?" asked the stunning young woman who sat close beside Lenny in the leatherette booth, absently tracing designs on his knee with one gold-lacquered, talonlike nail.

"A bad cook," Lenny told her. "A cook who doesn't give a shit about the food."

"Really? Why they call it that?"

"I don't know, honey."

"I do," Anthony surprised him by saying. "You ever heard of Willie Shoemaker?" The stripper—who was all of twenty-two—looked blank, but Lenny nodded. "He was a great jockey, but he made one granddaddy of a mistake in his career. He was on Gallant Man in the '57 Derby, and somehow or other he mistook the sixteenth pole for the finish line. Stood up in the stirrups and threw the race—Iron Liege won by a nose."

"What's that got to do with bad cooks?" asked Lenny, fascinated.

"Well, the way I heard it, this chef had bet his paycheck on Gallant Man. Lost it all and never forgave the jock. From then on, every time one of his cooks screwed something up, the chef would yell 'Shoemaker!' I guess it just spread. Anyway, no, Rickey and G ain't shoemakers—they're real good cooks."

Lenny had no idea if the Willie Shoemaker tale was true, but it was the kind of story New Orleanians loved to tell in bars. He made a mental note of the young cooks' names and tracked Rickey down at Escargot's.

Though he knew they were suspicious of his motives, Lenny had been impressed with them, and particularly with Rickey. There was a young man who wasn't going to let much of anything turn him aside from his goal. G-man lacked that intensity, but it was obvious that he would do whatever Rickey wanted him to, and Lenny suspected he was a stabilizing influence on Rickey. Also, for a couple of nobody line cooks, they had charisma. People sneered at the idea that a chef's personality should factor into a restaurant's success or failure, but Lenny knew it was important.

Lenny didn't kid himself about his basic abilities. He could cook, but there were better chefs in New Orleans, and most of them weren't doing half the business he did. Lots of potential customers were intimidated by their own ideas of fine dining. They thought the menu would be in French, they wouldn't know which fork to use, they'd be scorned by highfalutin maître d's. If they saw the chef on TV acting like a regular guy, even poking a little fun at his own reputation, they were more likely to come. He didn't plan to put Rickey and G-man on TV just yet, but he thought people would like them. They were personable, good-looking, even reasonably well-spoken for a couple of kids who'd grown up in the Lower Ninth Ward. They said "dis" and "dat" and "ax a question" and "t'row out da gawbage," but that was OK in the restaurant world; people still saw chefs as essentially blue-collar, though tinged with a glamour they hadn't had when Lenny was coming up.

People tended to assume Lenny was a culinary school graduate, as if anyone who'd gotten so far in the competitive restaurant world must have a degree. He didn't. Like Rickey and G-man, he'd begun cooking in his teens. The summer after high school, he got a pantry job at the Schooner, a busy seafood joint in Portland. At first he just made salads and did prep work, deveining shrimp, separating curly parsley into sprigs to garnish plates, slicing thousands and thousands of lemons. The chef-owner, Jerome McElroy, understood the necessity of catering to tourists but had a secret yen for the exotic. In the off-season, he'd make things like lobster terrine and Provençal fish stew. Lenny was so interested in these flights of fancy that Chef Jerome took a liking to him. The chef moved him to the hot line and occasionally let him make a dinner special. Lenny began to get his chops.

He stayed at the Schooner for four years, eventually becoming one of Chef Jerome's three sous chefs. The others were a waste case named Seth and a twenty-year-old girl named Diane. Lenny was the best of the three; Chef Jerome always scheduled him for the busiest nights and gave him more creative control than the other two. At the beginning of Lenny's fifth year there, Chef Jerome started talking about making him a partner in the restaurant. For a thousand dollars, Chef said, Lenny could have a ten percent share. It wasn't much money, but Chef was in his late forties, single and childless, and hoping to retire by the time he hit fifty-five. He was looking for someone he trusted to take over someday.

Lenny got some of the money from his parents and scraped together the rest. Chef Jerome promised him they'd draw up the legal papers soon. Lenny kept working the line, secure in the belief that he'd soon be part owner of a restaurant. He really thought he had it made.

One day the crew showed up for work to find the doors locked. Calls went unanswered. Everybody was owed at least a week's pay, and of course Chef Jerome had Lenny's thousand dollars. Diane, the sous chef, was gone too. It transpired that Chef had been sleeping with her for several months, she was pregnant, and they'd last been seen boarding a lobster boat rumored to do a brisk business running bales of marijuana to and from Canada. The Schooner turned out to be heavily mortgaged. There was even a lien on the property that Lenny hadn't known about.

No one ever got paid, and Lenny never heard from Chef Jerome again. One night he and Seth the waste case went out drinking, did a bunch of coke, wrote "THIEVING SCUM" on a sweet potato with Magic Marker, and hurled the makeshift missile through one of the Schooner's big plate-glass windows. It was a pointless act of vandalism that Lenny never regretted, since it got most of the anger out of his system. He understood that the chef had been completely unhinged by sex with a twenty-year-old, and that the twenty-year-old would leave him broke, alone, and in Canada. Lenny couldn't even stay angry at Diane: he'd seen what women cooks had to put up with working in kitchens dominated by men who didn't appreciate female encroachment on their turf.

He didn't hate Chef Jerome or Diane. Lenny liked to think he was incapable of such an unproductive emotion as hate. What bothered him, and soon came to obsess him, was the fact that he had fallen for it. He couldn't stand the thought that someone had tricked him and gotten away with it. Since he'd stupidly let the chef slide by without signing the papers that would give him part ownership of the Schooner, there was no proof that Lenny had ever had any rights at all. He was tormented by the memory of certain phone conversations in which he and Chef Jerome had discussed the deal. If only he had a record of those conversations, he would have proof. The fact that there was nothing left worth proving seemed beside the point. The ideal thing would be to have one's entire life on tape. When someone tried to lie to you or fuck you over, you could just rewind to the relevant part and prove them wrong.

All these years later, Lenny thought of Chef Jerome with something resembling fondness. After all, the guy had taught him almost everything he knew about cooking. Lenny went into the Schooner a scared pantry bitch and came out a roller. He'd found that most cooks had a similar figure in their past, someone who'd given them permission to be serious about food. Rickey's had been Paco Valdeon of the Peychaud Grill; it was obvious when Rickey talked about the guy.

Lenny knew Rickey didn't trust him, and there was no reason Rickey should, not yet. Lenny wouldn't have been as impressed with someone who trusted him right away. That would come in time, though, and they'd all make a lot of money, and the balance of righteousness would come that much closer to being restored.

He drained his wineglass, reached over to the faucets, and turned on the water as hot as it would go. He put his hand under the gushing stream and held it there, kitchen-callused palm taking the heat but not feeling the pain. Lenny knew people called him the Nixon of the New Orleans restaurant world, but he believed he had far more in common with G. Gordon Liddy.

chapter 6

A subtle, musky perfume filled the kitchen of the Apostle Bar. Rickey stood looking at a ramekin full of uncooked white rice in which three knobbly grayish-black objects were half buried. One was the size of a Ping-Pong ball, the other two slightly smaller. He'd found the ramekin sitting on the counter when he and G-man arrived for their shift a few minutes ago. Rickey poked at the rice with his forefinger, and the fragrance intensified, making his mouth water.

G-man came in from the storage room buttoning his white jacket. "What's that?"

"Black truffles."

"You're kidding. Dried?"

"No, fresh."

G-man let out a low whistle. "That's like two hundred dollars' worth of truffles, maybe a little less if Anthony got a deal. Lenny must have warned him about our meeting."

"He's gonna have to do more than buy me truffles if he wants me to stop being pissed at him." Rickey leaned over the ramekin and stirred the rice again, inhaling deeply. "Damn, they're nice, though."

"So what you want to make?"

"Don't know. A potato cake Périgord, maybe, or some kind of bruschetta . . ."

They had stashed some of their cookbooks in the Apostle Bar's kitchen and were flipping through these when Anthony came in. "Hey, guys."

"Where y'at, Anthony," said G-man. Rickey muttered something and buried his nose in Richard Olney's *The French Menu Cookbook*.

"Rickey, how you like them truffles?"

"They're real nice." Rickey didn't look up.

"I thought you'd like to have 'em for your first night. They're flown in fresh from Italy."

"Gee, Anthony, I never would have known that. Thanks a lot for telling me."

"I guess you're pretty upset about Lenny, huh?"

"I'm not upset about Lenny."

Anthony looked relieved. "You ain't? That's good."

"No. I'm upset about your *big fat fucking mouth!*"

"Aw, jeez, Rickey, I'm sorry. I knew you'd be mad. I didn't even mean to say nothing to him—we were just out drinking one night and—"

Rickey picked up his cookbook and left the kitchen.

"He's really mad, huh?" Anthony said sadly.

"He'll get over it."

Once Anthony was busy in the stockroom, Rickey came back with his recipe picked out. "Richard Olney has these sausages with cognac. He says it's traditional to serve them with oysters on the half shell." He unclamped the small meat grinder from the countertop and put it in the reach-in to chill, which would improve the texture of the forcemeat.

"Cool. I think I'm gonna do risotto balls with lemon vodka. We can serve them with some kinda dipping sauce."

"Can you prep up while I go get some hog casings for my sausages?"

"Sure, I got it under control."

"Anthony!" yelled Rickey. "Let me use your car . . . Where the fuck is he?"

"He always leaves the keys by the register."

"You want anything at Zanca's?"

"Yeah, pick me up some nice black olives. I'll do a tapenade."

"You got it."

Rickey left, and G-man set up their mise-en-place, the arrangement of ingredients and supplies that would take them through the night. Then he picked up his clipboard and examined a copy of the prep list. To someone who had never worked in a kitchen, this would appear to be—and was, really—written in a strange code. The various items could be checked, circled, double-circled, question-marked, exclamation-pointed, or crossed off altogether, depending on what needed to be done that day. Also on the clipboard were a photocopied order sheet, a list of purveyors' names and phone numbers, a sheaf of blank paper for notes, and a copy of the Apostle Bar menu that would make its debut tonight.

After knocking out a few quick pieces of prep work, G-man made his risotto, sautéing Arborio rice in butter and stirring in small amounts of chicken stock until it was rich and creamy. When he added the diced truffles, their intoxicating fragrance wafted around him. For service, he would form it into balls, panfrying them until they were golden-brown.

Anthony came into the kitchen. "Hey, that smells great."

"Just took it off the heat. You want a little taste?"

"Sure."

G-man spooned a portion of risotto into a ramekin. "Here you go. If it's cooled off too much, I can nuke it."

"No, this is perfect. And it's good, too. This's Italian, right?"

"Yeah, Anthony, it sure is."

"Aw, don't look at me that way. My family's from Sicily. They never made nothing like this."

"I know it. My mom was Mary Rose Bonano before she got married. Great cook, but I was eighteen before I found out all Italian food didn't have red gravy and breadcrumb stuffing."

"Rickey told you, huh?"

"No, that was one thing I managed to find out on my own."

Anthony finished his risotto and went to the sink to wash his ramekin. That was the kitchen experience in him, G-man thought; most owners would have left the dirty dish in the sink for somebody else to deal with.

"I'm real sorry Rickey is so mad," said Anthony.

"Don't be. You might've done us a big favor. Rickey will figure that out sooner or later." G-man considered. "Probably later."

° ° °

On his first full day in the Apostle Bar's kitchen, Rickey was happy to be out of the place for a while. It was exciting to be in charge of a kitchen with G-man, but today was one of those January days that felt like the middle of spring, and he was glad he'd decided on a special that required a supply run.

Anthony's old Continental sailed along Carrollton Avenue. The radio was tuned to a classic rock station, songs so old and corny that they were almost cool again. "I am the space cowboy," the radio sang, "I am the gangster of love." Just before he reached the watercourse of Bayou St. John, Rickey took a left into a neighborhood of shabby Victorian houses, prefab warehouses, and potholed one-way streets. There were several restaurant supply houses around here, including Zanca & Sons Wholesale Grocers, where Rickey pulled in. The delicious smell of the place hit him as soon as he walked through the door, an oily herbal savor composed of a thousand different notes. Rickey passed through the work area to the warehouse, where the aromas were even stronger.

"Rickey! How you doing?"

The young man approaching him was Joe Zanca, great-grandson of Salvatore "Mr. Sal" Zanca, who had come to New Orleans from Sicily and opened a little Italian grocery in 1899. Joe ran this place with his two older brothers. Rickey had never seen any of the Zancas outside the warehouse and could not picture them elsewhere; their aprons were always striped with flour, their sleeves stained with olive oil, their forearms muscular from hefting big wheels of cheese and hocks of meat.

Joe was a small nervous man with wounded-looking dark eyes magnified behind wire-rimmed glasses and wide, sensitive nostrils that flared when he talked. He was Rickey's favorite Zanca brother because he made a point of knowing as much as possible about every item in the warehouse, perhaps to compensate for being the baby of the family, perhaps just fascinated by food.

"I hear you're opening a restaurant," said Joe.

Rickey supposed he might as well get used to dealing with the rumor. "I don't know where that got started," he said. "My friend G-man and I are just doing a new dinner menu at the Apostle Bar, that's all. You got any hog casings?"

"Course I do. Come on back to the cooler with me."

They walked through the warehouse, past bins of flour and sesame seeds, earthen jars of olives, barrels of dried fava beans and chickpeas. There were shelves stacked with tins of anchovies, jars of capers, wax-covered wheels of cheese, olive oil in every shade from pale gold to dark, mossy green. Rickey followed Joe into a big walk-in cooler where Joe located the sausage casings in a far corner.

"What else for you today?"

"I need some pork loin and a little fatback. And how about pistachios? You got shelled pistachios?"

"Naturally," said Joe. "Beautiful Syrian pistachios. We Italians first got the pistachio from Syria, did you know that? In Venice they used to call it the Syrian nut."

"No, I sure didn't know that."

"It grows all over Asia Minor, but the Syrians were the first ones to trade it."

Rickey, who wasn't even sure where Asia Minor was, nodded sagely. As Joe weighed out his fatback, he decided to tease the grocer a little. "How about pigs, Joe? Where'd they first come from?"

Joe didn't miss a beat. "Well, that's interesting. The pig may have been domesticated in Iraq about seven thousand years before Christ. You won't hear that from your Nation of Islam, but a lot of people believe it."

"Huh," said Rickey. "That's interesting."

"I think so. Can I get you anything else?"

Rickey remembered the tapenade G-man wanted to serve with his rice balls. "Let me have a couple pints of kalamata olives."

"Oh, those are nice."

Joe helped Rickey carry his purchases out and load them into Anthony's car. As Rickey started the engine, he heard Joe call his name. He cranked the window down.

"Some people believe pigs were raised by man as early as the Mesolithic era," Joe said. "I personally find that unlikely, but I thought you might like to know anyway."

After concluding his business at Zanca & Sons, Rickey drove over to the industrial area between the French Quarter and the housing projects of Treme. Many of the old seafood wholesalers here had closed down in the past couple of decades, but his favorite, Old Country Seafood, was still going strong. It was run by a Croatian family, the Vojkoviches, who were as taciturn as the Zancas were effusive. Rickey didn't mind the lack of conversation. Croatians had been working the same oyster beds in the Louisiana bayous since the late eighteen hundreds; they had the best oysters in the city and they knew it. Mrs. Vojkovich in the front office wore an oyster-shaped pavé diamond pendant with a huge gray pearl at its center.

"Eight dozen," was all she said to him, writing out a bill for Anthony. Rickey loaded the Styrofoam boxes into the Continental's trunk and headed back toward Tchoupitoulas.

At the Apostle Bar, G-man had set up the mise-en-place and finished all the prep work. He pulled a Tupperware container out of the lowboy and handed it to Rickey. "Horseradish cream sauce with a touch of Bushmills Irish whiskey," he said. "I thought it might be nice with your sausages and oysters."

Rickey tasted the fluffy white sauce. It had a definite zing, but the mellowness of crème fraîche kept it from being overpowering. "That's perfect," he said. "Thanks, G."

"How's Joe?"

"Knowledgeable."

G-man pureed kalamatas, capers, and anchovies with vermouth and extra-virgin olive oil while Rickey got ready to make sausages. He unwrapped the pork from its pink butcher paper and fed it through a smallish blade of the grinder. After seasoning this mixture with garlic, chives, salt, and black pepper, he added coarsely chopped pistachios, a generous splash of cognac, and a finely diced truffle. The last three ingredients he mixed in with his hands, working the forcemeat until it felt silky but not crushing the delicate truffles.

G-man finished his tapenade and went out to the bar. He came back with a small blackboard and a box of colored chalk. Sitting on a barstool near the reach-in, balancing the board on his knees, he wrote "SPECIALS" in blue chalk and outlined the blue letters in yellow. Beneath this he wrote "Pan-Fried Risotto Balls with Black Truffles + Absolut Citron Vodka—Served with a Vermouth Tapenade." Then he looked up at Rickey. "How you want your special written up?"

"Uh . . . 'Bordelais Sausages and' . . . no, wait . . . 'Cognac Truffle Sausages and Oysters and' . . . hell, G, I don't know. I can't think right now. Would you figure something out for me?"

"Sure." G-man selected a piece of green chalk and wrote "Oysters on the Half Shell and House-Made Pork Sausages with Cognac, Pistachios + Black Truffles—Served with Bushmills Horseradish Cream Sauce." Beneath the descriptions of the specials he tried to draw a couple of truffles, but they came out looking like small turds and he erased them.

Rickey glanced over at the board. "Hey, that looks nice."

"Maybe I got an undiscovered talent."

"I'd stick to cooking if I were you. It pays better."

G-man carried the board back out and set it on a ledge over the bar. Dinner service began in an hour. Currently, the only customers in the bar were two dockworkers drinking beer and arguing about the Super Bowl. They didn't look as if they would be interested in either of the specials.

At six, Rickey and G-man replenished their already pristine mise-en-place. At 6:15 they topped up the squeeze bottles of olive oil, red pepper rouille, and cognac mustard they used to garnish the plates. At 6:22 an order for a burger and a plate of cheese fries came in. "Fuck!" said Rickey. "That's all anybody's gonna want!"

"C'mon, dude, it's just the early dinner crowd. It's the early dinner crowd in a *bar*. They'll start coming in later. Don't worry about it."

At ten to seven somebody ordered the risotto special. From there, the dinner service took off. It was only a small rush—the Apostle was only a small bar—but they were definitely hustling. Rickey realized he had completely spaced out on how to plate his special. He knew the sausages and oysters should alternate on the plate, and that the sauce should go in a little monkey dish in the center, but he hadn't really thought about what to *do* with the oysters. If he put them right on the plate, the shells would leak dirty water onto the sausages. G-man was busy frying rice balls and dropping batches of wings; there was no help to be had from that quarter. Rickey spooned three small mounds of rock salt onto the plate and nestled an oyster into each one. It wasn't the perfect solution—the salt might bleed onto his sausages—but it would work on the fly.

"Pick up two sausages!" he yelled, sliding them into the window for Laura to deliver.

"Pick up one balls and two wings!" G-man said when she came for the sausage plates.

"What y'all think this is, a restaurant? Do I look like a waitress to you? I got drinks to make."

"Then get Anthony to help you run plates!" said Rickey. "This shit's dying in the window!"

She gave him a dark look, picked up two plates, and walked away. A moment later Anthony appeared and grabbed the rest of the plates, checking the accompanying tickets to see where they needed to go. "We got a nice little crowd out there, guys."

"Cool," said Rickey. He'd have time to be pleased about it later. Right now he had oysters that needed shucking, sausages that needed poaching, and a pair of artichoke dips under the broiler.

"We're getting killed!" said G-man happily. They weren't really, but he found that he had missed being able to say it.

Around nine, people settled down to serious drinking and the orders tapered off for a while. They used the lull to prepare for the second, smaller rush that would come between midnight and two. This rush was important because it was composed largely of cooks from other restaurants getting off the dinner shift. If they discovered that they could get something decent to eat at the Apostle Bar, their word of mouth would be invaluable, not just for business but for the kitchen's reputation. Many of these cooks stuck their heads into the kitchen to razz, harass, and insult Rickey and G-man by way of greeting.

"Who told you y'all could cook? Your mommas?"

"When you opening your own place? You saving me a nice job on the hot line, right?"

"Y'all ain't drinking no *beer* back there, are you?" This last remark came from Terrance, Rickey's former coworker at Escargot's, who knew all about the Tequilatown debacle.

The cooks ate, drank, played video poker, went home or on to other bars. Rickey started cleaning up while G-man handled the few orders that still trickled in. These were mostly for small-hour drunks who didn't want anything fancy, and the night ended as it had begun, with burgers and fries. When Anthony came in and said, "Y'all can shut it down any time," they were surprised to see that it was 3:30 in the morning.

"Damn," said Rickey. "We did it."

"Course we did it. You think we were gonna do anything else?"

"I knew we'd do it, but I was afraid nobody would show up."

They put away the food, washed the dishes, wiped down the surfaces. G-man scrambled some eggs and shaved the remaining truffle over them. His risotto was gone, but a few of Rickey's sausages were left, and he put those on the side.

Laura came in as they were starting to eat. They

hunched protectively over the plate, and she rolled her eyes. "I don't like eggs *or* mushrooms, OK? I'm just bringing this in. Anthony told me to give it to you." She set a bottle of Taittinger and two champagne flutes on the counter and left the kitchen.

"So are you still mad at Anthony?" G-man asked Rickey.

"Truffles, Taittinger, *and* a great dinner crowd for our menu's first night? I'm not mad at anybody." Rickey uncorked the champagne. They lifted their glasses and grinned at each other like a couple of kids.

"Here's to Liquor."

"Here's to Liquor!"

They drained the glasses and poured some more.

chapter 8

HOLY SMOKE, THIS IS GOOD!

By Chase Haricot, Restaurant Critic

With a few exceptions, you don't go looking for great eats in New Orleans bars. Nor do you expect to get gourmet food after 10 p.m.—until recently our late-night options consisted mostly of greasy-spoon burgers, po-boys, and eggs. The Apostle Bar, an unlikely-looking little place on Tchoupitoulas Street, aims to change both of these unfortunate truths.

The ambiance (or lack thereof) offers no clue to the presence of good food. The Apostle is a typical neighborhood bar decorated with statues of saints and photographs of Saints. The faint smell of beer hangs over the long, polished bar and ten tables like the ghost of preseasons past. Trade here is a mix of hipster and blue-collar: the patrons at one table may sport facial piercings, while those at another call each other "Cap."

Owner Anthony Bonvillano has worked in restaurants around the city, but he doesn't cook any more. He leaves the kitchen duty to his two chefs,

John Rickey and Gary Stubbs. Though you wouldn't know it from tasting their food, these young men seem to have come out of nowhere. They've been working together for years, and between them, have racked up stints at Reilly's, La Tour Eiffel, the Peychaud Grill, and many others. Neither has been officially in charge of a kitchen, but they seem undaunted by the task. "We're just having fun," Chef Rickey says. "Relaxing. Doing the kind of food we want to do, with total creative control. It's great."

And it frequently is. The menu is an odd mix of bar snacks and what Rickey calls their "upscale" dishes. Both have moments of excellence. Well before the new menu debuted, regulars were buzzing about the slow, spicy burn of the tequila chicken wings, served with a creamy blue cheese dipping sauce in which (for a change) you can really taste the blue cheese. The "martini" muffuletta sandwich (bigger than a burger, smaller than the behemoths at Central Grocery) is updated with a gin-laced olive salad. These will satisfy any late-night drinking munchies, but it's with the "upscale" food that the chefs really shine. Prosciutto-wrapped figs marinated in Calvados are addictive. The hot artichoke dip is a local standard, but touched with cognac, it's one of the best in town. Specials have included a succulent duck breast with arugula, spiced pecans, and Southern Comfort reduction, a delightfully tender Southwestern pork chop with zesty tequila salsa, and the most authentic Oysters Rockefeller I've had outside of . . . well, you know where they were invented. It's so rare not to find them smothered in limp spinach, and so nice.

Sharp-eyed readers will notice a uniting theme in the Apostle's dishes. Does the bar setting dictate the food's, uh, high spirits? Perhaps. "I've always made a point of cooking with whatever's around," Rickey says. "Here at the Apostle, I guess that's liquor. To tell you the truth, we never even thought about it."

Table service can be iffy—the lone waitress seemed to actively resent serving us, and we were relieved when Bonvillano took over—and desserts are pretty much nonexistent unless you can get excited about vanilla ice cream drizzled with the liqueur of your choice. However, these are tolerable glitches in an exciting new operation. Next time I'm up late and hankering for something good to eat, I won't think of sullen waitresses or dull desserts— I'll think of those figs in Calvados.

A sidebar gave the Apostle Bar's location, hours, and average prices. At the top of the sidebar were three red beans, denoting a Very Good restaurant. Four beans were Excellent and five were Superior.

"THREE BEANS!" said Mike Mouton. "I don't believe this shit! Did they take the guy in the kitchen and suck his dick? I always knew Rickey was a fag. Seriously, you think they sucked his dick?"

"Damn if I know," said Terrance's cousin NuShawn, who had had the misfortune to come into Mike's office carrying a Friday newspaper. Mike had heard that the Apostle was going to be reviewed this week and had snatched the paper from under NuShawn's arm. He showed no signs of giving it back, either.

"You don't understand. This punk used to work for me. He was always giving me a lot of shit. Even tried to assault me in the kitchen, but I showed him a thing or two."

"He makin good money now?"

"Probably. You know how these deals work. He's a prettyboy, NuShawn, just another prettyboy chef. That's what matters to these critics. They don't care if somebody's talented, just so he's photogenic."

NuShawn studied Mike's narrow perspiring face, Mike's blank bloodshot eyes that always reminded him of those cheap peppermint drops you could pick up free at the cash registers of low-end restaurants. He didn't know what this Rickey looked like, but he could see why Mike might be jealous of a prettyboy. Then his mind returned quickly to business, as it tended to do. "You think this guy need anything?" he asked.

"What? Goddamn it, NuShawn! Just give me what I ordered and get out of here!"

"Can I have my paper back?"

"Here's an extra dollar. Buy yourself a new one. Go on. Vamoose."

NuShawn put a wrinkled brown envelope on Mike's desk and left the office. Mike glared at the newspaper for a while longer, started to crumple it, then changed his mind and slid it into a drawer.

° ° °

Laura waved the paper in Anthony's face. "Look at this. They thought I was a waitress! I wanted to wait tables, I'd get a job at a real restaurant. You gotta hire a waitress, Anthony."

"Aw, Laura, it ain't that bad. We don't need a waitress. I'm always here to help you take out plates when it gets busy."

"I don't *want* to take out plates. I'm not a damn waitress. I'm a bartender. If they're ordering food, they're ordering drinks. I make drinks, remember? Sooner or later I'm gonna drop one of these hot plates in somebody's lap and you're gonna be sorry."

"You won't drop nothing. You're a good waitress."

"I'M NOT A WAITRESS!"

"I know it, Laura, I meant to say you're good at whatever you do."

Laura scowled. "What was wrong with just running a bar? Why are you letting those two jerks take over the kitchen?"

"I thought you liked Rickey and G-man."

"I liked G-man all right when he was here by himself, but Rickey doesn't know when to shut up. They egg each other on. I swear to God, a few more nights of listening to them yell out that window—*'Laura! Pick up! I got hot shit here!'*—I'm gonna go back there and kick their butts."

"That's just how cooks talk when they're busy. You want to be a waitress, you gotta get used to it."

Anthony realized his mistake when he saw Laura rolling up the newspaper, but he could not move quickly enough to avoid being smacked over the head with it.

° ° °

Lenny was in Gulfport for the weekend, consulting with the GM of a new restaurant at the Pot O'Gold Casino. It was a nice gig—he got a hefty consultant's fee, a free suite, and a thousand dollars' worth of chips, and he didn't even have to put his name on the joint. As he had requested, a New Orleans paper was sent up with his coffee each morning.

He grinned as he read the review. Chase Haricot was a friend of his, and Lenny had bent his ear about the new menu at the Apostle Bar, but it sounded as if the boys had won him over on their own. Lenny wasn't surprised. He'd already eaten there a couple of times, and the food was terrific.

He sipped his coffee. It was hot and strong, but it didn't taste right because it lacked chicory. Draining the cup anyway, he picked up his cell phone and called his business manager, Bert Flanagan.

"See if you can set up a meeting with those two cooks I was telling you about. Get De La Cerda to come, too." Oscar De La Cerda was Lenny's lawyer. "I think it's time we all had ourselves a talk."

° ° °

Rickey was on the phone with his mother.

"I bought me ten copies of the paper today!" she said in her helium-balloon voice, the one she always used when she was excited. "I give 'em to Claude, and Darlene, and Miz Morrison—that nice colored lady works by the corner grocery, you remember?"

"Momma, you ought to say black."

"Huh?"

"You ought to say Miz Morrison is black. Not colored."

"Aw, you know I can't remember that. Miz Morrison don't care. You sure you supposed to say black? I thought it was African-American now."

"I don't know about that African-American stuff. Any of the black guys I work with heard me say that, they'd laugh their asses off."

"Well, anyway, babe, I'm so proud of you. 'He ain't never been in charge of no kitchen before, but he's doing fantastic!' It says so right here in the paper!"

"Yeah, more or less."

"How's Gary? He's doing good?"

"Oh, yeah. I couldn't do this without him."

"You met any nice girls?"

Rickey refrained from heaving a deep sigh. He had come back from the CIA, moved in with G-man, and eventually reconciled with his mother. He knew she loved him and needed him. Brenda Crabtree (she'd reverted to her maiden name) made a flighty impression on people, but she was no dummy—she'd raised him while working as an accountant at a Ninth Ward restaurant, had made sure he got to school even if the school wasn't very good, had called Rickey's father in California and threatened him with court when the child-support payments didn't come on time. On the subject of her son's sexual orientation, though, she was deliberately stupid. It irritated Rickey that the devout Catholics of the Stubbs family had become far more accepting than unreligious Brenda.

He'd gotten her to stop asking what she had done wrong, and whether he thought things might have been different if his father had been around. He'd put an end to the clippings about the dangers of HIV by telling her point-blank that G-man was the only person he'd ever slept with, and if she thought G-man was sleeping around, she should take it up with him. But asking "You met any nice girls?" was an annoying habit Brenda had not yet been able to break. In her fantasy world, the ten years he'd spent with

G-man were some kind of awkward phase, and any day now her son was going to get married and give her a couple of grandbabies.

"No, Momma," he said. There was no point in taking it any further.

In a few minutes they said goodbye and hung up. Rickey looked over at G-man, who was lying in bed reading the new issue of *Gourmet*. "You think she'd leave me alone if we could have a kid?" he said.

"We *are* gonna have a kid," said G-man. "Its name will be Liquor."

chapter 9

Terrance and NuShawn were cruising on Terrance's night off. NuShawn had a badass ride, a Viper GTS that could supposedly do a ten-second quarter mile. Terrance had never let NuShawn show him.

They'd smoked a joint, eaten a package of cookies, checked out a hot new club on St. Bernard Avenue only to find it closed down after a shooting. That was one of the problems with hot new clubs in New Orleans: the moment they got too hot, some fool showed up with a gun. Terrance supposed it was the same in other cities. *Grand opening? Grand closing!,* as Chris Rock said in one of his more caustic comedy routines.

"Nothin goin on," said NuShawn. "I got places to go, people to see."

"You can drop me home, then."

"Hey, man, I thought we were hangin out. Why you want to go home early?"

Translation: NuShawn was kind of a small, reedy guy, and he liked having somebody Terrance's size with him on his "rounds." Terrance didn't care for that. Some of the people NuShawn dealt with kept their guns behind the sofa cushions; some just let them lie out on the table. Size was no advantage in such a crowd.

Terrance could take his cousin's company or leave it. Mostly he was out with NuShawn tonight because he'd stopped seeing a woman last week. Or, if truth be told, the woman had stopped seeing *him*. At any rate, it was Sunday, the big night of a kitchen worker's weekend, and he didn't feel like sitting home.

"You hungry?" he said.

"Shit! All you ever wanna do is eat. Every time we go out we gotta eat three or four times."

"This is different. I know the cooks at this place. They'll fix us something special. It's a nice quiet place. If you don't want to go, just drop me off—I'll get a cab later."

NuShawn pressed the Seek button on the radio and listened to several stations before settling on one whose signal seemed to consist entirely of throbbing bass. "They gonna fix us a special meal?" he said finally.

"I bet they will."

"We gotta pay for it?"

"Course we gotta pay for it."

"Well, what the hell good is that?"

Terrance prevailed, but when they walked in the door of the Apostle Bar ten minutes later, he kind of wished he hadn't. All the tables were full of people eating, and customers were three deep at the bar. A harried-looking waitress ran plate after plate from the window to the tables.

"Real nice and quiet in here," said NuShawn.

"I never seen it like this. Must have been that review in the paper. Lemme look in the kitchen a minute."

"You go in the fuckin kitchen, I'm leavin! Last time you went in the kitchen at a place, I ended up sittin there for about nine hours!"

"Just lemme glance in," said Terrance, and left NuShawn standing at the end of the bar.

Neither Rickey nor G-man looked up when Terrance came through the swinging door. Their eyes moved only between the food they were making and the solid line of tickets that hung in the window. They looked hot, sweaty, and pissed off, but Terrance knew they weren't really angry about anything; it was just the habitual expression of the cook in the weeds.

"Y'all all right?" he asked.

Rickey gave him the briefest of glances. "We already 86'd three things, one of my burners isn't working, and all the pots are dirty. We're taking it in the ass."

Terrance moved to the sink. It was heaped with dirty pots, at least one of which, he could smell, had been scorched on the bottom. "I'll get these for you," he said.

"Thanks, T."

Terrance knocked out the pots in ten minutes. There was nothing else he could do to help, so he rejoined his cousin at the bar. "I just remembered about this place," said NuShawn. "This the place your boss was talkin about."

"He talks about a lot of stuff," said Terrance. "I don't want to hear any of it right now."

They ordered a couple of beers and watched a soundless basketball game on the TV over the bar. The crowd was thinning out, some people leaving, others moving to the back room where you could shoot pool. In a little while, Rickey came out of the kitchen carrying two plates. "Thanks

for doing those pots. I fixed you a couple of dinner specials."
He had a blue-green bandanna tied around his head. Ter-
rance noticed that the bandanna was the exact same color as
Rickey's eyes.

"How'd you know I had my cousin with me?"

"I didn't. I fixed 'em both for you. Hell, I used to make
those staff meals, I remember how much you eat. But you
can share, can'tcha?" Then Rickey seemed to remember
something. "You're Terrance's *cousin?*" he asked NuShawn.

"Yeah, man. Thanks for the food."

"Sure . . . Listen, I gotta get back to it. Y'all hang out if
you can, but we won't really slow up for another hour."

Rickey cast a final curious glance at NuShawn and
headed back to the kitchen. He probably wanted to pump
NuShawn for dirt on Mike. No way was Terrance encour-
aging that, though. NuShawn and Rickey were two of the
most trouble-causing people he knew. He probably
shouldn't have let them in the same *room* with each other.

"These some kinda little birds, or what?" NuShawn
said.

Terrance looked at his plate. Two boned-out quail rested
on a bed of wild rice. Four spears of roasted asparagus were
arranged around the rice in a box shape. The quail were
meltingly tender beneath a sauce that tasted of Southern
Comfort. Even NuShawn shut up and ate.

o   o   o

Rickey had had to pee for two hours. As soon as the tickets
cleared out, he went to the bathroom. He was still standing
at the urinal with his dick in his hand when Terrance's
cousin came in.

"Hey, man, that was some good shit. I never ate no quails before, but it was good."

"Thanks, uh—sorry, I didn't catch your name."

"NuShawn Jefferson."

"Thanks, NuShawn." Rickey zipped himself up and went to wash his hands. "We were sure glad to see Terrance in there. I miss working with him. He's cool."

"Yeah, he all right. Say, you got some guy name of Rickey working here?"

"That's me."

"Damn!" NuShawn took a step back.

"What?"

"Nothin. I know a guy who hates your ass, is all."

"Really? Is he a stupid fucking cokehead named Mike?"

"Yeah."

"So he even talks about me to his dealer? I feel honored. I don't guess you know what his problem is or anything, cause I don't."

"He say the same shit bosses always say. You slackin off, you got a smart mouth. Oh, and you supposed to be suckin some guy's dick in the newspaper. I got tired of puttin up with that kinda boss shit a long time ago. Went into business for myself."

"I'm tired of putting up with that boss shit too, NuShawn. But I love to cook, and it's hard to get cooking jobs without running into a lot of assholes like Mike Mouton. So what would you do if you were me?"

NuShawn considered. "I guess I'd start my own restaurant."

"Yeah," said Rickey. "I guess I would too."

"You need somethin?"

98 ° *Poppy Z. Brite*

"Got any weed?"

"No, just C."

"I guess not tonight. Thanks anyway."

He went back to the kitchen and told G-man about the conversation. "I wouldn't have minded a bump," said G-man.

"Fuck that. If it turns you into Mike, I'm never doing it again."

"That won't be any big loss, since you haven't done it in about three years anyway." G-man looked over and saw Rickey scowling at his depleted mise-en-place. "Dude, I don't get why you take Mike so seriously. Nobody else does. I mean, we got screwed over by Brian Danton at Tequila-town, and you don't hate him. So how come you care what Mike thinks? He's so stupid, he thinks you get a good review by sucking the restaurant critic's dick, for Chrissake."

"Brian Danton didn't go around *trashing* me," said Rickey. "He had a rule, we broke it, and he fired us. He had a reason for what he did, even if it was a stupid reason. But I didn't do anything wrong at Escargot's. I did a *good* job. Sometimes I think that's why Mike hates me so much. He just disliked me to start with, and I never did anything he could fire me for."

As twisted as this logic was, G-man could see it, and he nodded. Still, he couldn't help wondering if there might be more to it. His peaceful soul usually kept him from questioning things too deeply, but he didn't like the way Mike Mouton seemed to have fixated on Rickey.

o o o

Anthony came into the kitchen as they were cleaning up. He wore the hangdog look that usually meant he had something important to discuss.

"Busy night," was all he said at first.

"Sure was," said G-man.

"Nice crowd, huh?"

"Anthony," said Rickey. "No offense, but what do you want? I know you want something."

"Well, we're making so much money. I gotta give you both a big raise, cause you're the only thing bringing it in."

"Cool!" said Rickey. "You know what I'm gonna do? I'm gonna get a car. I never had my own car before. I'm gonna get me a crappy old car."

"I'm gonna get a real good knife," said G-man.

"Yeah, me too. A car and a Wüsthof knife."

"Uh, guys, if you could start spending your riches a little later? Like I said, I gotta give you a raise. But you can see this kinda business is too big for the place."

"It won't stay this crazy," said G-man. "It's the review. It'll die down some."

"Some, but not a whole lot, I bet. And we got Mardi Gras coming up. Y'all are gonna have some fairly nice money of your own. You could start putting it away toward your restaurant."

"I got a bad feeling where this is leading," said Rickey.

"Look, I know Lenny's manager called you to set up a meeting, and you said you weren't ready to talk to him again yet. I wish you'd think about talking to him."

"Fuck Lenny!" Rickey tossed an empty squeeze bottle into the sink with more force than was strictly necessary.

"That big fucking pork chop. He wants to talk to us, he can call us himself. Not some *manager,* like, *summoning* us. That pissed me off."

"It did," said G-man. "It really pissed him off."

"Lenny's kinda big-business that way," Anthony admitted. "He don't think about the effect. But listen, if he called you himself, would you talk to him?"

"I don't know," said Rickey sullenly. "Maybe." Behind his back, though, G-man gave Anthony a thumbs-up.

chapter 10

"The turtle soup is excellent," said Lenny. "It lives up to its reputation."

"Yeah, I had it before," said Rickey. He saw no need to mention that he had eaten at Commander's Palace only once, ten years ago, when his father had visited from California and brought him to lunch here. If he wanted to be a chef, his father had said, he should eat at the best restaurant in New Orleans. Of course every New Orleanian had his own "best" restaurant, but Commander's Palace was a hard choice to argue with. Serving fine Creole food in the Garden District since 1880, it had done what most of the city's other old-line restaurants had not: evolved with the times while preserving a deep sense of tradition. The older dishes on the menu did not seem stodgy; the newer ones did not seem like frivolous nouvelle upstarts. The food had a coherent voice, a harmony. From the turtle soup au sherry to the bananas Foster prepared tableside on a rolling cart, Rickey had never forgotten anything about that meal.

Upon entering the big turquoise-painted Victorian

building, you came into a pretty little foyer that was usually packed with tourists and rich locals. To your left was a cabinet full of awards the restaurant had won. To your right was an etched-glass window through which you could see the main dining room. Directly in front of you was the reservations desk. If you were a regular person, the maître d' might suggest that you go through the kitchen to the bar and have a drink while you waited for your table. If you were Lenny Duveteaux, you were greeted quietly but effusively and shown to your table at once.

The main dining room hadn't changed much in ten years. The patterned green carpet was still marshmallow-thick underfoot, the walls accented with dark wooden paneling and softly lit paintings of Louisiana swamp birds. Balloons and ribbons festooned the tables of parties celebrating special occasions. The hum of conversation and the clatter of dinnerware were lively but not distractingly loud. This room could seat about 120, but somehow it still had an intimate atmosphere.

Rickey was wearing the only jacket he owned, a navy-blue affair from high school, too short in the sleeves and uncomfortably tight across the back when he tried to button it. G-man, bereft, wore the dreaded green House Jacket provided to underdressed male patrons. His customary dark glasses didn't help the look. Lenny sported an expensive-looking white silk jacket and a candy-striped shirt with too many buttons undone. The other two men at the table, Lenny's lawyer and business manager, wore conservative business suits.

"So," said De La Cerda, the lawyer, "we've got quite a few things we'd like you to look at—"

Lenny held up his hand. "Not yet, Oscar. They want to check out the menu."

They had a round of Bloody Marys made with the restaurant's own Worcestershire sauce, then placed their orders. A few minutes later the waiter set small plates of butterflied shrimp in front of them. "Chef Jamie sends these out with his compliments, Mr. Duveteaux. Our shrimp and tasso Henican. Enjoy."

Rickey took a bite of the appetizer. The tender Gulf shrimp were spiked with tasso ham, tossed in a spicy beurre blanc, set atop a pool of five-pepper jelly, and garnished with pickled okra. The dish had a bright, complex flavor: first you tasted the sweetness of the shrimp and butter, then the gastrique's sourness and the tart burn of the peppers. Rickey suspected he might be in the presence of genius. This was a worshipful presentation of shrimp, not just bringing out its best qualities but actually improving them. Of all the cooks he'd known, only Paco Valdeon had had such a gift for exalting his ingredients.

Rickey finished his appetizer in four bites and glanced around the table to see if anyone was watching. When he saw that no one was, he used the side of his finger to scoop the remaining sauce from the plate. Just as he put his finger in his mouth, G-man looked up, saw what he was doing, and nodded emphatically.

Lenny looked at their two spotless plates. "You like that, huh? You do as well with this restaurant as I expect, you can eat here any time you want."

"If we do as well as you expect, we'll be at our own restaurant all the time," G-man pointed out. "So was that Crystal hot sauce in the beurre blanc, do you know?"

"Yeah, it was. Good palate."

The waiter brought the first courses. G-man had foie gras on brioche with a Sauternes sauce. Rickey had the turtle soup again.

"Sherry, sir?"

"You bet."

The waiter set down a small silver pitcher, and Rickey poured its contents into his soup.

"Another Bloody Mary?"

"Sure."

"Me too," said G-man. "Please."

The soup was as thick, salty, and savory as Rickey remembered. G-man passed him a bite of foie gras. Beneath its seared surface, it was meltingly tender. When Rickey looked up and saw Lenny watching them, he had the disconcerting feeling that Lenny knew they had eaten here exactly once between them.

That was one of the problems with Lenny. Rickey usually thought of himself as smart—smart enough to get by, anyway—but Lenny made him feel stupid, like somebody who didn't know a damn thing about food or restaurants. It wasn't anything Lenny did; he wasn't sure *what* it was. Maybe it was just that he had expected Lenny to be kind of a dope, and Lenny had turned out to be anything but.

He was getting a little drunk. He took a sip of his water, and a back waiter swooped in and replaced it with a fresh, ice-filled glass.

When the appetizer plates were cleared, Flanagan retrieved a leather portfolio from the floor and extracted a slim sheaf of paper. He glanced at Lenny, who nodded. Flanagan cleared his throat.

"First we'd like to show you some figures—we feel you should understand the potential here. These are last year's sales figures for the Duvet Corporation—the combined proceeds of Lenny's, Crescent, and Sundae Dinner."

He handed the sheet to Rickey. Rickey looked at the bottom and saw a figure he would never have associated with restaurants. The cost of a B-2 bomber, maybe, or the debt of a very poor Third World nation, but not restaurants. He passed the sheet to G-man, whose eyebrows rose above the tops of his shades.

Flanagan handed him another sheet. "This is a rough monthly breakdown of the restaurants' costs."

These figures—percentages of money spent on food, labor, utilities, and so forth—were a little more familiar. Food costs in all three restaurants hovered around 26 percent, a figure Rickey found low. "We'd want a little bit higher food costs than this," he said.

Lenny grinned as if he'd guessed Rickey would say that. De La Cerda looked at Flanagan, who said, "That's doable."

Flanagan removed another item from his portfolio, an eight-by-ten color photograph. "This is the property we'd like you to consider taking over."

Rickey studied the picture. For a few seconds it was just a photo of a building on an oak-lined portion of St. Charles Avenue. He knew it was on St. Charles because he could see the streetcar tracks in front of it, a leftover string of Mardi Gras beads dangling from the overhead wires. Then it hit him. "This is *Sundae Dinner.*"

"That's right," said Lenny. "I'm closing the place down. I want you to take over, make it into your restaurant."

"Oh no. Oh no no no." In his dismay, what little tact

Rickey had completely deserted him. "That place is gonna have the Bad Restaurant Curse. No *way* are we taking over that spot."

He knew Lenny understood exactly what he meant. The Bad Restaurant Curse was universally acknowledged among restaurant people. It could haunt locations for years after the first bad restaurant closed. There was a pretty little storefront over on Prytania, no less desirable than any of a hundred other locations in the vicinity. The first bad restaurant there was opened by a woman who had spent several years writing vicious restaurant reviews for the *Cornet,* a weekly free paper. Her menu was Asian Eclectic: eighteen-dollar noodle bowls, pot stickers in cilantro pesto, curried calamari. The place was universally shunned and went broke in a matter of months. The second restaurant was an earnest, mid-priced, family-run tapas bar. It reviewed well and the dining public seemed to *want* to like it, but it closed within a year. Now a young chef named Cole Parker had taken over the space, renamed it Poivre, and started cooking excellent French country food there. He seemed to be doing all right, but it could take years to see whether the Bad Restaurant Curse was truly broken.

To his credit, Lenny didn't try to act as though he had no idea what Rickey was talking about. Nor did he seem offended. "It wouldn't be a bad location for you," he said. "I know Sundae Dinner was a dumb idea, but my dumb ideas make more money than most people's good ones."

"That's true," said Flanagan. "He's raking it in. Duvet Corporation just includes the three restaurants. He also gets cookbook royalties, product endorsements, consulting fees, a lot of miscellaneous stuff."

"I got offered the chance to do a show on the Food Network," Lenny said. "I didn't do it because I would've had to spend too much time in New York. But I could have. I'm not bragging . . . well, not too much. I just want you to understand where these things can lead."

"We don't want to do a TV show," said Rickey. "We don't even want to have three restaurants. Just one. Just one damn restaurant that isn't piggybacking on somebody else's reputation."

Lenny templed his hands in front of him. "Rickey, haven't I made myself clear? I don't want you to piggyback on my reputation. I specifically *do not* want that. I see Liquor attracting mainly a local crowd. I wouldn't even want New Orleanians to know I was associated with it. They hear my name, they'll assume it's just some flashy tourist joint."

"You don't think people will find out you're backing us?" said G-man.

"Sure they will, eventually. But if we handle it right, you'll already have a crowd of regulars by that time. They'll want to keep eating there, so they'll justify my involvement by seeing it as exactly what it is—you using my money without letting me fuck up the place."

"That's kinda harsh," said Rickey.

"I'm doing one type of thing, you're doing another. There's plenty of room for both."

The salad course had been served while they were talking, but no one had touched it. Now Rickey looked at his plate and saw a glistening pile of romaine lettuce with golden-fried oysters arranged around the periphery. He picked up his salad fork, speared one of the oysters, and ate it. It was perfect—the seasoning, the breading, the oyster itself. He was starting to feel demoralized, both by Lenny and by the parade of exquisite food. What the hell made him think he could open a restaurant anyway?

"Wow," said G-man, who had a salad of fried chicken, roasted red peppers, and Bibb lettuce. "This blue cheese dressing is almost as good as mine. Not that I'm *bragging* or anything."

It was hard to tell with the dark glasses, but Rickey was pretty sure G-man had just given Lenny a sly look. If so, Lenny either hadn't caught it or didn't care. "Yuh," he said through a big forkful of crabmeat, "your chicken wings are terrific."

"Aw, they're just bar food," G-man said modestly.

"Nothing wrong with great bar food."

"I like some good buffalo wings," said De La Cerda, and everyone nodded as if this were a scintillating conversational gambit.

The salad plates were cleared, the chef came out to say hello to Lenny, the pace of the restaurant whirled around them, and Rickey ordered another Bloody Mary. He knew he was drinking too much, but he felt too depressed to stop. Depressed wasn't even the word; he felt *torn*. One part of his mind was busy resenting Lenny and the two suits. Another part realized that Lenny was, in fact, making them a very generous offer; that part was experiencing a craven urge to accept Lenny's backing on Lenny's terms and make a shit-load of money. Yet another part—perhaps the most basic— was simply enjoying the meal, wishing he and G-man could be sitting here eating it without having to talk to these clowns.

So it could not be said that he was precisely in his right mind when he sat up in his chair, stared Lenny in the eye, and said, "*I just can't do it.*"

For the first time, Lenny looked a little nonplussed. "Do what?"

"Open there. Where Sundae Dinner is—was—whatever. I can't do it, Lenny. I know you want to help us. That's pretty cool. I used to think you were kind of a jerk." From the corner of his eye he saw G-man wince, but he kept talking. "You're OK, though. I could probably go into business with you. I could even listen to your advice, although I'd probably ignore most of it. I could do all that, maybe. But I can't open my restaurant in the Sundae Dinner space." He poked the table with his forefinger, clumsily, three times. "Can. Not. Do it."

"Can I say anything to change your mind?"

"No. No way."

"OK. So you open somewhere else."

". . . Huh?"

Lenny shrugged. "It would've been easier to use property we already have, but it's not essential. We'll break the lease on that building, find a new place, transfer whatever equipment you can use—you don't have any objection to using some of the *equipment,* I hope?"

"No," said G-man, seeing that Rickey was speechless. "Course we don't."

Flanagan and De La Cerda sat silent, impassive. Rickey guessed they had known Lenny was prepared to make this counteroffer and had just been keeping their mouths shut waiting to see if it happened.

Now Rickey felt, if not exactly trapped, then obligated somehow. He'd come into this meeting with his mind as open as he could make it on the subject of Lenny and his money. He'd been horrified by the Sundae Dinner possibility and convinced that Lenny wasn't really interested in them at all; he just wanted them to revitalize his crappy gimmick restaurant. Now Lenny had countered with evidence that this wasn't the case at all, that he would do whatever it took to win them over.

As the waiter returned to the table with the entrées and began to remove the metal hats from the five plates, Rickey gazed at Lenny with grudging, drunken, but genuine admiration. Maybe they could work with this guy after all.

° ° °

By the time they left Commander's Palace, Rickey was not so much drunk as saturated—with vodka, with great food, with information and possibility. He was only vaguely aware of saying goodnight to Lenny and the suits. The cab stand was right across from the kitchen door, and he hoped no one they knew was working in that kitchen right now, maybe stepping out for an after-service smoke, only to see G-man pouring Rickey into a cab.

As they rode uptown, Rickey thought about how nice it was to be able to afford a cab. Then he thought about how terrible it would be to throw up in one, especially after such a meal. He closed his eyes, slid down in the seat, and tried not to think at all until they got back to Marengo Street.

He hung up his jacket, draped his shirt and pants over a chair, and fell into bed. The last two courses of the meal—

potato-crusted Lyonnaise drum and bread pudding souf-
fle—still weighed heavily in his stomach, but he no longer
felt sick. Though he knew he ought to be thinking about
Lenny's offer, he couldn't get his mind off the food. It didn't
need any clever hooks or gimmicks. It was simply awesome,
about as good as he imagined food could be.

G-man came in and began to undress. "That drum was
so *moist,*" he said. "The potatoes were golden, but the fish
wasn't dry at all."

"Yeah, I was just thinking about that."

"It's the potato crust. The water in the potatoes crisps
them and steams the fish at the same time. Real simple, but
smart."

"You'd want to have your heat nice and high in a real
heavy pan."

"Was that a caper beurre blanc, or were the capers just
scattered over it?"

"Just scattered over it. But they were, like, *toasted* or
something."

"Toasted capers," mused G-man, sitting naked on the
edge of the bed. "They do some wild shit."

"They really do. It's traditional, but it's also wild as hell.
I'd love to do stuff like that."

"Looks like you're gonna get your chance."

"Oh, God," Rickey moaned. "We didn't actually *agree* to
anything, did we?"

"What, you don't remember signing that contract?"

"Dude—"

"I'm just fucking with you. We didn't agree to anything.
You told Lenny you'd call him. That's it."

"So what do you think?"

"I think we should do it. I've thought we should probably do it all along—you know that."

Rickey put his hands over his eyes. "It makes me feel like a whore."

"Well, would you rather stand out on Burgundy Street and give three-quarters of your money to some pimp, or would you rather have your own whorehouse?"

"What do you mean?"

"I mean we *are* whores, in a way. We work ourselves half to death for other people's pleasure, and we give up big chunks of our lives to do it. How many Thanksgivings and Fat Tuesdays have we worked? How come we got no savings, no health insurance? When did we ever have a vacation? And going to Gulfport for the day doesn't count."

"We gotta make a living," Rickey mumbled. His head was beginning to ache.

"You think whores say something different? My point is, you want to open this restaurant, and I don't see any other way to do it. If we're gonna be whores, let's milk the johns good instead of settling for five bucks a throw."

With that, G-man stretched out on the bed and went quickly to sleep. It appeared to be an untroubled sleep, and Rickey envied it.

chapter 11

The madness that gripped New Orleans for two months of each year had finally receded. It was now possible to drive somewhere without first consulting parade routes. No one but the occasional clueless, straggling tourist still wore beads. Public drunkenness was as prevalent as ever, but no longer mandatory. Mardi Gras was over.

Rickey had dropped a thousand dollars—the most money he'd ever spent at once—on a 1973 Plymouth Satellite with a two-tone paint job, black and gold. The color scheme, the ancient fleur-de-lis-shaped air freshener dangling from the rearview mirror, and a paper bag with cutout eyeholes in the glove compartment made Rickey think the car's previous owner had been a Saints fan. He hadn't seen one of those bags since he and G-man were kids, when the Saints had a 1-15 season and local sportscaster Buddy Diliberto started wearing a brown grocery bag on his head during his TV segments. A sizable contingent of fans followed Buddy's lead and became known as Bagheads.

At first it was thrilling to have transportation any time

they wanted it. He and G-man had been able to use the family cars when they lived with their parents, but since they'd moved out they relied on the streetcar, the city bus lines, and their own feet. Now they no longer had to limit their grocery trips to what they could carry. After they closed the Apostle Bar's kitchen, they'd sometimes drive out to Lake Pontchartrain and dangle their legs over the seawall, staring out over the dark polluted water and talking about their plans, often until the sun came up. When they needed something for a recipe, Anthony would offer the use of his Continental, and Rickey loved being able to say, "That's OK, I'll take *my car.*"

As Carnival season advanced on them, the magic of automobile ownership had worn off fast. Though their odd hours made Rickey and G-man less vulnerable to it than some, every New Orleans driver got caught by a parade eventually. There was nothing glamorous or cool about trying to find a way across St. Charles when Orpheus was rolling. On Ash Wednesday morning, Rickey ran over a broken vodka bottle and got a flat tire. He thought this was a bad omen, and G-man had to talk him down. "Dude—any other time of year, maybe so. The day after Mardi Gras, half the people driving on the avenue are liable to get that kind of bad omen."

"But it was a *liquor* bottle."

"What'd you think was gonna be laying in the street on Ash Wednesday? Coke bottles?"

For the first time in their lives, they had work responsibilities beyond putting out the food. They met with Lenny a couple of times a week to learn the rudiments of leasing property, buying equipment, hiring staff, and so on. Sometimes Bert Flanagan sat in on these meetings; more often it was just the three of them. The amount of knowledge they needed was overwhelming, but Lenny turned out to be a good teacher. He was patient and didn't mind explaining something two or three times if necessary. "I didn't understand any of this shit at first," he said. "The only way you really learn is by watching it and doing it."

One night G-man was at the Apostle training the new cook, A.J. Rickey was off, and around ten o'clock he decided to go over to Sundae Dinner. He had just about decided to recruit Lenny's chef de cuisine, a tall, bone-thin young man named Tanker. The silly-assed food made it hard to tell whether Tanker was a good cook, but Rickey liked his attitude. The first time they'd met, Tanker was working the Sundae Dinner sauté station. "How do you think of so many ways to make food into sundaes?" Rickey asked him.

"You really want to know?" said Tanker. "I take two ramekins and a buncha slips of paper. Whatever meats I got, I write them on one bunch. Then I think of things I can scoop, like, say, sweet potatoes and crabmeat mousse, and I write them on the other bunch. Then I pull one slip out of each ramekin and that's my special." He'd said this right in front of Lenny, who just laughed. Tanker did not laugh, but winked solemnly at Rickey.

Rather than unnerving him, this little glimpse into the bowels of Sundae Dinner made Rickey more confident about working with Lenny. Lenny was always looking for the next gimmick. He'd never quite found it here, but the gimmick at Liquor was already built in and Lenny liked it. Rickey and G-man would just have to keep him from trying to fuck around with it.

Tanker had showed him around the kitchen, which also

reassured Rickey: the place was huge, but set up so well that nobody seemed to scramble. Everything they needed was at arm's length. The stations were arranged in a way that made sense. The hoods and range tops were at a comfortable height. Rickey remembered Lenny's beautiful home kitchen and gave silent thanks that Lenny either knew how to design a workspace or hire somebody who did.

Tonight Rickey sat at Sundae Dinner's bar talking to Tanker and his girlfriend, Mo, the bartender. Tanker had just finished his shift and Mo was closing out the bar. Even in her regulation black pants and white button-down shirt, Mo managed to look as if she had just stepped out of a 1940s noir movie. She wore her long auburn hair rolled at the nape of her neck, and her dark red lipstick gave her a mollish look. She made blood-orange screwdrivers that were among the tastiest drinks Rickey had ever had.

"So what's Lenny got to do with this place you're opening anyway?" Mo asked.

"Nothing really," Rickey said. "He's an old friend. He's just showing us the ropes." He hated lying to other restaurant people, but he didn't want word of Lenny's involvement with Liquor to get out yet.

"Well," said Mo, "after seeing some of the stuff he makes Tanker cook, I hope he's not giving you too many tips on the food."

Rickey laughed. "What'd you make tonight? Wasabi mashed potatoes with chocolate sauce?"

"That might've been an improvement," said Tanker. "My big dinner special was crabmeat ravioli with a raspberry beurre blanc. Yeah, raspberry."

"Lenny's idea?"

"But of course, my good man."

"Listen, Tanker, what are you gonna do after this place closes? If you're looking for a job—"

"I got no idea," Tanker interrupted. "Haven't even applied anywhere. I'm feeling kinda fried, and we got a little money saved up. Me and Mo might get out of New Orleans for the summer. My folks used to take me to Colorado. It was nice—I'd like to go back sometime."

"They got mountains there?"

"Like you wouldn't believe! I didn't even know what they were at first. You ever been to the mountains?"

"Not hardly. I saw the Catskills when I was at cooking school, but other than that, I never been much higher than Monkey Hill in the Audubon Zoo."

"Uh-oh," said Mo. "Boss in the house." Rickey turned and saw Lenny coming through the graceful archway that separated the foyer from the bar.

"Hi, guys," said Lenny. "How many'd we do tonight?"

"Hundred and twenty-five," Tanker told him.

"God, this place is a mausoleum. You think people know we're closing? Is it in the rumor mill?"

"Not that I know of," said Tanker. "People got ESP about that kinda thing sometimes, though."

"That's for sure. Say, Rickey, you busy? I need to talk to you."

"I gotta go pick up G pretty soon."

"Why don't I ride over to the Apostle with you? I can cab it back here later."

"Well," said Rickey. He looked uncomfortably at

Tanker and Mo, who were watching this exchange with great interest. "Sure. You want to go now?"

"Unless you have something else to do."

"No, I'm ready. Let's go. Night, y'all."

"Night," said Tanker and Mo. They watched Lenny and Rickey walk out together, then raised their eyebrows at each other.

"What do you think that's about?" said Mo.

"Rickey's restaurant," said Tanker. "I think Lenny's some kinda silent partner, and you know what else? I think Rickey's gonna ask us to work there."

"Should we?"

"Maybe," said Tanker. "As long they keep Lenny away from the food."

° ° °

"Pretty funky car," said Lenny, sliding into the Satellite's passenger seat. "Where's your beads?"

"What beads?"

"I thought there was an unwritten law that every car in New Orleans had to have Mardi Gras beads hanging from the rearview mirror."

"I hate those things. In fact, I hate Mardi Gras."

"Spoken like a true local."

"I don't know about that. My mom's lived here all her life and she still loves it. Goes to a shitload of parades, goes out masking with a bunch of her friends on Fat Tuesday. But she's an accountant. She used to do the books for Lemoyne's, but she never worked in a kitchen. That's what made me start hating the whole Carnival season—the way it can put you in the weeds no matter how much of a roller you are."

"You might change your mind once you're the owner. You'll still work your ass off, but you'll see the profits coming in. Gives you a whole new perspective."

"Yeah, I can believe that."

When Rickey cranked the engine, a Snoop Dogg tape came to noisy life in the player. He snapped it off and pulled out of the parking lot. "So what'd you want to talk about?" he said as they drove up St. Charles.

"I wanted to see when you guys could go look at some properties. I saw a couple that I thought might work. How big a dining room are you thinking of? How many do you want to seat?"

"Sixty, seventy."

"That's pretty small. This place will draw big, I'm telling you."

"I don't want a huge restaurant," Rickey said firmly. "I thought a lot about this. I want a small crew, a place I can really control."

"Figures. I pegged you for a control freak the first time we talked. Anyway, I've got my eye on a few places—one in the Warehouse District, a couple Uptown, one in Mid-City. Mid-City still has some run-down areas, but it's coming back."

"I hate that expression," said Rickey. "*Coming back.* All it means is that white people are moving in. What happens to the people who lived there before? They're moving to the projects, and we're supposed to be all happy that the neighborhood's *coming back*?"

"That's very idealistic, Rickey. You sure you wouldn't prefer a career in political activism?"

"Fuck you."

"Well, come on. You're not kicking some poor black family out of the home they've lived in for fifty years. You're leasing a piece of property in a commercially zoned area, most likely a property that was empty before you got there, maybe even dangerous. Where's the harm in that?"

"I just don't want to improve the neighborhood so much that people have to start moving out."

"That's unlikely. But you're in business now. Be realistic."

More even than the expression "coming back," Rickey hated being told to "be realistic." As far as he could tell, being realistic had never gotten him anywhere. He hadn't been realistic in fourth grade when he made up the Job Week skit that cemented his friendship with G-man. He hadn't been realistic when he got himself kicked out of the CIA. He certainly hadn't been realistic that day in Audubon Park when he conceived the idea for Liquor. He thought of telling Lenny all this, but decided not to. Instead he just said, "I hear you."

"That's something people say when they're listening to me but not agreeing."

"I agree with you. Mostly."

"Well, I guess that's all I can ask for, huh?"

"Right," said Rickey, pulling up in front of the Apostle Bar. "It sure is."

° ° °

Mike Mouton was tired of hearing about the Apostle Bar's great new menu. He'd been hungry after work tonight and had decided to go check out the place, hoping it would be terrible so that he'd have a snappy comeback for people who raved about it. Unfortunately, his dinner was excellent: a special of melt-in-the-mouth pork rillettes with brandy-soaked dried cherries and a salad made from arugula and mâche. Mike didn't even know where to get mâche. Escargot's would never bother with such a thing.

He sat alone at a corner table, picking at the last shreds of food on his plate and keeping an eye out for Rickey. Even after eleven, the place was pretty crowded; he thought he could pay up and get out without taking a chance on running into Rickey or his partner. If the food had been bad, he might have glanced into the kitchen and made a mock-sympathetic remark about how hard it was to live up to a good review. He realized, though, that they'd just laugh at him.

He looked up to signal the waitress. Instead he saw Rickey coming through the front door with Lenny Duveteaux. Lenny's hand was resting lightly on Rickey's back, and they were chatting like old friends.

Mike looked away, but Lenny had already seen him and was heading over to his table. "Hey, Mike! How about this place? I think these guys are real rising stars."

"It was good," said Mike.

"Aw, I bet it was a lot more than good. Say, you know Rickey here, don't you? Didn't you guys use to work together?"

"Yeah," said Rickey. "We sure did." He looked down at

Mike for a moment, his eyes burning like twin blue lasers of hate. Then he turned abruptly and headed for the kitchen.

G-man was not particularly surprised to see Rickey looking pissed off. He was, however, a bit surprised at how hard Lenny was laughing.

"What the hell was that all about?" said Rickey.

Lenny wiped a tear from his eye. "I was just teasing him a little. Did you see the look—"

"Just teasing him! Don't you think he'll figure something out?"

"Restaurant people will find out I'm working with you, Rickey. You know how the grapevine works. Don't worry— it'll take awhile to filter down to the public."

"What's going on?" said G-man.

"Mike's out there. Lenny practically grabbed my ass in front of him." This assertion sent Lenny off into fresh gales of laughter. Rickey glared at him, then turned to G-man, who tried to suppress his own grin.

"Go ahead and laugh, you fuckers! Laugh yourselves into a couple of coronaries for all I care." Rickey picked up a basket of Ponchatoula strawberries, sniffed them, and tasted one. "These are nice. I saw some last week that were still a little too hard. What are we doing with them?"

"A.J.'s gonna make a strawberry shortcake," said G-man. "But back up a minute. You said Mike from Escargot's is out there? *Eating?*"

"I'm not surprised," said Lenny. "You hate somebody and they get a nice review, you go eat at their place hoping it won't be all that good. But we busted him. He was probably hoping to sneak out without seeing you guys, and Rickey and I just walked right in on him."

"What'd he have?" said G-man.

"I couldn't tell. He cleaned his plate." Lenny began to laugh again. A little reluctantly, Rickey joined him.

"Was he by himself?" asked A.J., the new cook.

"Yeah. Yeah, he was."

"He had the rillettes, then. I sent 'em out. That's the only single we've had in over an hour—all the rest were deuces and four-tops."

"Ha!" said Rickey. "Those rillettes are *killer*. I made 'em myself last week. Best thing I've cooked in ages."

"See?" said Lenny. "Gives you some satisfaction, doesn't it?"

"I guess," Rickey said doubtfully. As a matter of fact, Mike's visit *did* give him some satisfaction. When Lenny first played him the tape of Mike's phone call, Rickey had wanted to kill the guy or at least injure him severely. But that was his past coming out; in the Lower Ninth Ward you had to know how to fight just to survive your childhood. Mike was from a different world, and people in that world found an enemy's success much more burdensome than an ass-kicking.

Lenny decided to stay and drink with Anthony, and A.J. thought he could hold things down for the last couple of hours, so G-man left with Rickey and they were home by midnight. It was almost like a vacation. Rickey stopped on the porch and got mail out of the box: a gas bill and the new issue of *Gourmet*. He flipped the magazine open at random. "I hate this question-and-answer column. 'What is an egg wash?' 'How can I keep cheese from sticking to the grater?' They ought to have *Shoemaker* magazine for people like that and *Gourmet* for the rest of us."

"Do I detect a note of snobbery?"

"Yeah, talking to Tanker makes me feel like a snob. He knows a lot about food, G, maybe more than we do, and he's doing bullshit at Sundae Dinner. *Raspberry* beurre blanc? I ask you."

"Ugh."

"Why do people eat stuff like that?"

"Lots of them don't," G-man said reasonably. "The place is closing, remember?"

"Well, but Lenny's not stupid. How come he ever thought it was a good idea?"

"I guess nobody ever really knows what's gonna hit in this business. Lenny's first two restaurants were slam dunks. Maybe he got to thinking he couldn't make a mistake."

"I hope he's not making one with us. What if our gimmick is as stupid as Sundae Dinner's and we just don't know it?"

G-man shrugged. "What if it is? We'll still be serving really good food. It's not gonna be like Sundae Dinner. You can't ignore the gimmick there. People who don't like *our* gimmick can ignore it and still get a great meal."

"I guess," said Rickey. "It's still pretty scary, though. I mean, Lenny Duveteaux asking me when I want to go look at property for *my* restaurant."

"You'd be crazy if you *weren't* scared right now. Anybody who's planning to open a restaurant ought to be scared. Ought to have their head examined too, probably. But you're smart to be scared. Keeps you from fucking up."

"You don't seem scared."

"I think of Karl Malone," said G-man. "When I get scared, I think about the Mailman taking it to the basket.

Yeah, I see you laughing, but it works. Karl Malone doesn't stop to be scared of whoever's defending him—he just drives."

Rickey riffled the pages of his magazine. "I can't just drive," he said. "I mean, I can most of the time, but sometimes I start freaking out about everything. You know that."

"I guess I do."

"So you got any other suggestions?"

"Well . . . I still say an Our Father once in a while."

Rickey glanced up, but G-man was looking away. "You do? Seriously?"

"Yeah. I don't mean to, but I'll be thinking about some problem, and all of a sudden I'll find myself in the middle of one. Old habit, I guess."

"Does it help?" Rickey was curious.

"Doesn't hurt," G-man said a little uncomfortably. "It kinda drowns out the noise in my head."

"I'd love for something to drown out the noise in my head, but I don't think praying would work. I never even learned how to do it."

"You're making things too complicated," said G-man. "Remember our rule back in the Ninth Ward? The one that was guaranteed to get us through any situation?"

"'There is always alcohol,'" Rickey quoted. G-man got two bottles of beer from the refrigerator, opened them, and set one in front of Rickey.

Rickey picked up the bottle and took a long swig. "It's nice to have a night off, at least."

"We're so pathetic."

"Why?"

"We get home by twelve and we think it's a night off."

"You're right. We need to do something to relax."

"I got an idea," said G-man. "Let's open our own restaurant."

"Very funny. I got a better idea—let's fuck."

G-man blinked. "I'm not sure I remember how."

"You're a real comedian tonight, huh? OK, so we been a little busy lately. You think I could refresh your memory?"

"Yeah," said G-man, smiling. "I think you probably could."

°   °   °

An hour later, Rickey lay in bed feeling infinitely more relaxed and just a little sheepish. A sex life wasn't something a person should have to *remind* himself to have. Though they hadn't forgotten how, it had been way too long since they had really gotten it on.

G-man had surprised him with the remark about the Our Fathers. Rickey didn't approve of the practice—when they were teenagers, a priest had told G-man that it was better to live a celibate life than to act upon his feelings for Rickey, and Rickey had always taken that as a personal affront—but he rather liked the fact that G-man could still surprise him. It made him remember that G-man had a stubborn streak beneath his complacency, which turned him on. If G-man hadn't made the remark, Rickey supposed they might have gone another week or two without having sex. *How screwed up is that?* he wondered, but he wasn't really worried; when they did get around to it, they knew one another's bodies and hearts as well as ever.

He guessed the work might have something to do with their periods of sexual drought: not just the long hours and weariness, but the fact that they'd never really felt comfortable showing any kind of public affection. Things were changing—there were even female chefs infiltrating the boys' club now—but the restaurant kitchen was still an arena of great machismo, and while Rickey and G-man had never gone so far as to deny their relationship, they knew they were more likely to be taken seriously by their fellow cooks if they weren't obvious about it. Behavior like that could carry over into your private life, Rickey thought ruefully. It could get to the point where you felt more like buddies than lovers, and needed to remind yourself why you were sleeping in the same bed.

That would be one good thing about having his own restaurant: he wouldn't have to act according to anyone else's expectations. He and G-man could make out in the goddamn bar if they wanted to, though he doubted they'd ever stray that far from their longtime habit of discretion. Rickey wondered how his career would have gone if he'd just been open about his sexuality from the start. Indirectly, hiding it had gotten him kicked out of the CIA, and certainly that had made a difference. There was a lot more to it than what he'd told Lenny the first time they met, when Lenny asked him about leaving school.

It was true that he'd beaten up a guy. What he hadn't mentioned to Lenny was that the guy, Phil Muller, had been his roommate. They'd gotten along OK at first. Muller talked a lot of trash about New Orleans cuisine, but Rickey hadn't cared so much once he adjusted to the fact that everybody up north seemed to think New Orleans was just a remote, benighted region of America. Muller mocked Rickey for not being able to take the Hudson Valley weather, but it was semifriendly mockery, the kind that cooks exchanged all the time. And in truth, Rickey *had* complained a lot about the weather; his wardrobe was wholly inadequate for New York, and he had no money to supplement it.

They went out drinking with a group of students one night, and that was where the trouble really started. Drunk, lonely, and homesick, Rickey must have appeared obviously miserable. As they walked back to the dorm together, Muller asked what was wrong, and Rickey made the mistake of trying to tell him. He didn't say anything too obvious, but he told Muller about G-man, how they'd been friends forever, how they always tried to work in the same kitchens, how they were going to get an apartment together when Rickey moved back to New Orleans. "I just miss him really bad," he'd concluded.

For whatever reason, Muller wasn't as friendly with him after that. It might have had to do with the fact that Muller wasn't really a very good cook and always had to scramble to keep up with the classes; maybe he resented the fact that this kid from the swamps of Louisiana was outshining him. Maybe it was something else. Rickey started to hear from other people that Muller was talking shit about him, not kitchen shit but personal. He didn't think he really cared until he learned that Muller had read one of G-man's letters to him; then he wanted to kill the guy.

The fight happened in their Skill Development class the morning after Rickey found out about the letter—another student had told him; it turned out Muller was going around spreading the news. The morning's work included cutting up a chicken. As Muller made the first cut, his knife slipped and the chicken went skidding off the counter. Rickey bent down to pick it up. His hand accidentally brushed Muller's thigh, and Muller snarled, "Save it for your boyfriend, faggot."

Rickey didn't even remember deciding to hit him. He certainly didn't recall getting Muller by the throat and backing him up against the reach-in, as others in the class told him he'd done. Muller must have gotten in some blows too, because Rickey had a few bruises, but he didn't remember that either. He had a few disjointed memories of standing with Muller in the dean's office, the atmosphere of mutual loathing thick and noxious. But he didn't clearly remember anything until he got back to the dorm, called G-man, and said, "I'm coming home."

It was probably best that he'd returned to New Orleans without finishing school. He wasn't sure their relationship could have survived two years apart. But he still sometimes wished he hadn't been kicked out over an asshole like Phil Muller. There must have been other gay students. Certainly there had been students who weren't complete homophobes. If he'd been open from the start, maybe he could have roomed with one of them and avoided the ignominy.

Well, that didn't matter now. What mattered was the chance to make a fresh start—with cooking and with their romance. Dry spells notwithstanding, Rickey thought, it *was* still a romance. They just needed to remind themselves of that a little more often. Refresh their memories, as he'd put it earlier.

He rolled over and put his lips against G-man's ear. "Is your memory refreshed yet?" he said.

"Ummm," said G-man sleepily. "You know, I'm a pretty slow learner sometimes. Maybe we better go over that again."

chapter 12

At 10 a.m., any resident of the second block of Marengo Street could have observed the red Lexus with the license plate GUMBO-1 pulling up in front of Rickey and G-man's little shotgun house. Fortunately, most of their neighbors were either early workers or late sleepers, so Lenny parked his flashy car without attracting undue notice.

Rickey answered the door in a pair of boxer shorts. His hair was shockingly disheveled, and he clutched a steaming mug of coffee in one hand.

"You guys up?" Lenny asked.

"Kinda. C'mon in."

Entering the living room, Lenny looked around at the Salvation Army sofa, the books in milk crates, the well-used bong on the coffee table, and the bare walls as if they were pieces in some museum installation on the Lives of Kitchen Schlubs. "Wow, this place brings back a lot of memories."

"Of what—how you lived when you were poor?"

"Well, yeah."

"Take a good look, then. You want some coffee?"

"No thanks."

"We got clean mugs and everything."

"That's OK, I already had some."

"Well, come on in the kitchen anyway. It's comfortable in there."

The kitchen, in fact, was the nicest room in the house. Thinking of Lenny's own spectacular kitchen, Rickey was a little embarrassed for Lenny to see it, but he need not have been. The old red-and-white linoleum was clean, the tile countertops scrubbed to a near-translucence, the jars of spices and dry goods attractively arranged on the shelves. They didn't have a great deal of kitchenware, but what they did have was carefully stored and well-kept. Lenny's eye was drawn to a blue plate on the table. On the plate beneath an inverted glass mixing bowl was a brown ring of pastry with a sugar crumb topping. "What's that?" he asked.

"Coffee cake. G made it yesterday. You want a piece?"

"What's in it? Sun-dried cherries? Cornmeal batter?"

"No," said Rickey, annoyed. "It's a *coffee cake*. Pecans. Cinnamon swirl. You want a piece or not?"

"I'd love one," said Lenny. "And I believe I *will* have a cup of coffee if you don't mind."

Slightly placated, Rickey served him these items. Lenny took a big bite of the pastry. "That's fantastic. Tastes like a coffee cake should. See, a lot of people try to make a simple, classic recipe like that, they gussy it up until you can't even recognize the thing."

"How can you gussy up a coffee cake?"

"You'd be surprised. I dated this girl who always wanted to impress me. You know—can't cook nice, normal food for a Professional Chef. She never made me a coffee cake, thank God. But one day she asked me what I wanted for dinner, and I couldn't face any of her fancy shit, so I said, well, I'd really like a cheeseburger. I figured, what can you do to a cheeseburger?

"Famous last words. She spent two hours at the store, then came back and started making cheeseburgers. Only somehow they turned into ground lamb patties seasoned with chipotle peppers, and Roquefort instead of Cheddar, and for-Chrissake whole grain buns. I tried to act appreciative, but I really just wanted a cheeseburger. Know what I mean?"

"Yeah. People got no idea how much you'd love a plain old plate of meatloaf and macaroni."

"Who's having meatloaf and macaroni?" asked G-man, drying his hair with a towel as he came in.

"Maybe we can today," said Lenny. "I know a little place in Kenner where nobody cares who the hell I am, and isn't that a blessing. But first we need to look at some properties."

Everyone had another cup of coffee, Rickey and G-man finished getting dressed, and they went out into the New Orleans morning. The yard was ringed with sweet olives, drab-looking trees nobody noticed except in the spring, when their small white flowers filled the air with a fresh, luscious scent. For Rickey and G-man, the smell of sweet olives and mimosa flowers brought back childhood recollections of springtime. Many of the mimosas had died off in a mysterious blight some years ago, but the sweet olives remained to stir their memories.

The first property—a former laundromat on Maple

Street between the Tulane campus and the Carrollton neighborhood—was large and full of light, but had no room for a kitchen. "They told me this place was twice as big as it really is," said Lenny, disgusted. "Next."

The next place was in the Warehouse District, and the owner stood outside waving at them as Lenny pulled up in the freight zone. He was an old man with a vacuous smile and brown Sansabelt pants pulled too high over a burgeoning gut. "I'm Friedrich," he said, giving no clue as to whether it was a first name or a last. "You boys gonna open a restaurant?"

"We're thinking about it," said Lenny.

"That ain't no easy bidness. You think you just gonna be making food, but there's all kinda headaches you gotta deal with. My brother, he had a restaurant in Gentilly in nineteen-fitty-three, before the blacks ruint the area."

"What kind of restaurant was it?" asked G-man.

"Seafood. All kinda fresh seafood and plenty a'gravy. Not no little piece of fish on a plate with a handful of grass like you see today. Plenty a'gravy. I tell you, though, running a restaurant's harder than you know."

"I think we might be able to make a go of it," said Lenny.

"Yeah, all you young kids think you can do it, but it ain't no easy bidness."

"Is this a good way to lease property?" said G-man, honestly curious. "I mean, if you know what the people want the property for, is it really a good idea to tell them what a lousy time they're gonna have?"

The old man squinted up at him. "I tell you what I don't need. I don't need no young smartass telling me how to lease no property. I been leasing property since nineteen-fifty-three!"

"I didn't mean—"

"C'mon," said Rickey, brushing past them. "It's a shit-hole. Let's go."

"Don'tcha wanna look in the back?" Friedrich called after them as they got into Lenny's car. "Don'tcha wanna see my nice alley? This place would make a terrific restaurant!"

"God," said Rickey. He leaned back against the leather headrest and closed his eyes. "I'm tired already."

"Let's look at one more place," Lenny said. "Then we'll get some lunch before we see the rest."

They drove up the Claiborne Avenue overpass and headed for Mid-City. The next property was on Broad Street (its proper name was Broad Avenue, but nobody ever called it that) in a bleak-looking commercial neighborhood near the city government complex that housed the police head-quarters, the courthouse, the Orleans Parish Prison, and the morgue. Auto shops, bail bondsmen, and convenience stores dominated the area. There were some residential streets nearby, but the houses were very small and very poor. "This used to be a paint factory," Lenny said as they pulled up in front of the property, "but it was a restaurant before that. Apparently the factory people never bothered to tear out the kitchen—they had more room than they needed, so they just sealed it off."

The building was large, square, and unlovely, standing alone in the middle of a big blacktop parking lot. It had few windows and looked as if it would be very hot inside. Rickey felt like crying. "Let's check it out," he said.

There was a weatherbeaten awning above the double

glass doors of the front entrance. As they let themselves in, Rickey tried to imagine well-dressed hungry people coming through these doors, looking forward to a good meal. He could not do it, not at first.

But as he entered the building, something clicked.

He wasn't sure what it was. He certainly didn't fall in love with the place or anything like that. It was just a cavernous space not so different from the old warehouse they'd just looked at—maybe even dirtier. Somehow, though, Rickey could imagine tables in here. He could imagine thick green carpet, polished wood, leaded glass partitions separating the dining room from the bar. He closed his eyes, and though the place smelled of nothing but dust and age, he could almost smell perfume and clean linen, fresh bread, caramelizing meat juices, all overlaid with the astringent tang of liquor. He could almost hear tipsy conversations and the clink of silverware on china.

"You like this one, don't you?" said Lenny.

Rickey opened his eyes. Lenny and G-man were watching him, and Lenny was smiling.

"You got a feeling about this place. I know how that goes. I felt that way when I walked into the place that ended up being my first restaurant, even though the ceiling was practically falling in."

"It's kinda scary," said Rickey. He was a little breathless. "It's like that scene in *The Shining* where the guy thinks it's New Year's Eve in the ballroom. He can hear the people, he can *smell* them, but there's nobody there."

"Damn," said G-man. "You can hear people? You can smell food in here?"

"Not exactly. But all of a sudden I could imagine them really, really vividly."

"That's not something you want to ignore," said Lenny. "Let's take a look around."

They found a row of light switches near the doors. Illumination did not improve the space a great deal. The paint-making machinery had been cleared out, but empty cans were still stacked here and there in tall silver pyramids. Swaths of cobweb hung overhead like dirty netting. Beneath the grimy webs, though, Rickey was just able to make out the design of an old-fashioned pressed tin ceiling. It was hard to find those at any price nowadays, and even the reproductions cost a fortune.

"How much they want for this place?" he asked.

Lenny glanced at a piece of paper he was holding. "Dollar a square foot for a minimum three-year lease."

"But it's in such bad shape."

"I've seen worse. We'd want to get it inspected, of course, but it looks pretty sound—no floors caving in, nothing collapsing. We wouldn't have to do a lot of structural stuff."

"Where's the kitchen?" asked G-man.

"All the way to the back, the agent said. But it's supposed to be sealed off."

"We'll get in," said Rickey.

Their footsteps echoed on the cement floor as they crossed the big room. They passed through a doorway into a smaller anteroom full of broken-down metal shelves. This could be the bar, Rickey thought. Beyond it was another doorway covered with plywood. Rickey wedged his fingers under the edge of the plywood and yanked at it. Lenny and G-man winced at the shriek of rusty nails parting from plaster. "You had a tetanus shot lately?" Lenny asked.

"Course I have. We couldn't start work at Tequilatown without our vaccination certificates. I tell you, that Jesse Honeycombe has his ass covered." Rickey wrenched at the plywood again, and it came away from the doorframe. Beyond it was blackness and the dank smell of mildew. Rickey reached around the frame, felt for a light switch, found a brace of them and flipped them on.

Every surface in the kitchen was covered not just with dust, but with a thick layer of that gray fluff that seems to be born of well-aged dust. Gobbets of it dangled from the range hood and the light fixtures. A thick frosting hid the counter-tops entirely. An ancient, powerless reach-in stood against one wall, yawning emptily.

But as they looked, it began to dawn on Rickey that beneath the corpses of a million giant dust bunnies, this was not a badly designed kitchen. It was laid out in the shape of a large, squat H, with the hot line forming the middle bar. To one side of the H was an open area that would make a good pantry. Someone had even left a very nice copper-bottomed sauté pan hanging from one of the overhead pot racks. It was badly tarnished now, but still appeared service-able. Looking at that pan, Rickey got a strange feeling, as if the previous chef had stepped out of the kitchen and forgotten to come back for a decade or two.

He felt a light touch on his neck. If it had been cold, he would have jumped a mile, but it was warm. G-man had reached out and palmed the back of his neck, just once, and

Rickey knew exactly what he meant to communicate: *We could be looking at our very own kitchen right here.*

°   °   °

An hour later, they sat in a divey little place on Airline Drive eating plates of delicious meatloaf. There was no macaroni, but the sides of mashed potatoes and smothered cabbage made up for the lack.

"I think we should go ahead," said Lenny. "Talk to the agent who's handling the property. Get an inspection. Bring in my contractor and get an estimate on fixing the place up."

"You know," said Rickey. Pride made the words stick in his throat, but he forced them out anyway. "You know we don't have *any money at all,* right?"

"Rickey, how many times do I have to tell you? I don't want your money. There's a contract sitting on De La Cerda's desk ready for you to sign—it gives you guys 75 percent ownership of the restaurant. That means you make 75 percent of the profits. It also means you can override anything I say. Remember the first time you came to my house and I told you I was a rich dickhead? I wasn't lying. I like making money. I think we can all make a lot of it if I invest in you two. Hell, if I wasn't such a nice guy—for a rich dickhead, I mean—I might even be insulted by all this money stuff." Lenny finished his meatloaf and wiped the gravy from his plate with half a roll. He did not look insulted in the least.

Rickey turned to G-man. "What do you think?"

"I say we should do it."

"The kitchen looked all right to you?"

"It looked like something from the haunted mansion on Scooby-Doo. But the layout's fine, and we can fix everything else."

"OK then." Rickey put down his fork. "Let's go over to De La Cerda's office this afternoon. I'm ready to sign that contract."

chapter 13

Anthony Bonvillano was setting up his St. Joseph's altar. He hauled the wooden boxes out of the storage room, stacked them in three ascending tiers to symbolize the Holy Trinity, and covered them with pink and white altar cloths. He set the tall plaster statues of Christ and St. Joseph on the top tier and arranged a semicircle of votive candles at their feet.

For two days the Apostle Bar had been full of Anthony's relatives bringing in the traditional dishes and decorations for the altar. Now he began to place these carefully on the three tiers. There were stuffed artichokes, whole roasted fish, bowls of pasta, the sweetened breadcrumbs known as "sawdust" because Joseph had been a carpenter. There was a rosary made of white chocolate. There were little anise-flavored Italian cookies frosted in pastel colors and topped with sprinkles. There were a couple of whole lemons, a nod to the tradition that an unmarried girl who stole a lemon from a St. Joseph's altar would find a husband within a year. ("These lemons are bisexual," Anthony had told Laura when she said the tradition was chauvinistic.) There was a cut-glass bowl full of dried fava beans, also known as lucky beans: each visitor to the altar was meant to take one of these.

Perhaps most important were the specially decorated cakes and breads. There was a cake in the shape of a lamb, frosted white and finished with coconut for wool and jelly-beans for eyes. There was a book-shaped cake decorated with a picture of St. Joseph and the Holy Infant. There was a sheet cake with the inscription, "In memory of Anthony Francis Bonvillano Sr. and Mary Tomolillo Bonvillano, who Founded this Altar." The breads were baked in various traditional shapes: a sandal, a hammer, a saw, a shepherd's crook. This year, for some reason, Anthony's sister had made carefully hand-lettered index cards identifying each shape of bread. One of them was misspelled—SANDLE—but Anthony put it out anyway, figuring the saint would forgive mistakes in a labor of love.

He stepped back and examined his handiwork. It wasn't as fancy as some altars—there was a rich family in Metairie that did one ten feet long and twenty feet wide each year—but he thought it would do. Tonight the priest would come to bless it, and the Apostle Bar would serve a special St. Joseph's meal through the saint's day, March 19.

Rickey and G-man were supposed to be here right now, as a matter of fact. Buddy Diliberto's sports talk show had just come on the radio, and they were always at work by the time Buddy D came on. They'd been out with Lenny every day this week. Anthony supposed they'd be getting their own place soon. He had already decided to scale back the menu once they left, keeping the now-famous chicken wings but otherwise going back to ordinary bar snacks. The prospect of running a simple bar again was a relief to him. He had enjoyed having the two exuberant young cooks and their crazy, hugely popular menu in the same way he enjoyed Mardi Gras: it was fun for a little while, but tiring.

Anthony sat down and listened to Buddy mangling the names of likely Saints draft picks. Just as he was thinking about trying to call Lenny on his cell phone and see if Rickey and G-man were with him, they came bursting in. "We signed a lease!" said Rickey. "We signed a fucking lease, Anthony! We got a restaurant!"

"Well, we got a *location,*" said G-man. "It doesn't look much like a restaurant yet."

"Yeah, but it's a big-ass building and it's already got a kitchen and we're gonna fix it up real nice."

"Where is it?" Anthony asked.

"Corner of Toulouse and Broad, just down the street from the courthouse."

"Big, kinda boxy-looking white building?"

"Yeah."

"And there used to be a restaurant in there?"

"Yeah, the kitchen's still partly set up," said Rickey. "I don't know what kinda place it was, though."

"Italian," said Anthony.

"Really? You know anything about it?"

"Uh, no, no I don't. I just remember an Italian place being in there about twenty years ago."

Rickey and G-man went into the kitchen. Anthony remained at the bar, rubbing his forehead in consternation. They'd be too young to remember the thing, of course. They couldn't have been more than seven or eight when it happened. Lenny wouldn't know either, because he hadn't moved to New Orleans yet. Anthony had just been starting out in the business, and he remembered it well. It had been known among restaurant people as the Red Gravy Murder.

The restaurant, Giambucca's, was owned by a trio of mobbed-up guys who caught their general manager skimming profits. A huge amount of money was missing, something like two hundred thousand dollars, a sum that had seemed unimaginable to Anthony at the time. The GM, more concerned with the ponies at the Fair Grounds than with the restaurant, never even twigged to the fact that his bosses knew the money was gone. They must have figured the place was about to tank anyway; otherwise they surely wouldn't have killed him right on the premises. They'd tried to make it look like an after-hours robbery, but the police hadn't bought it. Most robbers didn't blast their victim once in each kneecap before blowing his head off.

Well, they hadn't killed him in the *kitchen,* Anthony rationalized. Not exactly. He thought it had happened in the walk-in.

He couldn't remember the name of the dead GM. It hadn't been Italian; an Italian guy, even if he were stupid enough to steal from the Mob, would have been more careful about it. He was pretty sure the guy had had a French name, and he knew some of the guy's relatives were still in the restaurant business. A brother was on the Downtown Development District board. A nephew managed a hotel kitchen in the Quarter. He thought Rickey might have even worked with the nephew. Maybe they'd hear about it someplace eventually. Anthony didn't think it was important, and he wasn't going to spoil their excitement by telling them now.

°   °   °

Rickey took the pan of salt cod out of the reach-in where it had been soaking in water since yesterday. Intending to make a brandade, he put some russet potatoes on to boil and started chopping garlic.

G-man was making sauce for the St. Joseph's pasta, a savory-sweet concoction of cauliflower, anchovies, raisins, and pine nuts. He consulted a cookbook, then looked over at Rickey. "You think it really matters if you break up cauliflower florets instead of cutting them?"

"No, I don't think so." Rickey opened the reach-in. "Aw, fuck!"

"What?"

"A.J. didn't shell these fava beans, and I just now noticed."

"Give 'em here. I'll do it if you'll deal with this cauliflower. It's the only vegetable I really hate."

"How come?"

"I think it looks like cancer."

"Dude, it does *not* look like cancer."

"How do you know? You ever seen cancer?"

"No, but it'd be all black and shit, probably."

"Well, ain't this a nice conversation?" said Anthony, coming in.

"G thinks cauliflower looks like cancer."

"No it doesn't," said Anthony. "Cancer's purple."

"I'm gonna sit up front and shell these favas," said G-man. "You guys are making me sick."

He carried the pan into the bar, made himself comfortable, and began splitting open the pods, then nudging the fat little beans out of the greenish-white plush where they nestled. After shelling, they would have to be blanched in boiling water for sixty seconds before their tough outer skins could be peeled off. "Favas and artichokes," his mother liked to say, "the only vegetables that make you lose weight cause you gotta work so hard to eat 'em." She never made a St. Joseph's altar, but her sister Teresa had one every year. G-man and the other kids helped put together the cookie bags: two fig cookies, two seed cookies, a piece of St. Joseph's bread, a prayer card, a lucky bean. Their hands would get sticky and they'd end up eating nearly as many cookies as they bagged. He remembered the house full of relatives and strangers on St. Joseph's Day, the smells of anise, burning candles, and thick red gravy bubbling on the stove. Mary Rose Stubbs would park in front of the little fenced yard, and as she hoisted herself out of her car, Teresa would come out on the porch flapping her hands and hollering, "Go away, lady! You ain't welcome here!" Then they'd both almost hemorrhage themselves laughing. He hadn't visited his Aunt Teresa's altar in years, but the furred texture of the fava pods brought the memories rushing back.

A.J. came in at seven to work dinner while Rickey and G-man finished making the holiday food. At ten, when the priest showed up to bless the altar, they had sauce ready to go on pasta, sautéed fava beans, stuffed eggplants and artichokes, Rickey's salt-cod brandade, and olive salad. "Go ask the priest if he wants a plate," Rickey told G-man.

"You go ask him. I don't want to talk to any priest."

"Why not? You think he can tell how bad you are just by looking at you?"

"I haven't talked to a priest in twelve years," said G-man. "I'm not in the mood to start now."

Rickey shook his head. "I'm *so* glad I wasn't raised Catholic. Hey, A.J., go see if the priest wants a plate."

"Aw, I don't feel like it."

"What? You're a lapsed Catholic too?"

"I don't see *you* running out there to ask him," G-man told Rickey. "Give it another couple of minutes, he'll be gone."

Rickey went up front. The priest, a big young Irish guy with startlingly green eyes, had finished the blessing and was talking to Anthony. "I'd love a plate," he said when Rickey asked him. "I been doing blessings all day and I haven't had a chance to eat anything but cookies."

"Fire one for the Father," Anthony called through the window.

"You know," the priest told Rickey, "I used to be a cook before I went to seminary."

"Yeah? Where'd you cook at?"

"Started off doing salads at Gertie Greer's, ended up working the broiler at Commander's."

"Didn't you, uh, were you, like, wasn't it—aw, never mind."

"No, what?"

"Well, you know, the way people talk in kitchens—didn't it ever bother you?"

The priest laughed. "You're not Catholic, are you?"

"No. I mean, my best friend was, so I kinda grew up around it, but no."

"Well, plenty of my parishioners are drunker and more foulmouthed than anybody I ever met in any kitchen."

"No shit?" said Rickey, honestly surprised. "Oh, fuck, I mean—oh, jeez, I gotta go check on your food."

"Nice talking to you," the priest called after him with no apparent trace of sarcasm.

"Dude," said G-man as Rickey came back into the kitchen, "are you *blushing*?"

"Fuck off."

"See why we didn't want to go out there? Even if a priest is nice, it's embarrassing to talk to him. Even if you're not Catholic, you still feel like you're in that damn confessional."

"Yeah," said Rickey. "I guess you do." Glad to be back in his element, he snagged a strand of pasta out of the boiling pot and tested it for doneness. "Hey A.J., you wanna dump this?"

With so many items on the menu, they were only serving a spoonful or two of everything. Rickey plated the pasta in the center, the stuffed vegetables and olive salad around the edges, and the brandade on a side plate with toasted rounds of Italian bread. A few minutes after sending it out, he peeked through the window to see how the Father liked it. The priest saw him looking and gave him a thumbs-up.

Later, Rickey went back up front and took a lucky bean from the altar. He noticed a shoebox covered with construction paper on a nearby table. Written on the construction paper was the legend **Petitions for St. Joseph.** Some blank slips of paper lay beside the box. Rickey grabbed a slip, unclipped a pen from his jacket, and wrote, "*Dear St. Joseph, I am not Catholic, if you really care about that. But I bet a lot* *of Catholic people will like our restaurant. So please let it do great. Thanks."*

He wasn't sure whether or not to sign the petition. After a moment of thought, he folded it in quarters and stuffed it through the slit in the top of the shoebox. Surely the saint would know who'd written it, if he was any good at his job.

chapter 14

"What's that *smell?*" said G-man. "I thought I was coming into my kitchen, but all of a sudden I'm in Pirate's Alley at 4 a.m."

"I'm testing a recipe," Rickey said. "Veal kidneys à la liégeoise."

"Why?"

"Elizabeth David says it's wonderful." Rickey held up a book called *An Omelette and a Glass of Wine*. "She's got a whole chapter about cooking with liquor."

"I think Elizabeth David is fucking with you."

"It's gonna be good."

"It's gonna be disgusting."

"Why? Be open-minded. Be open-tastebudded. Why is it disgusting?"

"Because it smells like *pee!*"

"Well, yeah," Rickey admitted. "But maybe it'll taste better than it smells." He covered the large sauté pan that contained the simmering kidneys, poured a generous measure of gin into a skillet, and tilted the skillet until the gas flame licked at its contents. Blue flames sprang from the surface of the gin. Rickey let it burn for a few seconds, then removed the skillet from the heat, took the lid off the kidneys, and clapped it over the gin to extinguish the fire. He crushed something with his marble mortar and pestle—juniper berries, G-man guessed—and added it to the kidneys, then uncovered the gin and poured it into the sauté pan.

"Now it smells like a drunk who pissed himself," said G-man.

"Well, we ought to get used to that—we're probably gonna have a few in our restrooms."

Without asking G-man if he wanted any, Rickey spooned the kidneys onto two plates. The organs had already been cleaned and sliced, and the pattern inside them reminded G-man of a cross between the spores of a mushroom and the sections of an orange. "You know," he said, "I really don't want to eat this."

"A good cook is a fearless cook." Rickey put the plates on the table. "Besides, I need your opinion."

"Why? We're never gonna serve this at Liquor. People in New Orleans won't eat kidneys."

"Why they got 'em at the store, then?"

"Probably they been sitting in the meat case for about a million years. I bet you're the only person who ever bought any."

Instead of answering, Rickey picked up his fork, speared a slice of kidney, and put it in his mouth. G-man watched him chew and swallow. "That's actually real good," he said. "I guess the pee makes it tangy."

"That does it. I'm having a bowl of cereal."

"No, dude, just try a bite. Please?"

Rickey made pleading eyes, big, blue, and innocent. G-man sighed and cut off a tiny edge of a slice. He pushed it around in the sauce, coating it as thickly as possible, then ate it.

"Well?"

"It's even more horrible than I thought it would be."

"Aw, you just don't have any sense of adventure. Gimme your plate. I like it."

G-man sat at the table and watched Rickey eat both plates of kidneys. At first he thought Rickey was just showing off, but Rickey wasn't one to finish two plates of food he didn't care for. "What do you like about it?" he asked.

"I don't know. The kidneys and the gin both have a kinda astringent taste, and the butter's sweet. What do you hate about it?"

"Everything."

"No, c'mon. Describe it."

"It tastes like a piece of liver marinated in a urinal."

The doorbell rang, and G-man went to answer it, glad to escape the smell in the kitchen. Lenny was on the porch. "You just missed the veal kidneys in gin," said G-man.

"Too bad. I love kidneys."

"You people are perverts."

"Listen," said Lenny, "I'm sorry I didn't call, but I was on my way uptown and I thought I'd see if you guys were free for dinner tonight. We need to start talking about the renovations."

"Don't you ever have to work?"

"Actually, I closed the kitchen at Crescent for the past

four nights if you want to get persnickety about it. So—dinner?"

"Rickey's off, but I gotta work at the Apostle."

"How long are you two planning to stay there?"

"Until we can make a living somewhere else, I guess."

"Well, listen, what if I put you on the Duvet Corporation payroll? Say I've decided to hire you and Rickey as consultants? That way you could devote all your time to Liquor. It wouldn't stand up to an audit"—Lenny lowered his voice—"but it might satisfy Rickey, since I know he won't let me just *give* you money."

"Lenny, he's gonna know you're just giving us money. He's not really gonna think we're consultants."

"I know that. But the consultant thing might let him take the money without getting his panties in a wad. You know how he'd react if I just said, 'Hey, I want to support you for the next few months.'"

"Yeah, that might not go over too well. But why didn't you just offer us the jobs? How come you're telling me all this?"

"Because I've never seen *you* get your panties in a wad about *anything,*" said Lenny. "I wanted to see what you thought of the idea first."

"It might work. I don't know. Why don't you ask him?"

"Ask me what?" said Rickey, coming in from the kitchen. "Oh, hey, Lenny."

"Hi, Rickey. Listen, we need to get moving with the renovation. You should be testing recipes and thinking about who you want to hire. How about you guys quit the Apostle Bar and I put you on my payroll as consultants?"

"OK."

"OK?"

"Sure. I figured you were gonna offer us something like that pretty soon. I accept if G does."

"It's fine with me," said G-man.

"Then I guess it's settled," said Rickey. "Hey, Lenny, I meant to ask you—I read about this walnut eau de vie from Hungary and thought it might be good in a salad dressing. You think we could find some?"

"I'll have De La Cerda check it out. He's arranged to import stuff for me before. He got me a crazy cheap deal on a bunch of black truffles from Toscano awhile back, and they were good, too."

"You didn't happen to sell any of those truffles to Anthony B, did you?" said Rickey.

"I didn't sell him any. I gave him a couple, three."

Rickey and G-man started laughing.

"What?"

"Nothing," said Rickey. "Find out what De La Cerda says."

"Will do. And I'll have Flanagan hook you up to the consultant thing. Say two thousand a month? Apiece, naturally. I know it's not much, but do you think you could get by on that until we open?"

"Yeah," they said, more or less in unison. Neither of them had ever made more than $1300 a month before, and usually well under that.

"OK, then, I better get going. Glad this worked out. I'll call you tomorrow."

"I don't think I've ever seen him look stunned before," said Rickey when Lenny had gone.

"I know exactly how he feels."

"What? You thought I wasn't gonna accept his offer?"

"Well, I sure thought you were gonna bitch about it first."

"Why bother? We're already table-dancing for Lenny. I'm supposed to complain if he wants to slip a little extra cash in our garter?"

"That's more disgusting than the kidneys."

"Well, it's true, and I don't even care any more. We're gonna fix that place up just like we want it, and hire a bunch of great cooks, and open a killer restaurant, and someday we're gonna buy out Lenny's 25 percent."

"You know, Rickey, you never stop surprising me."

"You thought the same thing as Lenny, didn't you? You thought I was gonna pitch a fit, but maybe the consulting thing would keep me from crying about it. You people think you know me so well, but I still got my little mysteries."

"You do," said G-man. "You certainly do."

"Hey, you know the first thing we should do with our four thousand dollars a month?"

"What's that?"

"Eat somewhere real nice without Lenny."

"You got a date."

chapter 15

Mike Mouton was happy. He had a brand-new bag. He locked his office door, poured some of the cocaine onto a pocket mirror, and chopped it up with a razor blade. It was clean white stuff, not yellowish and smelling of gasoline like some of the shit NuShawn had had lately. Just as Mike was about to hoover up the two fat lines he'd laid out, the phone rang.

"You seen the paper today?" his father asked, bypassing niceties like "hello" and "how are you."

"No."

"Somebody's opening a restaurant in the old Giambucca's place. Where your Uncle George was killed."

"That dump? Nothing's been in there for years."

"Says in the paper these two characters are fixing it up." Wilford Mouton, known to one and all as Pinky, had the gravelly baritone of a lifelong chainsmoker. Even over the phone, Mike could almost smell his cigar breath. "They been cooking in some bar, now they gonna open a real restaurant."

Suspicion touched Mike like a cold finger. "Does it give their names?"

He heard newspaper rattling at his father's end of the line. "Yeah. John Rickey and Gary Stubbs."

"They can't!" Mike slapped the desk, almost tipping the mirror with the cocaine on it. "That's impossible. They don't have the money to renovate that place."

"Must be somebody's helping them out, then."

Mike remembered his not-so-clandestine foray to the Apostle Bar, the disbelief and deep sense of injustice he'd felt when he saw who was coming in with Rickey. "Lenny Duveteaux," he said. "They've been palling around together."

"Hell, if Lenny's helping them, I guess they got enough money to open *two* restaurants if they want to. Say, Michael, you told me you were friends with Lenny. Why you didn't get him to help you open some nice little place?"

"I don't want to open a restaurant."

"Yeah, yeah, I know. You keep saying you're happy in that dead-end job I got you. You wanna work for somebody else your whole life, I guess there's nothing I can do about it. Hell, at least these kids got some initiative."

"They don't!" Mike shouted into the phone. "They don't have anything but dumb luck!" But Pinky had already hung up.

Uncle George, thought Mike. *Uncle George tortured and shot like a dog in the cooler of a Wop shithole on Broad Street, and now goddamn Rickey opening a restaurant there.* Mike Mouton's childhood had been a lonely time. His mother—who'd died when Mike was seventeen—was always more interested in Mike's two sisters. His father treated him like a project he'd started and then lost interest in, some needle-point pillow or model ship whose continued presence was an embarrassing nuisance. Mike had never been the kind of kid who made a lot of friends; something about him put people off. It was as if they could smell something bad on him even though his house was clean and his mother made him shower every day. Pinky's sour cigar smoke, maybe. His Uncle George was the one person who seemed to like him all right.

Unfortunately, the Moutons didn't like Uncle George. "He might be my brother," Mike's father often said, "but he's no kin of mine." Though he was supposed to be managing Giambucca's, George Mouton didn't care about the restaurant business, or about money at all except as something that could be bet on horses. He talked about hitting the big one someday, but he seemed to feel that the win would be an end in itself rather than a means to fortune and leisure. When he took Mike to the Fair Grounds with him (Mike soon learned to tell his mother he was going to the library; she believed he was very well read), it was easy to see that the place just made George happy. He loved the smell and the sheen of horseflesh, the bustle of the grandstand, the bugle playing "Call to Post," the characters who populated the track. Mike liked all these things too, but what he liked most was the company of his uncle, the one person who seemed to enjoy being with him. Looking back, he sometimes wondered if George had been friendless too, if he'd simply felt less like a loser in someone else's company, even that of his teenage nephew. But that was unprofitable thinking.

Even more unprofitable was Mike's suspicion, faint but persistent, that his father had tipped off George's bosses to his theft. The owners of Giambucca's had hardly been meticulous with their receipts; that was why George had been able to skim so much. He'd started with small sums, but it seemed so easy that he soon graduated to large ones. At least, that was what Mike had been able to piece together. He knew his father had been tight with the owners. George was an embarrassment, and Pinky Mouton hated to be embarrassed. Pinky was a businessman—CEO of a restaurant supply chain for twenty years, he'd been appointed to the board of the Downtown Development District in retirement—and George was bad business.

However, Pinky had probably figured they'd just quietly knock George over the head and throw him in the Mississippi. The splashiness of the murder had shocked the whole city. It made the front page of the *Times-Picayune* for three days straight, and the follow-up stories lasted for months. Pinky was furious. Mike, then twenty years old, found a tiny bit of comfort in the knowledge that George had managed to embarrass his brother one last time.

Mike snorted his two lines and went to the hotel lobby for a newspaper. Back in his office, he pulled out the entertainment section and turned to the restaurant review. Seeing a single red bean at the top of the column, he hoped for one wild moment that it was a hatchet job on Rickey's new place, but of course that wasn't open yet. The review dissected an expensive place in the Quarter that could not decide whether it wanted to be French or Italian. According to Chase Haricot, rude waiters represented the former option and overcooked pasta the latter. The one bean was for the gorgeous river view. The information about Rickey appeared in a sidebar of restaurant news:

> **New Orleans is losing its best late-night din-ing option, but not for long. Chefs John Rickey and Gary Stubbs, who revolutionized the kitchen at the Apostle Bar with their spirit-enhanced recipes, will open their own restaurant this summer. Rickey and Stubbs are currently overseeing renovations on the property at North Broad and Toulouse Streets, formerly Giam-bucca's Home-Style Restaurant. No word on the new name or menu, but let's hope they keep the prosciutto-wrapped figs in Calvados.**

Mike caught himself grinding his teeth. He wasn't sure if it was a side effect of the coke or just an externalization of his dislike for Rickey. His face burned as he remembered how Rickey had kneed him in the crotch and pushed him up against the cooler. Probably Rickey had gotten some kind of illicit charge from that. The little faggot obviously had it in for him—first the assault; then taking up with Lenny Duveteaux and turning the powerful restaurateur against Mike; now this. Mike felt certain that Rickey knew George Mouton had been murdered on the property and had chosen to open his restaurant there for that reason. He was thumb-ing his nose at Mike on a grand scale—not just Mike, but Uncle George too.

He heard his father's voice again. *At least these kids got some initiative.* They had even turned his own father against him—not that that took much effort. One of these days, though, his chance was going to come. Pinky, Rickey and his fag partner, Lenny Duveteaux—they would see what Mike was really made of.

He took his new bag from the desk drawer and began to lay out two more lines.

°   °   °

"A *murder?*" said Rickey. "What? *When?*"

He was standing by the pay phone at the Apostle Bar. The pay phone also served as the house line, and Anthony had just looked into the kitchen to tell him he had a call from somebody at the newspaper.

"Nineteen-eighty," said the writer. "People called it the Red Gravy Murder."

"What do you mean, murder?"

He caught Anthony's eye. Anthony glanced away, but not before Rickey had seen the guilty look on his face.

"I mean, there was a *murder* in the *restaurant,*" said the writer patiently. "Gangland-style killing—man shot twice through the brain. In the cooler, I think. Nobody told you about it?"

"Absolutely not."

The writer gave Rickey a basic rundown of the events. "I can't remember the guy's name," he concluded. "I can probably look it up for you."

"What, so I can name a dish after him?"

"Hey, that's a pretty good idea."

"Look, mister—what'd you say your name was again? Who are you, anyway?"

"Sid Schwanz. I write horse racing stories and a column

in the Living section. I thought I might do a feature looking back on the murder—it was a pretty big story."

Rickey leaned against the wall next to the phone. His bandanna was slipping down over his eyes, and he pushed it back up. "Mr. Schwanz, this is the first I've heard of any murder. I could use some time to think about it first. What kinda hours you keep?"

"The latest."

"Well, why don't you come to the Apostle tonight around twelve? Let me buy you a drink and we'll talk about it then."

"Sounds good."

"You won't write anything before then?"

"Not a word, Chief."

Rickey hung up. He hated people who called him chief instead of chef, thinking they were being witty.

"What's up?" said Anthony too casually.

"What's up is that somebody once got killed in my restaurant, and I think you knew it."

"Aw, Rickey, you guys had just signed the lease. You were so excited. I wasn't gonna ruin it by telling you that garbage. Anyway, the buildings in New Orleans are so old, somebody's probably died in most all of them."

"Maybe so, but I bet most of them didn't have a guy get his head blown off in the kitchen."

"Did that writer tell you it happened in the kitchen? I didn't think it happened in the kitchen."

"It happened in the walk-in."

"Well, that ain't exactly the kitchen."

Rickey turned his back on Anthony and fed some coins

into the phone. He called home, but there was no answer; G-man had the car and must be out somewhere. He called Lenny, but Lenny's cell phone wasn't on, so he left a message.

He went back in the kitchen, grated two pounds of Cheddar, and mixed up a cheese straw dough with Calvados. While the dough was chilling, he made caponata. It was a weird combination, but he'd tried it before and it worked. As he was rolling out the dough, G-man came in. Seeing that Rickey was making cheese straws, he said, "What's wrong?"

Rickey told him.

"Damn," said G-man. "You talked to Lenny yet?"

"I couldn't get hold of him."

"Dude, are you OK?"

"No," said Rickey. "I'm really not." He sat down on a beer keg, put his apron over his face, and began to cry. He hadn't known he was going to do it, but once he got started, it was hard to stop.

G-man sat beside Rickey and put an arm around his shoulders. "Come on. It's gonna be OK. We've been through worse things than this. Come on, now."

"I know," said Rickey, sniffling. "It just seems like every time we move forward, something horrible happens. Maybe we're not meant to have a restaurant."

"That's silly. You think Lenny had it easy when he opened his first place? Remember how he told us he'd just signed the lease when his contractor found termites in the attic, and it turned out the owner of the building had paid off the inspector not to say anything about them? They had to tent the building for a week and it cost, like, five thousand dollars, but look at him now. This is just a little setback."

"You think?"

"I know it."

Rickey let out a long, shaky sigh and buried his face in his hands. G-man sat quietly beside him massaging the back of his neck, the only thing that almost always calmed Rickey down. He noticed a pillow-snarl in Rickey's hair and gently untangled it with his finger. Anthony's head appeared in the window, then disappeared just as quickly.

"You want something, Anthony?" called G-man.

"Nuh-uh," said Anthony without looking in again. "Got an order, is all."

"Well, put it up."

Anthony's hand came around the edge of the window and stuck a ticket in the rack. "You want me to come back there and make it?"

"No," said G-man. "I got it." He gave Rickey a quick kiss and got up to make the order, a martini muffuletta and fried okra rellenos.

Rickey went to the sink to wash his face. He felt embarrassed, not because he had cried in front of G-man—he'd done that plenty of times before—but because he'd let this murder thing get under his skin so badly. G-man was right; they'd been through worse. What was more, they probably had worse still ahead of them. He needed to toughen up. He decided that, one way or another, he was going to keep Sid Schwanz from writing that story.

o   o   o

G-man had only stopped by the Apostle en route to the gro-cery store. After making sure Rickey really was all right and promising to return before midnight to meet with Schwanz, he decided to go on his way. As he was leaving, Anthony followed him outside and said, "I guess Rickey was pretty upset."

"Well, yeah, it kinda sucks to find out somebody got murdered in your kitchen. But he'll be fine."

"I guess you were just—I mean—I didn't mean to act, you know, like there was anything funny going on."

G-man took off his shades. It was a sunny day and the light hurt his eyes, but he wanted to get a good look at Anthony. "Funny?" he said.

"When you had your, uh, your arm around him and all."

"Anthony—"

"Now don't get mad, I ain't saying—"

"Anthony."

"What?"

"I had my arm around Rickey because that's what you do when your friend is upset."

"Yeah! Yeah, sure, that's all I—"

"But listen close: we *are* a couple, Rickey and me. Have been for years."

"A couple of what?"

G-man folded his arms across his chest and leaned against the car, waiting.

"You mean—"

"I mean exactly what you think I mean. Probably more, too. I hope you don't have a problem with that, but if you do, it's not gonna keep us up nights."

"No, jeez, of course not," said Anthony, rubbing his hand over the thinning hair on top of his head as he always did when something made him uncomfortable. "I like you guys. It's none of my damn business."

"You got that right," said G-man, climbing into the Satellite.

Anthony went back in the bar and sat watching a game show on TV, but his mind was elsewhere. How could he have known Rickey and G-man for years and not realized such a thing? Maybe his ex-wife was right; maybe he really was a dumb bunny. When he could no longer help himself, he got up and peeked into the kitchen. Rickey looked just the same as ever. He felt Anthony's eyes on him and turned around. "What?"

"Nothing," said Anthony, retreating.

When he finished his cheese straws, Rickey felt a little better. He decided to make a dinner special of pecan-crusted catfish with rum butter, knocking out the prep just as A.J. came in. Word had gotten out that Rickey and G-man would only be cooking at the Apostle for a couple more nights, and the place was packed with people wanting their favorite dishes one last time. Rickey was glad to be busy; it took his mind off the upcoming conversation with the newspaperman.

Lenny called at eleven. "Sorry I didn't get back to you sooner, but I didn't want to bug you in the middle of the dinner rush. We had a fire over here during lunch."

"A fire!"

"Nothing too serious. It's my own fault, really, for not having the air conditioning ducts cleaned a long time ago.

One of my waiters was making bananas Foster at the table, and he got a little too enthusiastic with the rum. Flames shot all the way up to the ceiling and ignited a bunch of crap in the ducts."

"Damn."

"It's not too bad. I'll have to get the carpet cleaned and replace a few tables. What really sucked was that we had to evacuate the restaurant. About thirty parties got their lunch for free—whatever they had time to eat, anyway."

"It's been a great day all over," said Rickey, and related what the newspaper writer had told him.

"Shit," said Lenny. "Right there in the kitchen?"

"In the walk-in."

"I thought a dollar a square foot was pretty cheap for that property. Well, listen. I'll be happy to help if you want, but I really think you guys should handle this one yourselves. You don't want people knowing I'm a partner in this restaurant, then you better get used to dealing with the press. It's your place. When stuff like this comes up, you need to decide how you want to deal with it."

"I already have," said Rickey. "I was upset before. Now I'm kinda philosophical about the whole thing."

"That attitude will get you far, my friend."

At 11:45, Rickey left A.J. to handle the kitchen. He sat at a table sipping a double shot of Wild Turkey. G-man showed up and ordered the same thing for himself, and together they formulated a plan. When Sid Schwanz came in a few minutes after midnight, they were ready for him.

"Gentlemen?" he said, approaching their table. He was an amiable-looking guy in his midforties, with whiskey blossoms in his cheeks (a good sign as far as Rickey was concerned) and a pronounced limp.

"Probably you noticed I'm kinda gimpy," he said when they had all introduced themselves. "See, I spend a little too much time at the Fair Grounds, and I tend to gravitate to the stables. Horse stepped on my foot in the backstretch. Broke every damn bone in it."

"All of them?" said G-man. "I thought there were, like, two hundred bones in the foot."

"It was a big horse. Broke every damn one of 'em. Hurt like hell, a'course, and all my toenails turned black and fell off."

"You want something to eat?" said Rickey. "I got a nice dinner special. Catfish pecan."

"Yeah, I don't mind if I do."

Rickey went back in the kitchen and fixed the plate himself. When he came back with it, G-man had gotten Schwanz a drink. Pretty soon Schwanz was halfway through the piece of fish and looking happy. "So you're local boys," he said.

"Yeah," said Rickey. "G's so skinny, people sometimes think he's a tourist until he opens his mouth, but we were born and raised in the Lower Ninth Ward."

"No kidding? I grew up down that way, in Holy Cross. Where you went to school?"

In New Orleans, this always meant high school. "Frederick Douglass," said Rickey.

"Whoo! Pretty rough school. My daddy went there when it was still Nicholls. Me, I went to Holy Redeemer."

"Looks like you need another drink, Sid," said G-man. "What was it again?"

"A Horse's Neck. Little something I drink at the Fair Grounds. Maker's Mark and ginger ale with lemon."

"So," said Rickey when G-man had come back with a fresh round of drinks, "I guess you probably know we'd rather you didn't write about the Red Gravy Murder."

"I wouldn't worry if I was you," Schwanz said. "People remember the case, and if they don't, they gonna find out sooner or later. Just look at it as a little advance publicity."

"Well, that's not really the kinda publicity we want before we even get up and running. We'd like to have a chance to build a customer base before people start associating our place with a gangland killing."

Schwanz shrugged. "Whatcha gonna do? I'm not in the restaurant business. I'm in the news business, and I see a story here."

"We understand that," said Rickey. "That's why we're willing to make you an offer." He took out two copies of a document they'd prepared before Sid Schwanz's arrival and handed one to the newspaperman.

"'Drunkard's Agreement,'" Schwanz read aloud. "'This document entitles the bearer, Sid Schwanz, to one year's worth of free drinks at the restaurant of John Rickey and Gary Stubbs, provided that Mr. Schwanz publishes no stories about the Red Gravy Murder during said year. This agreement is nontransferable and does not include meals or gratuities.'"

"You gotta tip our bartenders," said G-man. "Otherwise they'll take it out on us."

"Chiefs," said Schwanz, "you drive a hard bargain. But not that hard. I accept."

A few minutes after Sid Schwanz limped out of the

Apostle, Lenny came in. There were black smudges of ash on the cuffs of his check pants and across the front of his white jacket. At first Rickey couldn't figure out what looked strange about him. Then he realized he'd never actually seen Lenny in chef's clothes before, except on TV.

"Never in my life have I needed a drink this badly," said Lenny. Almost before he had finished speaking, Anthony appeared at the table with a large vodka tonic. Lenny took the glass, drained it, and put it back in Anthony's hand. Anthony returned to the bar and got him another one, then joined them at the table.

"I thought the fire wasn't too bad," Rickey said.

"It wasn't. But remember I told you we had to evacuate the place? Well, it turned out not everybody left. Looks like one of my crackhead dishwashers took the opportunity to stay in the building and go through the employee lockers."

"You catch him?"

"No, but he skipped out before his shift was over, and a bunch of people found their money missing. I gave them a hundred bucks apiece. Most of them didn't lose that much, but they all helped clean up the mess from the fire. I figured they had it coming." He leaned back in his chair and pressed the heels of his hands into his eyesockets. "What the hell do you want to open a restaurant for, anyway?"

"I don't really know," said Rickey. He found himself liking Lenny better than he ever had before; Lenny seemed smaller and more human than usual. "Just crazy, I guess."

"I guess. How'd it go with the guy from the paper?"

Rickey told him about the Drunkard's Agreement, and Lenny started laughing so hard he almost choked on his drink. "That's the best thing I've heard all day. How'd you think of that?"

"We just tried to figure out the common ground between cooks and newspaper reporters. Something we could appeal to. The only thing we could think of was liquor."

"Think he'll stick by it?" said Anthony.

Rickey shrugged. "Not much we can do about it if he doesn't. It's not legally binding. But if he wants his free drinks, he will."

"He'll stick by it," said Lenny. "I've known some journalists in my day. There's nothing they like better than free drinks. You're a genius, Rickey."

"It was G's idea too. He was the one who told me to try and think of the common ground."

"Our diplomat," said Lenny, patting G-man on the back.

"You're in a pretty good mood," G-man told him, "considering how your day went."

"Perspective, guys. It's all in the perspective. My building's still standing. Nobody's dead. One of my pastry chefs just got engaged, and she told me she almost left her ring in her locker but decided not to at the last minute. So at least I don't have a brokenhearted pastry chef, and I don't have to replace a diamond. I'm looking on the bright side of life. You'll learn all about it soon enough."

"I can't wait," said Rickey. "It sounds like a fucking picnic."

chapter 16

I n the time it took to renovate the building at North Broad and Toulouse, a veritable alphabet soup of restaurants opened and closed in New Orleans.

There was African Bounty, whose menu seemed a cruel vegetarian parody of East African food. Instead of rice or cornmeal porridge, either of which would have been reasonably authentic, most of the dishes were served over whole wheat pasta. The building had no air conditioning, only one portable fan directed at the kitchen door. When diners in imminent danger of heatstroke attempted to direct the fan's weak current toward their tables, the waitresses would rebuke them as if they had attempted to walk out without paying the bill.

There was China Bayou, an attempt to mesh the cuisines of Louisiana and Canton. Alligator-and-cream-cheese wontons were the least of the horrors. The dish generally thought to have heralded the restaurant's downfall was the chef's specialty, kung pao crawfish. Nothing was inherently wrong with this dish, but there had recently been a big media flap about Louisiana restaurants buying cheap Chinese crawfish instead of local ones. Everyone seemed to assume China Bayou's crawfish were card-carrying Communists, and nobody wanted to be a pinko.

There was Durum, a multi-culti pasta place reviewed by Chase Haricot, who found a ladybug in his house salad. He called this to the attention of the waiter, who blithely told him, "Oh, that happens a lot. Good thing you didn't come in the winter—we find earwigs then!" The exchange was repeated verbatim in Haricot's review.

There was Eau, a French Quarter café backed by and decorated with pictures of three supermodels. The menu, heavily loaded with salads, was dull but not actively offensive. Bulimia jokes were believed to have rung the death knell for this one.

There was Iko Iko, a tiny, musty space decorated like the living room of a thrift-shopping addict, which enjoyed a brief spell of trendiness before repeat diners finally noticed that the "famous" fried chicken had approximately the same effect on their digestive tracts as those fat-free potato chips that had been all the rage a few years back.

There was Iafrate's, a Creole-Italian place that seemed like a sure bet until an outbreak of salmonella swept through its customers. When tested, the undercooked lasagna contained enough organisms to kill the entire crowd at a New Orleans Brass hockey game.

There was the Krazy Kajun, a Bourbon Street tourist mill whose Liquid Smoke-flavored red beans and rice, scorched etouffee, and eraserlike fried alligator nuggets proved too vile even for tourists with a few of those colorful yard-long daiquiris inside them.

There was Lhasa, a Tibetan restaurant whose owner

took great pleasure in entertaining diners by playing his violin and singing medieval ballads. Sadly for him, the diners did not share his pleasure, and the charbroiled mutton and butter tea failed to keep them coming in.

There was Maman's, a po-boy place that frightened people away by hanging big, inexplicable photographs of the Stealth bomber in the dining area.

There was Riesling, a would-be Alsatian restaurant that offered no mustard with its limp choucroute garnie. If mustard was requested, the chef would send out a squeeze bottle of the same Zatarain's Creole you could buy at the grocery store.

There was the Rue de Difference, a breakfast-and-burger joint owned by a pair of old queens who were a bit too fond of slot machines and video poker.

There was Sauvage, a New Louisiana Eatery whose chef blew all his local credibility by putting fresh basil in the maque choux. Its harsh herbal bite rendered the classic corn-and-okra combo sickly-sweet and pallid. Most culinary pundits concurred that the owners had already doomed the place by using the word "eatery."

There was Vaca Felíz, a Mexican cantina with terrible frozen margaritas. In a city of drinkers spoiled rotten by the drive-thru daiquiri, frozen margaritas could make or break a Mexican restaurant.

There was Yancey's, where the chef showed off his nouvelle training by serving an appetizer called Deconstruction of Gumbo: one boiled shrimp, one piece of stewed okra, and a small heap of toasted flour on a plate whose edges were dotted with filé powder and Tabasco sauce. By the time the chef was fired, the damage to the customer base had already been done.

And there was Zen, a pan-Asian bistro with European influences. Unfortunately, the European influences included a plate of French fries with four mayonnaises: sate, five-spice, cilantro-lime, and the especially loathsome coconut. This plate of fries cost 7. Nothing so vulgar as a dollar sign sullied the menu; the price was simply 7. A small foie gras appetizer was 12.5, and entrées ranged from 18 to 32.

Rickey kept a list of all these restaurants (and a few other, less disastrous ones that opened during this time) in a purple spiral-bound notebook. As the places closed, he crossed them off the list. He kept waiting for one that would worry him, but none ever did.

chapter 17

With the help of Lenny's contractor, Rickey and G-man took a long, critical look at their future restaurant and decided where to knock out walls, raise the floor, put in restrooms, and such. They also started thinking about how to decorate, but the finer details would come after the heavy work was done.

They called a bunch of night porters who were eager to pick up some day work and spent a week hauling trash out of the building. Their more fearsome finds included crack vials, a piece of yellow crime scene tape, and an old mattress covered with scorch marks and worse.

Lenny was not present for the trash-hauling, but he did find them a test kitchen so they could start trying out recipes on a larger scale than they were able to do on Marengo Street. Rickey wanted to use Lenny's home kitchen, but Lenny nixed the idea. "That kitchen is my baby," he said. "No restaurant cooking allowed." Instead, he rented them a vacant, fully equipped kitchen deep in the bowels of the casino at the foot of Canal Street. Gambling hadn't gone over as well as expected in New Orleans, and the casino's restaurants were faring even worse than its games. Lenny got the space cheap.

Rickey and G-man stocked the test kitchen and started making food. Lenny sometimes brought people by to eat, but mostly they fed themselves and their friends. Terrance came by one day and asked for a version of fettucine Alfredo. They made two, one with white rum and one with Advocaat, a sweet Dutch egg liqueur. They did not judge either version to be a success, but Terrance ate big plates of both. "I was a lot skinnier before I found out about fettucine Alfredo," he told them. "Damn, I love this stuff."

"It's a waste of calories if you ask me," said Rickey. "I'm gonna eat all that cream and butter, I'd rather have dessert or maybe some nice barbecued shrimp."

"Well, see, you just don't appreciate the dish."

"How's Escargot's?" Rickey asked. "How's Mike?"

"How you think Mike is? Sweaty, coked-up, and mean. One of the dessert ladies chased him through the dining room with a knife last week."

"Cool! Why?"

"Aw, he was riding their asses for not working hard enough, and she smart-mouthed him a little. She said 'You think we're your kitchen niggers?' and Mike said yeah."

"No way!"

"You know he did."

"Yeah, I believe it. This happened during service?"

"Course. Mike's gonna fuck up real bad, he always makes sure to do it during service."

"Terrance, you gotta get out of there. You need to move up in the world. You ever worked the grill before?"

"No, not really."

"I'll train you. Can you hold out for a couple more months?"

"I been holding out four years with old Mike. I guess I can stand him a little longer."

Another day, Rickey called Tanker and invited him to cook with them. He and Mo were leaving for Colorado the following week, but he came downtown anyway—mostly, Rickey thought, out of curiosity. "I don't even know if we're coming back to New Orleans," he said. "We might just stay out there."

"Sure you're coming back," said Rickey. "All they eat in Colorado is elk and venison. You'll be crying for a piece of fresh Gulf fish within a month, and you'll call us up going, 'Rickey, if only I'd listened when y' all made me that nice offer . . .'"

"You guys are so full of shit," said Tanker good-naturedly. Without even seeming to pay attention to what he was doing, he had just made the most beautiful salad Rickey had ever seen. Perfectly torn pieces of redleaf and butter lettuce were mounded on a big white plate. The lettuce was topped with a small heap of sweet potato hay, and three pastel shades of creamy vinaigrette—purple, green, and gold—decorated the edges of the plate.

"You *like* making salads?" G-man asked Tanker. From his tone, he might have been asking, "You *like* drinking that gray scum that forms in the gutters on Mardi Gras?"

"Love it," said Tanker. "I started doing 'em because nobody else ever wants to, and they ended up being one of my favorite things."

"I don't care what we have to do to get this guy," G-man said to Rickey. "We gotta have him."

"See?" said Tanker. "That makes you want me. How come? Why does everybody hate salads so much?"

Rickey and G-man looked at each other, shrugged. "I don't know," said Rickey. "Salads are just weak. You got somebody who can't do anything else, you put him on salads."

"Yeah, and you get crappy salads." Tanker brandished his creation. "Hire somebody with talent, you get ones that look like this."

"We're trying to hire *you,*" Rickey said. He was a little tired of Tanker's waffling, but the guy was such a good cook that Rickey was willing to play the game. He'd already confessed to Tanker that Lenny was backing them, just so Tanker would think he was an up-front kind of guy. Tanker hadn't seemed too surprised. "How much do you want?"

"I'll think about it."

After they ate lunch, G-man made a batch of bread dough studded with green and black olives that had been soaked in gin. If it worked, it would be a sort of ultrarefined version of the martini muffuletta. Rickey and Tanker got very involved with a recipe for orange-fennel osso buco from the *Union Square Café Cookbook*. Tanker's idea was to replace some of the orange juice with Grand Marnier. They started making a gastrique sauce, and soon the kitchen reeked of hot vinegar. G-man left his dough to rise and took the elevator up to street level.

Downstairs, it had been about as noisy as a kitchen with just three cooks can be: their trash talk, the Ramones blasting on the boombox, ambient sounds of pots and utensils, gas jets, motors. As soon as G-man walked onto the gaming floor, though, the kitchen seemed like an oasis of tranquility. Slot machines jangled, played music, simulated explosions. Dealers chanted numbers and raked in chips with their long canes. Gamblers parked their meaty asses in front of the machines, chattering to each other in strange accents. It was peculiar, G-man thought, how most New Orleans tourists were thinner than the locals, yet the tourists who came to the casino were so often fat.

He headed for the first exit he saw, which took him out onto Tchoupitoulas. An elderly husband and wife in shorts and multiple strings of Mardi Gras beads passed him on the casino steps. Eyeing his check pants and white apron, they said, "Evening, Chef."

"Evening. Where y'all from?"

"Nashville."

"Well, have a good time. Be careful." As he spoke, he wondered why so many otherwise degenerate locals reflexively urged such tourists to be careful. It was just that they seemed so helpless, at once thrilled by the city and completely out of their league. And they insisted on wearing those damn beads, which might as well be signs around their necks reading **PLEASE ROB ME.** They were innocents in a strange land, and G-man hated to think of anything bad happening to them.

"Can you recommend a good place to eat tomorrow night?" the man asked. "Something fancy?"

"Sure, uh, Commander's Palace is real good, you've probably heard of that, and if you want to go a little more casual there's Poivre up on Prytania—"

"Are those in the French Quarter?" the woman asked. "We were thinking of the Quarter. We want to see the real old New Orleans."

G-man hesitated, then went ahead and recommended Lenny's. They would probably like it better than any of the other places he'd mentioned.

"Lenny's!" said the man. "We already tried to get in there. They were booked for the next two weeks."

"You really want to go to Lenny's?"

"Oh, we'd love to," the woman said. She smiled, and beneath her sensible cap of tightly permed gray hair, her face took on a dewy teenage glow.

G-man pointed to the cell-phone antenna sticking out of the man's shirt pocket. "Let me see that thing."

He dialed the front-of-the-house line at Lenny's. The phone was answered by Helmut, a young maître d' who had eaten at the Apostle Bar several times when Rickey and G-man were still cooking there. G-man chatted with Helmut for a few moments, then said, "I was wondering if you could find me a deuce sometime tomorrow night."

"Sure! That's for you and Rickey?"

"No, it's for these two nice people I just met. They're from Nashville, and they said they had trouble getting a table when they called before."

As G-man had intended, Helmut understood this to mean *They're a couple of clueless* turistas, *and I'm taking pity on them.* "Can they do 8:45?" he asked.

G-man relayed this request to the couple, who nodded excitedly. "What's your name?" he asked.

"Shannon Wilson Bell," said the man, raising his voice

and enunciating each syllable as men his age often seemed to do when introducing themselves.

"Well, I heard *that,*" said Helmut. "Bell, party of two, at 8:45 tomorrow. Can I do anything else for you?"

"I don't think so, Helmut. Thanks a lot."

"Are you free for a drink sometime?"

"It's been pretty crazy lately. I'll try to come by with Rickey."

"Come without him if you like," said the maître d', and rang off.

The couple from Nashville went into the casino, still waving and thanking him effusively. G-man sat on the steps marveling a little at the fact that he could call one of the most famous restaurants in the city and get a table for two people he didn't even know. Things certainly had changed a lot for him and Rickey in the past few months. Growing up in the Lower Ninth Ward, then struggling to live on the income from various cooking jobs, G-man had assumed he would always be a broke nobody. That was fine; as long as he mattered to Rickey, he didn't need anyone else to know his name, and he didn't care if they lived in a fancy house or a shotgun shack.

Rickey didn't want to be broke, though, and he sure didn't want to be a nobody. "What if we get famous?" G-man had asked him. "It could happen. Lenny's really gonna hype us."

"Then we'll be famous for something we're damn good at," Rickey said. "Where's the problem?" That was what it came down to, G-man thought. Rickey wanted a car and good knives and meals in fancy restaurants, but most of all he wanted to be acknowledged. He'd worked hard to become a serious cook, and G-man knew he still had regrets about not finishing his program at the CIA.

G-man was a serious cook too, but he'd never been driven by pure passion for it as Rickey was. He'd gotten into the business because Rickey wanted to, but he hadn't really been "in the life," as Paco Valdeon used to put it, until Rickey left. That was when he learned that the grind of a busy kitchen could keep him from thinking painful thoughts, and that sometimes the kitchen is the only place where a cook knows what the hell he's supposed to do.

If he craned his neck a little, G-man could see an old vacant building on the other side of the Poydras Street intersection. He was not surprised that no one had bought the building and renovated it, because he knew what horrifying shape it was in. It had once housed the Pirate Lafitte Grill, site of his first serious kitchen job.

The fall when Rickey left for New York had been the worst time of G-man's entire life. He was eighteen, directionless, and desolate. He was sure he and Rickey were through; they'd agreed to try and stay faithful, but G-man felt certain Rickey would meet people far more attractive and interesting. He smoked pounds of bad pot, drank oceans of well-brand liquor, quit a crappy lunchtime line job at a sandwich joint shortly before he would have been fired for chronic lateness. His morale was nonexistent, and he took a job washing dishes at the Pirate Lafitte. When it was slow, the cooks made the dishwashers do prep work. The chef soon saw that G-man knew what he was doing and promoted him to the line.

Chef Irvin was one of those mysterious café-au-lait-colored men who populate New Orleans, their complexions and features unclassifiable by even the most rabid segregationist. After a few days, G-man decided he was mostly black; his speech suggested it, and he used racial epithets more freely than any sane white man would have dared. In fact, Chef Irvin had the foulest mouth G-man had heard before or since, and that was a remarkable superlative in the restaurant world.

He held another record, too. He was the fastest cook G-man had ever seen, unnaturally fast; at times it seemed like he had six or eight arms. He drove his crew to an insane pitch, not pushing them beyond their limits so much as making them push the limits themselves. Nobody could shuck oysters or put out plates faster than Chef Irvin, but everybody wanted to try. He would egg them on: "You motherfuckin pussy-boy, where's my seafood platters? I made ten fuckin platters in the time it took you to make that one. You little bitch-ass piece a'shit, you keep cookin like that, you gonna lick out my ass for dessert. Where's my softshells?" All this was delivered in a rather dry and affable voice, as if he were discussing the ball game he'd seen on TV last night. You knew you were in trouble not when Chef Irvin cursed at you, but when he called you by your real name. He had a nickname for everybody. That was where G-man had gotten his—Rickey had sometimes called him G when they were growing up, but before Chef Irvin, he'd mostly just been Gary.

The Pirate Lafitte Grill was nothing special, just another fried-stuffed-or-broiled seafood joint popular with downtown business types and tourists who wandered across Canal

Street. The equipment was ancient and filthy, and there was a hole in the kitchen floor through which you could see the building's cracked foundation. But it was where G-man got his cook's hands, his knife-callus and hatchmarks and burn scars. It was where he learned to keep up with an unexpected rush, where the skin of his fingertips toughened enough that he could pick up hot plates and food just out of the fryer. It was where he became a cook rather than a piece of half-assed kitchen meat. When Rickey came home a few months later, he was surprised to find that G-man had gotten an education too.

Chef Irvin had died of lung cancer a few years ago. When he heard about it, G-man pictured the chef standing at the pearly gates giving St. Peter what-for: "You bitch-ass gatekeeper, how come you think I want to get into your motherfuckin Heaven? I don't give a fuck about all that harp and halo bullshit. Go on, motherfucker, send me to Hell, all my friends probably ended up there anyway . . ."

The afternoon was winding down toward the blue hour when twilight began to settle over the city. There was a breeze off the river and a light scrim of clouds overhead. It was May now, the last spell of temperate weather they were likely to see for many months. G-man sat on the steps for a while, then went back into the casino and descended to the test kitchen. The vomity smell of the gastrique had been replaced by the aroma of roasting fennel and beef marrow. His dough had risen nicely. Just as he was putting the loaves in the oven, Lenny came by with a box of goodies that included some Plugra butter. The four of them sat in the semicircular booth at one side of the kitchen eating osso buco and olive bread slathered with Plugra. The expensive butter had a smooth, sweet flavor that perfectly complemented the marrow they scooped out of the veal bones. "I think I gained five pounds since we set up this kitchen," Rickey said.

"You can take it off later," said Lenny. "Just think of eating as part of your job right now."

"I *always* think of eating as part of my job," said Tanker. "I never gain a goddamn ounce, though."

"Me either," said G-man.

"You wait," Lenny told them. "You're young yet."

"I won't mind if I do," Tanker said. "I always been too skinny. Mo says I need malteds."

"Malteds?" said Rickey. "What's that?"

"I don't know. Something her grammaw in New Jersey used to give the kids when they'd been sick."

"Malteds," said Lenny. "Malted milk. It's like a chocolate shake with malt powder. You never had one?"

The three younger men shook their heads. "Must be some kinda Yankee thing," said G-man.

"I ought to take you guys to New York. You need some education."

"I already been to New York," said Rickey. "I didn't like it."

"Yeah, well, New York sucks when you're broke. Tell you what. Sometime next year, after you start making some money from Liquor, we'll go up there just to eat. I'll introduce you around, take you to the good places."

"Damn!" said Tanker. "Look at their faces, Lenny. These are a couple of dyed-in-the-wool yat boys. You're gonna have a hard time prying them loose from New Orleans."

"We're no yats," said Rickey. "You gotta be old to be a yat."

"Bullshit," Tanker told him. "Here, take my foolproof yat test." He scrawled five words on a paper napkin— SURE, ALL RIGHT, ROOM, TULANE—and pushed it across the table. "Read that out loud."

"Shore. Awright. Rum. TOO-lane," Rickey read.

"You're as yatty as they come."

"What's a yat anyway?" said Lenny. "I know it's somebody who talks like you guys, but I don't know why you call it that."

"*Hey Lenny, where y'at?*" chorused the three New Orleanians, more or less in unison.

Lenny laughed. "OK, I get it. I think you're trying to change the subject, though. How can you learn about food if you refuse to travel? What am I going to do with you two?"

"Sign the checks and leave us alone," said Rickey. "Don't be sending us to New York and shit."

Tanker blinked. "Harsh, man."

"Aw, they say that sort of stuff to me all the time," Lenny assured him. "I'm used to it. Is there any more olive bread?"

G-man got up and unwrapped another loaf from the nest of clean towels keeping it warm. Rather than slicing the loaf, he just stuck a knife in it and set it in front of Lenny. With the knife's handle sticking straight up, it looked like something Hagar the Horrible would order. "There you go," he said. "It won't be any good tomorrow, so knock yourself out. Tanker, you wanna take some home?"

"Don't you want it?"

"We been eating so much of our own cooking here, we

don't eat at home any more. There's nothing in our fridge but some old jars of mustard and a bottle of vodka."

"You could make a dinner special with that," said Lenny.

"Fuck off," Rickey told him, unmaliciously, without looking up from the last shreds of meat on his osso buco.

"You like that," said G-man.

"I think it's one of the best things I ever made. It was mostly Tanker's idea, though. I'm telling you, we gotta get this guy."

"You hear me arguing?"

Tanker tapped his fork on the table to get their attention. "It just so happens I been thinking about this," he said. "*If* I come back from Colorado, and *if* you still want to hire me, I'd like to work with you. I like the way you cook. But I'm tired of being on the line. I want to do something totally different. Make me your pastry chef."

"What?" said Lenny. "You really are nuts, Tank. You want to go from chef de cuisine to pastry puff?"

"Yeah, yeah, you big-dick badass chefs, you always gotta rag on the dessert guys. I got talked out of going to pastry school for that exact reason, and I still regret it. I love desserts. Never outgrew 'em."

"You got any dessert experience?" said Rickey.

"Just at home. I got a nice hand with the pie crust— that's a rare thing if you ask me—and I learned to make ice cream last year. I can do dacquoise, meringue, Lady Baltimore cake, baked Alaska—"

"You made baked Alaska at home?" asked Lenny.

"Sure."

"I'd give him the job if I were you."

"What about our salads?" said Rickey. "I thought you were gonna make us these gorgeous salads."

"I'll make you some salads," Tanker assured him. "I won't be able to help it—the ideas just come to me once in a while. I'm a fucking prima donna about salads."

"Somebody needs to be," said Lenny, "most of the ones you get in this city."

"And I guess New York is the goddamn salad capital of the world?" said Rickey.

"Well, not quite. You want great salads, you ought to check out California wine country."

"Forget it."

"What do you have against traveling?" said Tanker. "Don't you know there's things out there you'll never get to eat unless you go find 'em?"

"Yeah, but I told you, I already traveled. I didn't like it."

"I bet you were just homesick."

Rickey shrugged.

"And I bet you didn't eat anything good."

"Well, some of us went into the city one weekend. Me and my friend Dave Fiorello and a couple other people from Skills. We were all poor, and we heard you could eat real cheap in Chinatown. There was this fish . . ." Rickey's eyes took on a faraway look. "Some kinda cod. I didn't think I'd like it—I mean, it wasn't a Gulf fish. They took it right out this tank in the front of the restaurant, steamed it, and brought it to the table still on the bone, with the head and everything. Didn't do much to it—just some soy, ginger, and scallions—but they didn't need to. I had some good fish in my life, but I never tasted anything else that fresh."

"He wrote me a whole letter about it," said G-man.

"See?" said Lenny. "I know you love New Orleans. I understand that. I came here once and never left. But you have to broaden your horizons."

Rickey and G-man got up from the table and started clearing the dishes.

"Better leave it alone for now, Lenny," said Tanker. "They aren't listening any more. All they see is that Grey-hound Scenicruiser going down the highway into the heart of darkness, and they don't want any part of it."

chapter 18

Rickey parked behind the building—he was actually starting to think of it as Liquor—and walked around to the Broad Street side. He usually entered through the kitchen door, but the renovations were far enough along that he wanted to see what the place looked like coming in the front, as diners would.

Lenny's contractors had already finished with the front of the house and moved into the kitchen. Now the decorators were working on the front. The walls had been replastered and painted hunter green. Thick carpet pads were laid in preparation for a lush, dark green carpet. When Rickey and G-man met with Lenny's dining room designer, the woman had tried to talk them into lining the foyer with mirrors, hanging a big, swirly abstract metal sculpture in the middle of the dining room, and painting the walls orange— she called it "burnt sienna," but the chip she showed them was definitely orange. Apparently people did scientific studies on these things, and one of the studies showed that this color made people eat more.

"We want them to eat more because they like our food," Rickey said, and the woman smiled pityingly at him. He'd finally fired her when she suggested ripping out the tin ceiling and painting some kind of Roman orgy scene in its place. The firing hadn't gone over too well with Lenny.

"You can't just tell my people they're canned," he said, calling fifteen minutes after the woman had left.

"I sure can. Ask your designer."

"I wish you'd talked to me first."

"Why? No way we were gonna be able to work with her. C'mon, Lenny—she wanted to turn my ceiling into the side of a Mardi Gras float."

"Rickey, I admire the fact that you know what you want, but you never seem to consider the possibility that anyone else's ideas might have merit."

"The side of a Mardi Gras float has merit? What crawled up your ass anyway? Wait a second—that designer lady—are you fucking her?"

"That doesn't have anything to do with it."

"Or are you just trying to, and I screwed it up for you? Which is it? Cause I know it's one or the other."

"Trying to," Lenny admitted. "God, you're such a smug little shit sometimes."

"Well, sorry. You want me to call her? I'm still gonna turn down her stupid ideas, but if you think it'd help to let her come back in here and wave some more paint chips around—"

"Nah, forget it. I've been asking her out ever since she designed Crescent, but she won't go for it. She thinks she's some kind of high-class professional, ought to be dating a doctor."

"Then she's even dumber than I thought. You're not my type, Lenny, but you're definitely a catch."

"Thanks so much, asshole. I think I'll go ask out a stripper to soothe my poor, battered ego. I'm their type for sure."

"What, rich?"

"Yeah."

Lenny hadn't stayed mad, though. Rickey had to admit the guy's equanimity was pretty amazing. He'd always heard money caused as many problems as it solved, but doing what he loved and making millions of dollars at it seemed to agree with Lenny. Maybe he'd always been like that, and his attitude had helped him get rich. Either way, it was a theory Rickey wouldn't mind putting to the test. He didn't have much equanimity of his own, but surely G-man had enough for both of them.

Rickey went into the kitchen and spoke to the contractor's crew, who were installing new countertops on the back line. He knew they didn't like it when he hung around, but he made a point of stopping in every few days, just to make sure they weren't stacking two-by-fours on the stovetops or anything. They weren't, so he entered the walk-in and looked around for what must be the fortieth or fiftieth time, wondering exactly where and how that guy had died, and what he had looked like afterward. Rickey and G-man had witnessed a fair amount of violence growing up, but a guy tortured and shot to death by the Mob had to look way worse than anything they'd seen.

The fridge had been cleaned out, of course, but it still seemed as if there should be some sign of what had happened here. Indelible bloodstains, maybe, or a tarnished face that appeared on the inside of the door and could not be scoured away. Thoughts of the murder would probably continue to haunt Rickey every time he entered the walk-in. He wished he'd never heard about the whole thing, but now that he had, he found himself wanting to know more. He wondered if he should call Sid Schwanz. No, it was probably best not to remind the newspaperman of the story he'd forfeited until they actually had free drinks with which to ply him.

Leaving the restaurant, he drove over to Annunciation Street to check on the neon sign they were having made for the roof. "Carlos is working on that one right now," said the counter girl at Signed Sealed Delivered. She led Rickey into the studio, where the signmaker was heating glass tubes with a tool that looked like a larger version of the little blowtorch a pastry chef would use to caramelize his crème brûlée. "It's coming along real nice," Carlos said without looking up. The sign was not a masterpiece of subtlety, but Rickey hadn't intended it to be. The word *Liquor,* eight feet long, was spelled out in a swooping but legible script. The lettering would be pink when the gas was running through it. In the upsweep of the R would be a blue martini glass containing a green olive. Rickey had doodled this logo on a cocktail napkin at the Apostle Bar one day and had never told anyone how beautiful he secretly thought it was, not even G-man. It was tacky in a way, he knew, but it also had a kind of retro elegance he associated with the downtown New Orleans of his early childhood. He remembered riding down Canal Street in the car with his parents, seeing all the spotlit billboards atop the buildings, gazing up at the Walgreens and Canadian Club signs with their neon and glittering cascades of gold light, thinking it was pure magic.

Now he was so close to Crescent that he might as well
stop in and see if Lenny was there. Lunch service was over
and they wouldn't really be gearing up for dinner yet. Maybe
Lenny would have time for a drink. Rickey wouldn't mind
shooting the shit with him for a little while. It was hard to
believe that just a few months ago he had been so dismissive
of Lenny. There was no way they could have gotten this far
without him. Even if somebody else had been willing to put
up the money, Rickey couldn't think of anyone who would
have been able to guide them through the whole thing like
Lenny had. Other people would have gotten sick of their
naïveté or impatient with their bad attitudes. These days, so
close to opening the restaurant, Rickey actually found
Lenny's presence comforting.

There was no comfort at Crescent today, though. Someone had tipped Lenny off that the health inspector was coming, and the whole day crew was scrubbing, boiling, and
throwing things away. "You go on and have a drink in the
bar," Lenny told him. "I'll get away for a minute if I can."

"Don't worry about it," said Rickey. "I didn't want anything really." He sat in the bar and drank an espresso, gazing around at the orange walls and strangely shaped metal
sculptures. He felt glad he'd fired that designer, and wished
Lenny could find someone better to lust after—maybe
another restaurant designer who could redo this weird-
looking place.

Most of the cooks who heard that Rickey and G-man
were opening a restaurant had said, "I bet it'll be a crazy
joint," or something to that effect. Rickey guessed Liquor
would be kind of a crazy joint, but he had no desire for it to
look crazy. It seemed to him that every restaurant opening

nowadays had to have the sheet-metal artwork, the light sculptures in the bar, the hard shiny surfaces so all the noise could bounce around and around until the sound level was well-nigh unbearable. Rickey had never once imagined his restaurant looking like that. He figured the food could be as wild as they wanted to make it, but above all else, the restaurant itself should be comfortably elegant. He believed people chose their favorite restaurants for two reasons: either they wanted to feel fashionable or they wanted to be comforted. The first set of people would eat at one or two places for a while, then move on to the next hot ticket. The second set, if you kept feeding them well and giving them the atmosphere they craved, would eat at the same places all their lives. At Liquor, the trendy crowd would come in for a look-see, but he wanted to snag the lifers. He believed he understood their mindset, whereas the trendy people were something of a mystery to him. For instance, they flocked to Crescent, but they treated Lenny's as if it served a side order of salmonella on every plate just because the tourists ate there.

He finished his espresso and looked into the kitchen. Everybody was still running around wiping surfaces with disinfectant and checking temperatures in the food-storage areas. "I gotta go," he mouthed to Lenny, who was standing at a sink halfway across the kitchen rinsing the salt off a Smithfield ham. Lenny nodded and made an I'll-call-you gesture with his thumb and pinkie finger.

There was one more errand Rickey needed to run today, something he'd been feeling guilty about. When he and G-man were out drinking with Tanker and Mo the other night, Mo had said something about calling her mom on

Mother's Day. It turned out that Mother's Day had slipped right past Rickey and G-man. Rickey drove over to St. Charles Avenue, parked in front of Scheinuk the Florist, and bought two big bouquets. They'd deliver the flowers tonight, probably eating dinner at G-man's folks' house and then having a glass of Tia Maria with Rickey's mother. Brenda loved her Tia Maria.

"Cash, check, or credit?" said Mr. Scheinuk.

"Can you take a debit card?" With his new high income, Rickey had applied for a Visa, but it hadn't been approved yet.

"Absolutely. We take any kind of plastic. Well, except for gas cards and the like."

"So I guess I can't use my old K&B card, huh?"

The florist laughed. "I love those things. I still got my Maison Blanche card."

"I got me a Krauss card," chimed in one of the ladies working in the back.

"I got a menu from the Blue Room in the Fairmont," said the other lady. "The shrimp cocktail cost a dollar and a quarter!"

"I bet you'd still eat there if they were open, huh?" said Rickey.

Behind her cat's-eye glasses, her face grew radiant at the thought. "Course I would!"

"It's not the same city any more," said the florist. "Canal Street full of high-rise hotels. Schweggman's turned into Sav-A-Center. K&B sold to Rite-Aid, and done took down all the purple signs, too."

They all shook their heads sadly; the loss of K&B had

seemed to pierce New Orleans hearts deepest of all. The locally owned drugstore empire had made purple its trademark: not just the signs but the bags, the shopping carts, the wrapping paper and prescription labels had all been a vivid hue known as K&B purple, and it saddened people to think future generations would not know this color. The stores had even carried several kinds of K&B brand liquor, mostly inexpensive and not half bad.

"It ain't the same," one of the ladies echoed.

Lifers, Rickey thought. *Bless their hearts and send them to my restaurant.*

chapter 19

L enny sat in the bar after service at Crescent, drinking pastis with Chris, one of his waiters. He'd been cooking with the aniseed-flavored aperitif for years, but hadn't drunk it until Chris showed him how one night. You poured a measure into a tall, narrow glass, then added cold water from a pitcher on the side. As the water mixed with the spirits, it brought out the volatile oils, causing the whole thing to turn gorgeously opalescent. They always drank a brand called Mon Pastis that Chris had talked their liquor guy into ordering. To Lenny it tasted about like Herbsaint or Pernod, but Chris swore it was far superior to either.

Lenny didn't really care; what mattered to him was that the stuff acted as a balm of Gilead on his aching back. Back problems came with the job, but a few glasses of pastis created a lovely melting feeling that started at the nape of his neck and seemed to drip down his spine like warm butter. Compulsively he poked his finger into the flame of a votive candle, then withdrew it, then put it back. The small pain helped him to more fully appreciate the relief offered by the liquor.

"I swear you can see the future in this stuff," said Chris, who was pretty drunk.

"What?"

"When you pour the water in and it starts swirling around, gets all milky—look." Chris had just poured himself a fresh pastis. Now he held it up to the light for Lenny's inspection. "You can *see* shit in there."

"I think you're right," said Lenny, holding up his own glass.

"Yeah?"

"Yeah. I think I see a wasted waiter."

"Aw, you just don't appreciate the true beauty of pastis."

"I do," said Lenny, rolling his shoulders and stretching his back. "I really do."

As he drained his glass, Lenny saw a figure hovering in the archway between the bar and the dining room. It was the night porter, Polynice, a forlorn presence in his snap-front dishwasher's jacket and filthy-cuffed checks. "Scuse me, Chef," he said. "There's a phone call for you in the kitchen."

Lenny glanced at the bar clock. It was 1:40 in the morning. "For me?" he said.

"They axed for you special. Said it was important."

"It better be." Lenny went into the kitchen and picked up the phone. "Yeah?"

"Is this Lenny?" said a voice he didn't recognize. It sounded muffled, as if the guy had his hand over the receiver. This was obviously going to be the perfect end to a lovely day.

"Yeah, it is. Who's calling?"

"Did you know there's a warrant out on John Rickey?"

"What?"

"A warrant. For his arrest. You can't get a liquor license if there's a warrant on you—but you know that, right? What else you think Rickey hasn't told you?"

"Look, pal, if you don't even have the balls to identify yourself before you start slandering people, I'm hanging up right—"

The line went dead. Lenny took the receiver away from his ear, stared at it for a long moment, banged it back into the cradle. "Shit," he said. Polynice edged past him, dragging a huge bag of wet garbage toward the back door. He met Lenny's eyes for an instant, then looked away. As Polynice went through the door, Lenny saw that the garbage bag had leaked a trail of unspeakable ooze onto the freshly hosed-down floor.

With the heel of his hand, Lenny pounded the wall beside the phone. "Pencil-dick sonofabitch shithead bastard!" he said. He turned around to find that he now had an audience of two: Polynice by the back door scared to come in, and Chris, who had come in uninvited, lurking near the service bar peering at him through the bread shelves.

"It's OK, guys," he told them. "Just a real motherfucker of a day. Maybe even a grandma-fucker."

The two young men answered him with solemn nods. They were kids, but they'd worked in the business long enough to know about grandma-fucker days and tread lightly around people who'd had them.

By 2:30 Lenny was on Canal Boulevard headed home. He didn't have the energy for the Gold Club or any of that nonsense. Tonight it would only make him feel pathetic, and with good reason. He just wanted to swallow his last two aspirins of the day and go to bed alone. Right now he'd be thrilled if the heavens opened up and God told him, *Thou shalt not speak to another human being for at least three weeks*. Rickey and G-man didn't think he worked; well, wait until they'd had a few days like this.

Thinking of the bong he'd seen on their coffee table, he contemplated driving over there and asking them to smoke him up. They kept late enough hours that they might still be awake. Lenny had quit everything but caffeine and alcohol years ago and had lost all his connections. He guessed he could find something, but when you owned the place, you hated to ask your runner or your dishwasher to score you a bag of weed. The way things were going tonight, it would probably make him paranoid anyway.

He wondered if he had reason to be paranoid. The weird phone call had unnerved him a little. Because it had come into the kitchen rather than his office, he didn't have it on tape, and this bothered him; he wanted to listen to it again and see if he could recognize the voice. Of course, he'd immediately thought of Mike Mouton. Mike was capable of pulling such a stunt. He'd seen the way Mike looked at Rickey that night at the Apostle Bar. Rickey was everything Mike was not: young, talented, good-looking, full of promise. There was something seriously wrong with a guy who would hire somebody like that, then expend so much energy on hating him.

Lenny eschewed hatred as unproductive, but he harbored a strong dislike for Mike Mouton. When he first moved from Maine to New Orleans, he'd worked with Mike at the Fontainebleu, a hotel restaurant on Canal Street. Mike was an assistant manager there, and Lenny was pretty sure he'd been skimming money. That wasn't too cool, but it wasn't Lenny's main problem with the guy. What he really hated was the way Mike would suck up to you, then turn around and bite you on the ass. It wasn't just Lenny; he did it to everyone. He'd implied that the executive chef had some kind of problem with Lenny's cooking, then denied the implication when it turned out there was no problem. He'd loved to hang around the kitchen and make innocuous little remarks about how the last guy had done a thing, as opposed to how the current guy was doing it.

After Lenny left the Fontainebleu for a sous chef job at another place, he kept hearing weird, malignant rumors about himself, rumors that could not only be traced back to Mike Mouton but seemed to actually describe Mike rather than Lenny. "You're not hard to work with," a cook would say. "Somebody told me they heard you were hard to work with." Or, "You don't do coke? Someone told me you did a lot of coke." Or, "Somebody said you didn't like working with black dudes." Ugly stuff, and pointless: Lenny had never done anything to Mike except be competent where Mike was incompetent. He tried to ignore it, figuring he could prove more by behaving decently to his colleagues and employees than by confronting Mike. But he kept track of it and never forgot a word. Now, with Liquor getting ready to open and Mike trying to interfere, it looked as though the old nastiness might be coming home to roost.

His low opinion of Mike didn't cause him to discount the possibility that the caller's claim could be true. He would call De La Cerda tomorrow and have him check it out. Lenny had already decided he was willing to lose money on Liquor. He didn't expect to—on the contrary, he expected to rake it in—but it was bad business to invest in such an uncertain venture unless you could afford to lose the money. Lenny could, but he wasn't willing to lose it due to stupidity, his own or anyone else's.

◦ ◦ ◦

De La Cerda called with the information the next afternoon, just after the health inspector left. Crescent had aced the inspection and Lenny was in a much better mood now. He hoped De La Cerda wasn't about to ruin it. "What's up?" he said, checking the red recording light of the tape machine attached to his office phone.

"Well, your mystery pal was right—there is a warrant on Rickey. But it's a ticky-tack thing—an open container violation."

"That's it?"

"That's it. He's clean otherwise. Not even a speeding ticket."

"He's only had a car for about six months," said Lenny. "Give him time." He hung up, feeling both relieved and disgusted. What kind of person would go to the trouble of finding out about such a small, stupid thing, then use it to try to get a guy in trouble? It wasn't just malicious; it had overtones of the psychotic.

He made some more calls, helped his sous chef prep for the evening, then left to meet Rickey and G-man for an early dinner at Poivre. They needed to go over the licensing requirements they'd soon be required to deal with. Lenny arrived first and had a drink at the bar. Poivre was a beautiful little jewelbox of a restaurant, all gilded glass and dusty-rose walls, seating about forty. The chef was an affable young man as handsome as a movie star. There were small oil lamps and fresh flowers arranged in antique glass bottles on the tables. For a few minutes Lenny entertained the idea of having a tiny restaurant; he sat there developing a whole fantasy about how relaxing it would be. He knew he was kidding himself, but this was the kind of place that made you imagine owning a restaurant could be relaxing even if you knew better.

He was so absorbed in his little fantasy that he didn't know the boys had arrived until Rickey came up beside him and nudged his elbow. "You look like you just had a wet dream."

"I guess I did in a way," said Lenny. "It'll never happen, though."

They joined G-man in one of the booths. "How'd the inspection go?" Rickey asked.

"Fine. We got a ninety-seven."

"Rickey and I once worked at a place that got a sixty-eight," said G-man. "The manager hung it upside down, so from a distance it looked like an eighty-nine."

They ordered, and their appetizers came out quickly. Lenny waited until Rickey had taken his first bite of blue crab quenelles before he said, "So, Rickey, did you know there's a warrant out for your arrest?"

"Huh?"

Lenny repeated what he'd said, rather enjoying the look

on Rickey's face. It was a fairly mean thing to do, but he was irritated. Not because Rickey hadn't told him about the warrant—he'd probably forgotten all about it—but because they needed to get out of the habit of doing such silly, careless shit. They weren't slackers any more, and their habits had to change.

"No there's not," said Rickey, then thought about it. "Oh, wait. Shit."

Lenny waggled his highball glass in the air. "Does this refresh your memory?"

"Yeah, but it wasn't a glass, it was a beer can. We were working at the Peychaud Grill and a bunch of us went drinking out on the golf course at Audubon Park . . . I think that's what it was."

"You think, huh?"

"There's about a year of my life that I barely remember," Rickey admitted. "I finally had to cut back on the booze a little."

"I remember that," said G-man. "It wasn't pretty."

"Oh, like you were the model of sobriety back then."

"I wasn't *sober.* Nobody at the Peychaud was sober. I just wasn't as drunk as you were."

"OK," said Lenny. "So you got a piddlyshit open container citation. They even let you drink on the street here as long as you use a plastic cup, but I guess that was asking too much. So help me understand why you didn't just pay the fine."

"I didn't have any money, so I didn't show up for my court date."

Lenny was starting to get a slight headache. He ate one

of his fresh marinated sardines in rouille before he spoke again. Finally he said, "Did you know you can't get a *liquor license* if there's a *warrant out on you?*"

"Uh—no. I mean—no." Apparently seeing that his position was indefensible, Rickey switched tactics. "How'd you find out about this, anyway?"

Lenny told him about the phone call and how he'd had De La Cerda check it out.

"Fuck!" said Rickey. The maître d' glanced over at him, and he lowered his voice. "It's Mike. It's gotta be. So he knows you're working with us. How you think he found out about the warrant, though?"

"It wouldn't be hard. He could have put out the word for dirt on you, probably told people he'd owe them a favor if they found something. He's too dumb to realize it, but he actually did *you* a favor—otherwise, this would have bitten us in the ass when you applied for the liquor license and they ran your background check. You're lucky that's the worst he could find. It *is* the worst he could find, right?"

"I guess he could tell people we're a couple of alcoholic stoner fags."

"Yeah, but that'd just be the truth," said G-man.

Lenny waved an impatient hand. "Nobody's going to make a big deal over that kind of stuff. Is there anything else of a legal nature he could dig up?"

Rickey thought about it. "No. I've done some embarrassing stuff, but that's the only time I got caught."

"What about the Monkey Hill thing?" said G-man.

"Dude, we were like sixteen. It doesn't count if you're under eighteen. Does it?"

"No," Lenny said hastily. He didn't think he was up to hearing about the Monkey Hill thing.

"Well, look. I'll deal with this warrant tomorrow." Rickey got a hopeful look. "Unless you already had De La Cerda take care of it?"

"I did not have De La Cerda take care of it," said Lenny, measuring his words carefully. "You need to learn to handle this kind of shit. Owning a restaurant isn't just about having cool ideas and making cool food. You have to take care of business."

"Like Elvis," said G-man. Lenny shot him a look, but he just smiled.

"OK, sure, like Elvis if you say so. It doesn't matter. What matters is that you two start taking things seriously."

"I do take things seriously," said Rickey. "I'm trying to be responsible. I never had to be responsible except on the line, and when you're done there you can just fuck off the rest of the time. But I *am* trying."

"I know you are. But you won't get your licenses by trying. This is real life. You have to *do* it—you can't just try."

"Like Yoda," said G-man.

Lenny turned on him. "What the fuck is *with* you?"

"I don't know. Everything reminds me of something else today." G-man shrugged. "We got some good weed. It does that to me sometimes."

"Yeah, I was just reminding myself why I don't smoke that shit any more, you waste case."

"Thanks, you anal-retentive dickhead," said G-man amiably.

The entrées came then, and the sweet richness of Cole

Parker's pot-au-feu calmed Lenny's jangled nerves until he felt just about normal again. Still, he was glad for the few minutes when everybody was too busy eating to talk. He remembered his wish of last night, that God would forbid him to speak to anyone for three weeks, and realized it wasn't enough. He needed six weeks at least.

chapter 20

*P*erdido is the Spanish word for "lost," and after spending thirty minutes circling the same two traffic-choked blocks in search of a parking space, Rickey found it appropriate that City Hall was on Perdido Street. He had never set foot in any of the downtown government buildings before, but he was already starting to nurture a deep and abiding hatred for them.

"Why don't we just park in one of the pay lots on Loyola?" said G-man. "It's not far."

"I'm a citizen of New Orleans, goddammit. I'm on business. I want one of those meter spots."

"What for? So the meter can expire while we're still in the courthouse, and we can get a twenty-dollar ticket? If you don't like the pay lots, let's park at the Superdome."

"I want one of those meter spots," Rickey said stubbornly. As he turned onto Lasalle again, a Ford Escort pulled out, and Rickey wedged the Satellite into the tiny spot it had vacated.

"You got quarters, even?" said G-man.

"Course I got quarters." Rickey plugged a handful of change into the meter and set off toward the city court building.

They paid Rickey's substantial fine without incident, then walked across Duncan Plaza to City Hall. The boxy blue-green building loomed over the plaza like some squat and malign tiki god. "Don't make me go in there," said Rickey.

"I don't think we got a choice."

Obtaining a liquor license was contingent on passing one's health inspection, which couldn't happen until the kitchen was completely set up. The inspectors had to check the coolers, the ice machine, the number of hand sinks, and a thousand other things large and small. Today Rickey and G-man were just picking up the forms they had to complete in order to apply for the liquor license and the occupational license that would allow them to do business. After submitting the paperwork, they'd both have to pass a background clearance and get fingerprinted. It was all fairly mind-boggling.

The City Hall lobby had a lazy, half-deserted feel, rather like Rickey imagined a minor government office in some small Third World country. Two men sat at an information desk talking about baseball. A large U-shaped glass case monopolized the center of the lobby, containing nothing except a rather sparse arrangement of the New Orleans city flag, three puny-looking gold fleurs-de-lis on a white background. A stand card such as one might see advertising beer on a restaurant table announced that the flags were for sale in a variety of sizes.

"De La Cerda said to go to the Department of Revenue," said Rickey, scanning a board of listings. "Room 1W15."

"Where's that?"

"1W15? It's on this floor," said a woman passing them on her way to the elevators. "Go down that hall right there. It'll be the last open door on the left."

"Thanks," said Rickey, surprised. He hadn't been expecting any help.

The room was easy to find. It looked a little scary—glassed-in windows on either side like the payment department of a Ninth Ward discount-furniture store—but there was no line at the central information desk, and the young woman in charge smiled as she handed them the forms. They didn't even have to sign a clipboard. "That was too easy," Rickey said. "There's gotta be a catch."

"I think the catch comes later, when we actually send in the paperwork. These guys are just working stiffs like us."

"I guess," said Rickey. He had been ready for interrogation at the very least.

They still had a bunch of errands to run, so they bought sandwiches and sodas at the City Hall snack bar and went to eat in Duncan Plaza. With its trees and little gazebo, the plaza was actually kind of nice, though the same could not be said for the City Hall sandwiches. As Rickey and G-man ate, three women on a nearby bench talked animatedly among themselves, almost seeming to argue at times. Rickey tuned them out at first but began to listen as he realized they were talking about restaurants.

"What I don't like is the bad *service* there. That one lady, she always so sarcastic. She call you *ma'am,* like she supposed to, but the way she *say* it . . . 'Can I help you, *ma'am*? Here go your drink, *ma'am*' . . ."

"They got that good hot sausage po-boy, though."

"Girl, I know it. Why you think I still go there?"

"You know where I go? Mr. Pete's by the Superdome. I like their chicken."

"Y'all been to that sushi place opened up on Poydras?"

"Ooh, girl! I don't eat no raw fish."

"It ain't just raw fish—they got shrimp, crab, salad, them little beans in the pod—"

"Where you like to get a steak?"

"My husband took me to Gertie Greer's for our anniversary. Expensive, but ummmm, ummmm . . ."

"They got the potatoes au gratin on the side? I love me some potatoes au gratin."

"Yeah, they got five kinds of potatoes, grilled mushrooms, fresh asparagus . . ."

Rickey and G-man looked at each other. Where else could you eavesdrop on office girls and hear them talking about potatoes au gratin and fresh asparagus?

Plenty of restaurants failed in New Orleans. Rickey's purple notebook was proof enough of that. But very seldom did a place close because diners hadn't given it a chance. They would eat almost anything once, and if they liked it, they'd come back for more.

° ° °

Later that night, Rickey was lying in bed looking through the papers he'd collected. After lunch they had visited offices on Poydras and Loyola Streets to pick up their state forms.

Oscar De La Cerda had offered to do all this for them, but Rickey figured it would cost Lenny about four hundred dollars for the lawyer or his assistant to park in a pay lot and walk around to the various offices. That was just ridiculous. Not counting lunch, it had only cost Rickey $20.75. He slid the blaze-orange parking ticket out of the stack of forms and laid it on the nightstand, where it would remind him to write a check to the city tomorrow.

G-man came in from the kitchen and stood in front of the window air conditioner. His hair was damp and chaotic, and there was a V-shaped sweat stain down the front of his T-shirt. "I wish we would've known the A.C. in the kitchen was broken before we decided to make pizza," he said. They had picked up some Vidalia onions and Creole tomatoes at a truck stand during the course of their errands. If you caramelized the onions, spread them over the crust, then sliced the tomatoes thinly and laid them on top so they would roast in the oven, you didn't even need cheese.

"We could've *bought* a new A.C. for what that goddamn open container fine cost me," Rickey complained.

"Yeah, but we gotta have that liquor license."

"How long till the pizza's ready?"

"About fifteen minutes." G-man pulled the sweaty shirt over his head and leaned closer to the air conditioner. "Can you pull it out? I'm gonna get in the shower."

"Sure." Rickey put away the forms and went into the kitchen. It felt like a hothouse and smelled like sweet onions. He checked to make sure the pizza crust wasn't getting too brown, then opened a bottle of beer and sat down at the table. He'd been trying to put it out of his mind, but now

Rickey began to think about the phone call Lenny had gotten from Mike. It wasn't logical, the way he felt about this. He knew Mike was an idiot, and even sort of understood why Mike hated him. Rickey thought of a bumper sticker he'd seen once: *It's not my fault you suck*. But if you sucked as bad as Mike did, blaming someone else for your suckiness must be preferable to realizing it was nobody's fault but yours.

Still the thing rankled. He'd done a pretty good job at Escargot's, considering how badly the place was run and how demoralized most of the crew was. He'd worked well with Terrance and the others, helped the kitchen run—if not smoothly—then at least better than it had before he got there. When he had to quit, he'd given Mike two weeks' notice and trained the new saucier. And how had Mike repaid him? By goading him into a stupid dustup on his last day, then talking shit behind his back, digging up old dirt, trying to make Lenny suspicious of him.

But what could he do? He already knew he could kick Mike's ass, but it would be assault. You couldn't get a liquor license with assault on your record. He couldn't spread any nasty rumors about Mike; restaurant people already knew the truth about the guy, which was worse than anything Rickey could make up. Anyway, underhandedness was not Rickey's strong suit. He'd have no idea how to start a rumor and make people believe it.

That left murder. He grabbed another beer and lost himself in an increasingly wild fantasy of how he could kill Mike with no trace. He knew a couple of places in the Lower Ninth Ward where he could probably buy a stolen gun for a hundred dollars. He'd break into Mike's car, lie in wait, and force him to drive out to St. Charles Parish—that part would be satisfying, with Mike apologizing and begging and all—then shoot him through the brain, dump his body in the swamp, maybe sink the car too. There were any number of people who might like to do all this to Mike. Rickey wouldn't even be the primary suspect.

How would he get home, though? He couldn't let anyone see him walking back from the very area where Mike's body might later be found. G-man would have to come pick him up. That was where the fantasy abruptly fell apart. G-man would never be a willing party to murder.

The oven timer went off. Rickey pulled out the pizza and set it on a rack to cool. He'd been ravenous a few minutes ago. Now he just felt faintly sick. What he really wanted was another beer, but he saw that he had already finished two.

He went back into the bedroom. Instead of taking a shower, G-man had turned the air conditioner as high as it would go and fallen asleep with the fan trained on him. There was no escaping it. All through May you could try to tell yourself it wasn't *that* hot yet. By June, the 90-degree days, the 90 percent humidity, the thriving mosquitoes, the stinging caterpillars, and the shitty smell that rose from the baking asphalt all combined to make you admit that you were heading into the thick of another New Orleans summer.

Life was damn depressing sometimes.

Rickey turned off the light and lay down on the bed. G-man rolled over, propped himself up long enough to flip his pillow to the cool side, and said, "Mmmpizza ready yet?"

"Yeah, but I'm not hungry any more."

"I am," said G-man, and went back to sleep.

Rickey lay awake in the dark. He wanted to go to sleep, but every time he closed his eyes, his mind started racing. What else had Mike said about him? Would he find out that his phone call hadn't turned Lenny against Rickey? If so, what would Mike do next? Was the giant cockroach that had run under the stove earlier still there? Would it come out and contaminate the pizza Rickey had left sitting on the counter?

After what felt like hours of this, Rickey got up, went into the kitchen, covered the pizza, and opened another beer. He had a lot to do tomorrow—he had a lot to do every day now—and he needed his rest, but Mike had robbed him of it. He gritted his teeth as he realized that would make Mike happy. In this way, Mike's tactics were working. Rickey hated for such people to have power over him. He'd never forgotten Phil Muller, his CIA roommate, and had never stopped feeling a surge of helpless anger whenever he thought of the guy. Now he wondered if Mike Mouton was going to haunt him the same way. The worst part was that he'd never meant to make an enemy out of either man.

Sometimes sitting up all night drinking was the only way to stay sane. Rickey didn't much like doing it by himself, though. He contemplated cooking something else, not because he wanted anything so much as because the sound of the clattering dishes might wake G-man. Eventually, though, he turned off all the lights except the little one over the stove, settled down at the table, and sat drinking alone in the nighttime heat. The blue horror of dawn was visible through the windows by the time he felt able to stagger back to bed.

chapter 21

G-man awoke with the feeling that he had left something unfinished. When he went to put the coffee on, he remembered what it was: the pizza he'd made was sitting on the counter covered with plastic but otherwise untouched. He wondered why Rickey hadn't eaten any. Then he saw the twelve empty beer bottles by the sink.

Sighing, G-man fixed two cups of coffee and took them into the bedroom. Rickey was just waking up, wincing at the weak afternoon sunlight that filtered through the shutters. "No coffee," he whispered, lacing his fingers over his eyes. "No coffee."

"Why—" G-man was speaking at normal volume, but Rickey looked as if he might cry, so he lowered his voice to match Rickey's. "Why'd you drink so much? You drank all the beer in the fridge."

"Ah! Don't say that word!"

G-man laughed. He'd been through this hundreds of times, but Rickey was still pretty funny when he was hung-over.

"You're never gonna drink again, right?"

"Right . . ."

"Gonna be pretty hard making all those recipes with *liquor,* then."

Rickey pushed himself out of bed and stumbled to the bathroom. G-man sat on the edge of the bed and wondered why people ran the water in the sink when they were throwing up. It didn't mask the sounds of throwing up; it just made them wetter.

After a few minutes Rickey returned, red-eyed and damp-haired, and burrowed back under the covers.

"You'll feel a little better now," said G-man.

"Thanks." Rickey ran his tongue over his lips. "I'm so *thirsty* . . ."

"You want a snowball?"

Snowballs were a hangover remedy they had discovered by accident when they were seventeen. After a night of drinking vodka and Kahlua, they were rounded up and taken to a Metairie home-improvement store by Rickey's mother, who wanted them to load her car with several huge bags of sand she intended to dump into a pothole in front of her house. She knew they were suffering, but she had no sympathy. "You got your daddy's tolerance," she told Rickey. "That man never could hold his liquor. On our very first date, I drank two cocktails for every one of his."

"That must have charmed the pants off him, Momma."

Somehow they got the wretched sand into the car. On the way home, they groaned about their exhaustion and thirst so much that Brenda stopped and bought them strawberry snowballs from one of the brightly painted wooden stands that went up all over New Orleans in the summer. G-man didn't know if it was the coldness of the shaved ice, the quick sugar fix of the syrup, the fluid replacement, or some magic X factor, but they both felt better afterward: so much better that they not only filled in the pothole, but loaded the extra sand into a wheelbarrow, took it over to G-man's sister's house, and poured it into his little nephew's sandbox.

Leaving Rickey with a glass of water on the nightstand and a pillow over his head, G-man got in the car and drove the short distance to their favorite snowball stand, Hansen's Sno-Bliz on Tchoupitoulas. Hansen's had been in business since the 1930s and had moved into an actual, permanent building at some point. Hurricane Betsy had wrecked it in the sixties, and photographs of the devastation were displayed on a colorful piece of posterboard alongside accolades for the snowballs. G-man was scanning the long list of flavors—strawberry was best for a hangover, but he favored chocolate spearmint himself—when someone poked him in the small of the back and said, "Hey, stranger."

The guy was wearing Versace sunglasses and a tight tank top instead of a suit, so it took G-man a second to place him: Helmut, the maître d' from Lenny's. "Hey, Helmut," he said. "How'd my Nashville tourists like their dinner?"

"Oh, they were *thrilled*. They said it was the best meal they'd ever eaten, and you were just the *nicest* young man to fix it all up for them. What are you doing now?"

"Getting snowballs," said G-man as old Mr. Hansen handed the cups to him. "What are *you* doing?"

"Same as you. I live right around the corner. Would you like to come by?"

"Thanks, but I gotta take this to Rickey. He's not feeling too good."

"Hungover, eh?"

"Yeah."

"You know, you could do a lot better." Smiling, Helmut flicked his tongue across the top of his pink snowball.

"Better than what?"

"Than that uptight prick for a boyfriend."

"What are you talking about?" said G-man, appalled. Was that how people saw Rickey—as an uptight prick? Surely most people didn't, but he guessed he could see how a waiter might. (In typical back-of-the-house fashion, G-man thought of the maître d' as a glorified waiter.) Still, wasn't it rude to say so? Was this how people flirted nowadays, by saying horrible things about each other's partners? Helmut was only about five years younger than G-man, but he made G-man feel like an old fogey.

"Never mind," said Helmut, seeing the look on G-man's face. "I guess it's true love. Can't blame a boy for trying, though."

"I really gotta go," said G-man. He drove home balancing the snowballs against the side of his leg, since the Satellite was too old and primitive to have a cup holder and Rickey hadn't gotten around to installing one. The encounter with the maître d' made him feel vaguely guilty even though he knew he had done nothing wrong.

Rickey sat up in bed, grabbed his snowball, and plunged the plastic spoon deep into it. "Oh," he said after sucking down several spoonfuls of finely shaved ice. "That hits the spot."

"Eat up, then. It's gonna make you all better."

"Like I even deserve to feel better. I'm such a moron, G. How come I had to sit there and drink every damn beer in the house, and on an empty stomach too?"

"I was wondering that myself."

"Aw, hell, I bet you know exactly what I was thinking about."

"I had to guess, I'd say you were brooding about Mike. Maybe even reminiscing a little about Phil Muller."

"Course I was. I tried not to, but I couldn't help it." Rickey finished his snowball and set the wax cup on the nightstand. "I can't let Mike just get away with it. I can't!"

"Rickey, you're gonna be in charge of a kitchen pretty soon. People will be trying to fuck with you all the time, and sometimes you'll have to bust them for it, but sometimes you gotta let things roll off your back. Why not start with Mike?"

"Cause I don't know what he'll do next. What happens when he figures out he didn't turn Lenny against us? What if he realizes he actually did us a favor, the dumb shit, and that pisses him off even worse? What I'm gonna do then?"

"Guess who I saw up by the snowball stand," said G-man, not sure if he was trying to change the subject or just driven by a vestigial urge to confess. "Remember that guy Helmut?"

"What, the host from Lenny's?"

"Yeah. I think he was flirting with me."

"You just now figured that out?"

"Huh?"

"That little bitch has had a boner for you since the first time he ate at the Apostle Bar. It's so obvious. He looks at you like he hasn't eaten in three days and you're a hot roast beef po-boy."

"He does?"

"Fucking A he does," said Rickey. "I never liked that guy. I used to give him small portions."

"I'm glad you're not jealous or anything."

"Why the hell would I be jealous of a poodle-groomed, designer-label, front-of-the-house fag like that?"

"I'm not saying you would. I know you wouldn't. C'mon, give me that." Rickey had picked up his empty snowball cup and crumpled it savagely. Droplets of red syrup flew out and landed on the sheet. "Now look what you did. Give me the goddamn cup."

"Sorry." Rickey relinquished the mangled cup and lay back on his heap of pillows. "I don't think that snowball worked. I still feel like shit."

"You're full of hate, that's all."

"I know," Rickey said wanly. "It eats away at me sometimes."

o o o

While Rickey was drinking beer in his kitchen, Mike Mouton was drinking Ay Carambas in the bar at the Hotel Bienvenu. An Ay Caramba was made of tequila, Triple Sec, and blood orange juice. They cost seven dollars, but Mike got them free because the bartenders believed, wrongly, that he had some sort of control over their jobs.

He wasn't thinking so much about Rickey tonight. Instead he was angry with NuShawn, who had crapped out on a promised delivery. It wouldn't matter to NuShawn; no doubt he had plenty of other customers, all of whom were paying exorbitant prices for adulterated goods. He was probably making better money than Mike, which was a crime in every sense of the word. If you looked at it a certain way, you could even say Mike was doing NuShawn a big favor buying from him. Yes, goddammit, that was true, and everybody was scared to talk about it—maybe they thought it was politically incorrect or something. Well, he wasn't afraid of being politically incorrect. "Hey, Kevin," he said to the bartender, "did you know people are actually doing drug dealers a favor by buying their shit?"

"My name's Kendall, Mr. Mouton."

"Yeah, OK—*Kendall.* You ever think about that?"

"About what? People buying drugs?"

"It's like they're performing a public service. See what I mean?"

"No, I'm sorry, I really don't."

"It's very simple," said Mike, thumping the bar with his fist. "People who buy drugs are actually helping these little assholes make a living, when otherwise they'd be out sticking guns in people's faces, probably killing somebody."

Kendall nodded and walked to the other end of the bar. Mike did not judge this to be an adequate response. "Hey, come back here!" he yelled. "I'm not done talking to you!"

"I'm busy, sir."

"I can see you're not! Get your ass back here."

Returning to Mike's end of the bar, Kendall busied himself polishing glasses. "So what do you think of my theory?" Mike said.

"I think it stinks."

"What the fuck did you just say to me?"

"Mr. Mouton, my son had a drug problem. My wife and I found out he'd been using crack cocaine and got him into a program. He'd been clean for six months when he was killed in a drive-by shooting. He would've been twenty-one this year. I think your theory exposes you for the imbecile you are."

"I agree," said a man drinking a Hurricane at the bar.

It was too much: insulted in the space of a minute by a black bartender and a Hurricane-drinking tourist. Mike lunged halfway across the bar and would have punched Kendall if the tourist had not grabbed him from behind. The man was flabby but bulky, and Mike couldn't pull away. "OK, buddy," the tourist said in a flat Midwestern-sounding accent. "Looks like you've had enough. Let's hustle on out of here."

Easing up a little on his grip, the tourist walked Mike to the bar's entryway and gave him a gentle push. "Get yourself home, buddy. Catch a cab."

"Fuck you!"

"No need for all that. There's a guard right over there. Would you like me to call him?"

Mike glowered at the man, but was silent.

"All right. Don't come back in here. Go home." *Goo hoom,* in that strange flat accent. There were foreigners everywhere.

The tourist walked back into the bar. Mike loitered for a few minutes by the big art deco stained-glass window at the bar's entrance. Eventually he slunk off across the lobby.

"Thanks, man," said Kendall. "Thought I was gonna have to go for the panic button."

"Why didn't you just slug him?"

"Not worth it." Kendall picked up a glass and began to polish it with his towel, looking deeply into the convex surface. "What good would it do? Can't help my boy any. Can't afford to lose my job. Comes a time when it's just not worth it."

"Christ," said the tourist. "I'm sorry."

"Aw, no, I'm sorry. Sorry you had to catch that ugly scene on your vacation. Where you from?"

"Toronto."

"Tell me something. You like that ice hockey? I only ask because I went to one of the hockey games they had here, and for the life of me, I can't see the fun in a game where the score can end up being zero to zero."

The Canadian opened his mouth, closed it, and shook his head. He liked these New Orleanians, but they kept drawing him into conversations like this one, where he didn't even know how to begin. Sometimes it seemed as if they were living on a whole different planet.

　　　　　　　°　°　°

Ignoring the tourist's advice, Mike got his car out of the parking garage and drove home. People kept blowing their horns and flashing their headlights at him. He gave them the finger and kept driving. Not until he pulled into Redwood Glen, his Metairie apartment complex, did he realize his brights were on. He must have been blinding people the whole way. Well, fuck them.

Mike hauled himself up the redwood stairs of his building and let himself into one of six identical redwood doors. His apartment was neat but cheerless, almost regimented-looking. On the table by the door, a flashing red number 1 showed in the message window of his answering machine. He hoped suddenly and wildly that NuShawn had called, even though he had never given NuShawn this number. He pressed the Play button.

"Irene?" said an old woman's hoarse voice. "You there? Irene, that you, babe? I got me some nice shrimps over by the Langenstein's. I'm gonna berl 'em up tonight. Call me, you wanna have some, hear? . . . Irene, you there, honey? When you got this machine? I'm hanging up now."

"You stupid bitch," Mike snarled. He put his hand on the answering machine, intending to throw it across the room, but stopped at the last possible second. He'd been breaking too many things while he was fucked up; it was getting expensive. Instead he kicked the leg of his sofa as hard as he could. It should have hurt, but he felt nothing. The incident with Kevin—no, *Kendall*—and the tourist gnawed at him. He hadn't known the bartender's son was murdered. How could he be expected to keep track of every little thing that happened to the employees of the Hotel Bienvenu? People like that usually brought trouble upon themselves anyway.

Mike slumped on the sofa for several minutes. Then he got up and went into his bedroom. In here, a single small window looked out over the parking lot. The bats and insects around the sodium lights made weird, swooping shadows on the bedroom walls. Mike sat on the edge of the bed and opened the drawer of his nightstand. There was only one object in the drawer, a Luger semiautomatic pistol. He lifted it out and turned it over and over in his hands. The rubber grip was sticky against his right palm, the barrel smooth and cold against his left.

He pressed the pistol's muzzle into his forehead and sat like that for a long time. His forefinger stroked the trigger but put no pressure on it. He imagined his father's reaction on hearing that he had blown his brains out. Would Pinky be sorry for all the slights and hurts, sorry for what he had done to Uncle George, or convinced of his longtime suspicion that Mike just couldn't hack it?

As always, the latter possibility eventually seemed to outweigh the former ones, and he put the Luger back in the drawer. There were six beers in his refrigerator. Mike drank all of them before he was able to sleep.

chapter 22

L enny and Rickey were at Liquor taking delivery of several pieces of kitchen equipment. A reach-in cooler, a new flattop, and an ice machine had already come in on enormous dollies, and a few other, smaller items were still arriving.

"I got you a present," said Lenny.

"What?" said Rickey, instantly suspicious.

Lenny reached into the attaché case he was carrying and pulled out the smallest cell phone Rickey had ever seen. It folded down to a shiny black rectangle not much larger than a credit card. He dropped it into the palm of Rickey's hand, where it fit perfectly.

"Aw, Lenny, I told you before, I hate these things. I refuse to turn into one of those dickheads always yapping into a phone just to show how important they are."

"What, like me?"

"Hell yeah, like you."

"Well, it's got nothing to do with how important you are. I'm tired of not being able to get in touch when I need to. You know how many times I tried to get you yesterday to see about this delivery?"

"I told you, I was home. I just had some kinda twenty-four hour flu and couldn't come to the phone."

"The flu, huh?" Lenny looked closely at Rickey, and Rickey looked away. "Flu in a bottle, most likely. And where was G-man?"

"You must've called while he was at the snowball stand."

"Jesus." Lenny rolled his eyes. "Whatever. Just take the phone and use it."

"I'm not gonna use it in restaurants. People who do that are the world's biggest assholes."

"I agree."

"And I'm not gonna use it while I'm driving. I got enough distractions without a phone stuck in my ear."

"I wouldn't ask you to endanger yourself. Or anyone else, for that matter. Look, open the cover here—see this little LCD display? When you turn the phone off, the carrier takes messages for you, and the screen shows how many you have."

"If I gotta have one, G should get one too."

"What for? You two are always together."

"Not right now we're not," Rickey pointed out. "I'm here, and he's at the test kitchen training Terrance. What if I needed to get in touch with him?"

"OK, OK, I'll have Flanagan pick up a phone for him tomorrow. Christ, it's like having a couple of kids—one of you gets something, the other one has to have it too."

"Thanks for the phone, Dad."

"Sure. Thanks for reminding me why I never got married."

° ○ ○

Beneath the casino, Terrance was trimming the fat off a small ribeye steak. "You said save this fat?" he asked. "Don't throw it away?"

"Right," said G-man. "You're gonna use it to add flavor to the meat."

"It looks disgusting."

"Terrance, I've watched you eat four plates of fettucine Alfredo. You think a little steak fat is disgusting?"

"I don't like the way it quivers."

"You know, this could be a problem for a grill guy."

"I'll get over it. I don't love scraping plates, either, but I been washing dishes at Escargot's for four years."

"I guess you got a point. OK, now you want to lay out your cubed fat on the grill, cover it with a layer of peeled garlic cloves from your mise, and put your filet on top. You know, Rickey has some idea that we're gonna do this with Wagyu beef, but I don't see how. People in New Orleans aren't gonna pay fifty bucks for a steak."

"Fifty bucks!"

"Yeah, he says Lenny can get it wholesale for twenty a pound. Then we gotta mark it up. I don't think it'll fly."

"Well, that's why Rickey needs you. He lets his imagination get the best of him sometimes."

"Tell me about it. Now, take one of these metal hats and put it over your steak. The fat's gonna start melting and the garlic's gonna perfume the meat. Right now you can stand here and count off two minutes, but during service you'll be doing a lot of other stuff, so make sure you know how long two minutes is."

"I know how long two minutes is. I watch a lot of hoops."

"Yeah, you cook it for two basketball minutes, it's gonna turn into shoe leather. Two minutes by the clock, OK? Then you lift the hat and give it the cognac." From Terrance's mise-en-place, G-man grabbed a bottle of cognac fitted with a bar-style pour top and upended it over the ribeye. A blue flame danced across the grill.

"Damn!" said Terrance.

"It's cool. Now put the hat back on and let it go for two to six more minutes, depending on how the customer ordered it."

"Ain't that kinda short for well-done?"

"That'd be eight minutes altogether, which is way too long. But anybody who pays for a nice steak and then orders it well-done isn't gonna know the difference."

"Hey now, I like my steak well-done."

"You ever ordered one in a restaurant?"

"No, I seen the shit they do to 'em. Throw 'em over their shoulders, throw 'em in the deep fryer, throw 'em on the damn floor." Terrance wrinkled his nose. "I hope you don't expect me to do nothing like that."

"I promise we'll never require you to throw anybody's steak on the floor."

They grilled a second ribeye and sat in the semicircular booth to eat. Watching Terrance saw at his meat, G-man wondered how anyone could prefer a well-done steak, but he knew he would sound like a food snob if he pressed the matter further. Instead he said, "You put in your notice at Escargot's?"

"No, and I ain't looking forward to it. Mike's gonna

make my life miserable for the whole two weeks, just like he did to Rickey."

"So don't give notice."

"You mean just don't show up one day? Nah, I don't work like that."

"You can show up. Around lunchtime, when he's too busy to think much about it, tell Mike it's your last day. By the time it really gets through his skull, your shift'll be over."

Terrance sighed. "That just ain't the way I operate. I'll give him notice, let him fuck me around for two weeks, and leave knowing I'll never have to see him again."

"What's up with Mike these days, anyway? He ever say anything about Rickey?"

"Not that I've heard, but he don't talk to me too much. Why?"

"I don't know," said G-man, deciding not to mention the phone call Lenny had received. "Mike seemed kinda obsessed with him for a while there. I guess it worried me a little."

"I wouldn't worry on account of Mike," said Terrance. "He hates Rickey, but he's a coward. He ain't gonna do nothing about it."

o   o   o

"Somebody complained about *what*?" said Rickey. He and Lenny were in Oscar De La Cerda's office, having received a call from the lawyer as the last of the kitchen equipment was coming in.

"The sign in the window," said De La Cerda. "The one you have to post for fifteen days, remember? The one that says you plan to serve alcoholic beverages? You post it so people in the neighborhood can complain about it if they want to. Well, somebody complained. Called up Sam Marx at the Finance Department and said they didn't want a restaurant moving in."

"Can they do that?"

"Sure they can *do* it," said Lenny. "It doesn't necessarily *mean* anything."

"Or it might mean we don't get our liquor license!"

Lenny and the lawyer glanced at each other. "Well, that's the worst-case scenario," said Lenny.

"Who made the complaint? Was it Mike Mouton?"

De La Cerda consulted a note on his desk blotter. "No, I don't think your crackhead pal lives in the district. The complaint was made by one Rondo Johnson of 1311 Lafitte Avenue."

"Mike's got something to do with this. I know it."

"Calm down," said Lenny. "Don't get paranoid. It can't be Mike's fault every time."

"It is this time, though. You posted those signs in your windows, right? When you opened your restaurants?"

"Sure. Had to."

"Did anybody complain?"

"Well, no. We had a few people call up and ask questions, but nobody ever lodged a complaint."

"See? I bet it hardly ever happens . . . What time is it?"

"2:30," said De La Cerda, bewildered by the apparent change of subject. "Why?"

"Lunch shift is over. And check it out—Lenny gave me this cute little phone. You got a Yellow Pages?"

De La Cerda pushed the phone book across the desk, shooting a quizzical glance at Lenny, who shrugged. Rickey looked up a number and dialed.

"Yeah, let me talk to Cole . . . Hey, this's John Rickey . . . Fine, great. Listen, you know that sign you had to put in the window before you opened? The one saying you were gonna serve liquor and all? . . . Well, did anybody ever actually call to complain? . . . Uh huh. OK, thanks, I'll let you get back to it . . . Sure. OK. Bye."

He hung up and turned back to the others. "That was Cole Parker at Poivre. He says nobody complained about *his* sign. Now I'm gonna call Devlin over at the Lemon Tree."

"Don't bother," said Lenny. "It doesn't prove anything. Even if this is the first time anybody ever made a complaint, that doesn't mean Mike is behind it."

"I don't see that it matters much," said De La Cerda. "We're not automatically fucked because one person complains. It just means the Finance Department will take his complaint under advisement when considering your application. The area's commercially zoned, so I don't think you have a lot to worry about. Of course, it would be best if we could get Mr. Johnson to withdraw his complaint."

"How do we do that?"

"You go talk to him."

"Just me?"

"I think it's best if you go on your own," said Lenny. "If you take G-man along, it could look like you're trying to intimidate the guy with numbers."

"What if *he* has numbers?"

"Do you want to do it or not? You could just wait and

see what happens. But who knows? Maybe you can charm the guy."

"If Mike got to him, he must be an asshole. I'm not gonna be able to charm him."

"It's not essential that you talk to him," said De La Cerda. "Like I said, I don't think you have much to worry about unless he starts stirring up the neighborhood association or something."

"I'm sure he will if that's what it takes," said Rickey. "He'll do whatever Mike makes him do. But what the hell. I'll go talk to him."

o o o

"No *way* are you going over there alone," said G-man when Rickey told him about the conversation. "What the fuck is Lenny thinking, anyway? I got a few things to say to him about this."

"What's the problem?"

"Are you kidding? Are you so caught up in the restaurant that you can't see anything else? You got no idea what you could be walking into, Rickey. You said yourself Mike probably set it up."

"Lenny doesn't think so."

"Fuck Lenny. *He* doesn't have to go knocking on some perfect stranger's door."

"I guess you got a point there."

"I don't think we should go at all," said G-man. "If De La Cerda doesn't think we have a problem, I say we just wait and see what happens."

"I can't just wait."

"Yeah, I figured you'd say that. In that case, I'm going with you."

"Whatever," said Rickey. In his heart, though, he was pleased. He had a bad feeling about this thing, and he hadn't looked forward to visiting Rondo Johnson on his own.

At eleven o'clock the next morning, they parked in front of 1311 Lafitte Avenue. Like all the houses in the neighborhood, it was a narrow shotgun built right up against the sidewalk. Once it had been painted pink. Now the spots where the paint had not peeled away altogether were the color of dirty flesh. Three concrete steps led up to a glass storm door decorated with aluminum birds. A **BEWARE OF THE DOG** sign was wired crookedly to the storm door, but no dog barked as they climbed the steps.

"What are we supposed to say to this guy?" asked G-man.

"Don't worry about it. I'll do the talking."

"What are *you* gonna say?"

"I don't know yet," Rickey admitted. He'd thought about it most of the night, but hadn't come up with anything that gave him confidence.

Before they could ring the doorbell, the storm door swung open. "Help you?" said a rusty nail of a voice that did not sound as if it wanted to be helpful in the least.

"Mr. Johnson?"

"I don't wanna buy nothing, I don't wanna hear about Jesus, I just wanna know what the hell you're doing on my stoop."

Rondo Johnson was an old white man, maybe eighty-five, maybe just weighed down by a lifetime of bad habits.

He was not fat by New Orleans standards, but the excess flesh that hung from his arms and his neck had a doughy, unhealthy look. The smell of dead cigarettes wafted from him, and Rickey could see yellow nicotine stains on the first two fingers of his right hand.

"Well, uh, Mr. Johnson, my name is John Rickey and this is Gary Stubbs. We're—"

"Unicef?"

"What?"

"You from Unicef? They already come by here at Halloween. I told 'em to go to hell—what I'm gonna feed African babies for? So they can come to America and ruin my neighborhood? We got enough—"

G-man interrupted the old man. "Actually, sir, we're the owners of the restaurant opening over on Broad Street." He managed the *sir* without a trace of sarcasm; Rickey couldn't have done it.

"You from the restaurant?"

"That's right," said Rickey. "You made a complaint about our liquor license."

"You're damn right I made a complaint. I done lived in this house forty years. I remember when that other place was in there. The Eye-talian place. It brought a bad element to the neighborhood. Just look what happened to that man."

"The other restaurant—uh, could we come in and talk to you for a minute?"

"No, you can't come in. How the hell I know you're who you say you are? You don't look like restaurant owners. You look like a couple bums. I already been robbed twice and I got a heart condition. I ain't letting you in my house."

"Where's your dog?" asked G-man.

"He got some kinda cancer. Lady next door said he oughta see a vet'narian, but I figure you gotta be crazy to spend that kinda money on a animal. I took him to the pound."

Rickey and G-man glanced at each other. This wasn't going well. "I'm sorry about your dog," said Rickey. "Anyway, uh, the other restaurant—there was a Mob connection, and the guy who got killed was stealing money from them. Nothing like that will be going on in our place."

"Don't guess you'd tell me if it was, would you?"

"Well—"

"Listen, boy. Nobody wants another restaurant to move in that building. We don't want the traffic and we don't want a buncha drunks coming in. We like things the way they are."

Rickey looked around at the dingy houses, the cracked sidewalk, the treeless, trash-strewn street.

"Everybody around here agrees with me, but I'm the only one who'll bother to speak his mind. I ain't afraid of you rich bastards. I'm gonna bring it up at the next neighborhood meeting, and take a vote, and we gonna talk to our councilman. We don't want no damn restaurant. Now get off my stoop."

The storm door slammed. The **BEWARE OF THE DOG** sign rattled. The aluminum birds trembled. Rickey made as if to knock again, but G-man caught his arm. "I think we better just go."

"Shit," said Rickey.

chapter 23

He wouldn't even let you in the house?" said Lenny. "He practically threw us off his stoop," said Rickey. "Said we looked like bums. Oh, and he took his dog to the pound because it had cancer."

"Lovely."

"We couldn't get anywhere with him. He said he's gonna turn the neighborhood against us, talk to his councilman, all kinda shit. So what do we do now? What's the next step?"

"Let me talk to Oscar and call you back."

Lenny hung up, checked the recording light on his tape machine, and called the lawyer. "What district is the Liquor property in?"

"Uh-oh. They didn't have any luck with Mr. Johnson?"

"No, and he sounds like a regular old bastard. I hate to send them back up against him."

"They're gonna have to lose their cherries sometime."

"Sure, they'll have to deal with all sorts of bullshit, but I don't want to make them do it now. Things are going so well. You know what they made the other day? Grilled lobster with a Wild Turkey sauce. Like they were inventing the wheel. I didn't even have the heart to tell them Jasper White did lobster with bourbon back in the eighties."

"Lenny. Let's get back to the old bastard. What do you want me to do about him?"

"Get me the name of the councilman first of all. I'll talk to him, see if he's heard from Johnson. Who knows? Maybe the old man's just blowing smoke."

"I thought Rickey and G-man didn't want you to get involved."

"Yeah, well, if it's that or lose the restaurant, they'll reconcile themselves to my getting involved."

"OK, I got the list right here. The guy for that district is Lance Taliaferro."

"I know Lance. I'll give him a call."

Still recording, Lenny dialed Lance Taliaferro's office. The councilman took his call at once and knew precisely what he wanted. "Sure, I've spoken to Mr. Johnson. Wish I hadn't—he's not very pleasant. Loves to talk about how much things have deteriorated since the blacks moved in—only he doesn't say blacks—but when it comes to this restaurant issue, he acts like the neighborhood's so nice and the place is gonna ruin it. Then he starts in about his heart condition. Is this your restaurant, Lenny? I heard it was a couple of young guys opening the place."

"Thanks a lot."

"No, I mean real young guys, like in their twenties. Couple of whiz kids."

"That's true," said Lenny, pleased that word was spreading. "These guys are friends of mine—I'm just trying to help them out. So how seriously should they take this complaint?"

"Well, if Johnson really wants to make trouble for them, he probably can. I don't have any problem with the restaurant, but I can't ignore complaints from my district. He's called me three or four times already. I disregard that, he'll put the word out for sure—could hurt my chances for reelection."

"Hey, even if you didn't get reelected, you'd have a great new restaurant in your district."

"Yeah, I'd like to see it move in. But I don't know how I can help you if this old character really wants to stir up the shit."

"You think there's any chance he's working for somebody?"

"What do you mean?"

"The owners believe they have an enemy. Maybe Johnson could be getting paid to complain?"

"Hell if I know. Even if he is, that's not illegal."

"OK," said Lenny. "Thanks, Lance. Come see me sometime."

"Will do."

He called Rickey back. Rickey answered the phone sounding stressed out. "Don't worry about this," said Lenny. "Calm down."

"Seems like people are always telling me to calm down lately."

"Maybe you ought to give it some thought, then. Seriously, don't worry about Mr. Johnson. I'm taking care of him."

"Really?"

"I wouldn't say so if it wasn't true. Try to relax. Go on with whatever you were doing. Make some more food."

"OK," said Rickey, obviously wanting to believe him. "Thanks, Lenny."

"Don't mention it."

Lenny hung up, and his tape machine automatically clicked off. Years ago, when De La Cerda first learned how Lenny taped all his phone calls, the lawyer nearly had a coronary. "Do you *want* to put weapons in the hands of your enemies?" he'd asked. "Is it your *ambition* to be indicted someday?"

"I'm a restaurateur, not a don," Lenny answered guilelessly. "Who'd want to indict me?"

Even De La Cerda didn't know the true extent of the tapes. No one did. There were things on them that could cause Lenny quite a bit of trouble if they fell into the wrong hands. To Lenny, the secure feeling the tapes gave him was well worth the risk. He still sometimes brooded about the way Chef Jerome had screwed him two decades ago in Portland. Nothing like that could happen to him now. He had proof of everything.

○ ○ ○

"Lenny says he's taking care of it," Rickey told G-man.

"What's he gonna do?"

"He didn't say."

"Well, what if he's gonna have the old man killed or something?"

"Fine with me."

"Damn, Rickey. Don't even say that."

"I mean it. Johnson's a hateful old fucker. He's not doing anybody any good, and he's doing *us* harm."

"I know the guy's an asshole," said G-man. "I still don't want him on my conscience."

"I'm *so* glad I wasn't raised Catholic."

"That has nothing to do with it."

"Give them to us by the time they're five years old, they'll be ours forever," Rickey taunted. He knew he was being obnoxious, but he couldn't seem to help himself.

"Why don't you shut up?"

"I can't. I'm too nervous about all this."

"Let's go by the Apostle and have a drink."

°   °   °

That same evening—not terribly late, but just late enough that most people wouldn't be expecting drop-in visitors—a pair of wide, tall, bald men knocked on Rondo Johnson's door. One of the men was white and one was black. Otherwise they looked very much alike. Because of the hour, Mr. Johnson received them with even less grace than he had shown his earlier company.

Unlike Rickey and G-man, this pair did not ask if they might come in. Without seeming to use any real force, they pried Mr. Johnson's hands off the storm door and slipped past him into the dingy living room. There they stood looking around and wrinkling their noses. The surfaces of the room were covered in yellowing newspapers, choked ashtrays, and fingerprint-clouded drinking glasses. Mr. Johnson's dog may have gone to the pound, but ancient evidence of him remained in the corners. "Nice place you got here," said the big, bald white man, his voice rich with sarcasm.

"Who the hell are you two goons? What you want?"

"We're from the neighborhood association."

"Like shit you are. I been living here forty years. I know everybody in the neighborhood association. They don't come barging in my house at all hours."

"This is a different association," said the big, bald black man. "We represent certain facets of the neighborhood with which you may not have familiarized yourself."

"What you talking about, boy?"

"My colleague's name is Mr. Reemer," said the white man. "I'm Mr. Payne. We're simply trying to explain our position to you. There's no need to get ugly."

"That's right, Mr. Johnson. No need for unpleasantness or hard feelings. You might say we come from an alternative neighborhood association—one favoring progress over decay."

"Alternative? This has to do with them two fruits that was here earlier, don't it? This is about the restaurant."

"Is there a restaurant opening near here?" Mr. Reemer wondered.

"I don't know," said Mr. Payne. "That'd be nice, though, wouldn't it? A good restaurant could really help this neighborhood. Be a shame if one old crank tried to ruin it for everybody else."

"Nobody wants that place!" cried Mr. Johnson. "It's gonna bring in a bad element!"

Neither man answered him. Mr. Reemer pushed aside some newspapers and, rather reluctantly, settled down on the couch. "I hope this thing doesn't stain my suit," he said.

"Hang on there, boy, don't get comfortable. You got

about two seconds to take yourselves out my house before I call 911—hey, what the hell you doing?"

This last was directed at Mr. Payne, who had crouched down and reached under the telephone table on the far side of the room. "I can't unplug this thing," he said. "It's so old it doesn't even have a jack—the wire just goes right into the wall."

"Interesting," said Mr. Reemer. "I haven't seen one like that since my grammaw died."

"Oh well," said Mr. Payne. "Sorry about this." He wrapped one meaty hand around the telephone wire and yanked it out of the wall, but he must have pulled too hard, for the whole table came crashing over. The old rotary-dial phone emitted a weak jangle.

"Hey!"

"Gonna look like he tripped over the wire," observed Mr. Reemer.

"I guess so, yeah. We'll just kinda lay him out by it."

"What you talking about?" said Mr. Johnson furiously.

"Well, let's think a minute," said Mr. Reemer. "Say you were coming in from the kitchen—that evil-smelling room back there *is* the kitchen, correct? And maybe the telephone wire's lying out in the floor, and you caught your foot in it. You could have a bad fall."

"Ought to be more careful," said Mr. Payne.

"A fall like that—it's extremely dangerous for somebody with a heart condition. I heard the shock could kill them before they hit the floor. You OK, Mr. Johnson?"

Mr. Johnson's face had gone very red, and he was clawing at his shirt collar. As they watched, he heaved himself halfway across the room toward the defunct telephone, dropped to his knees among the newspapers, and fell headlong across a stack of old Thursday Food sections. The two men got up and knelt on either side of him, not too close.

"I think he's trying to say something," said Mr. Payne. Mr. Reemer leaned over trying to hear the words, wincing as he caught a whiff of Mr. Johnson's breath.

"Meditation? I don't think that'll help, Mr. Johnson. It might have calmed you down some if you'd started years ago—maybe a little yoga, too—but I think it's too late for all that."

"He's trying to say 'medication,'" said Mr. Payne.

"Well, pardon me, Mr. Elocution Lessons. He's not speaking very clearly. How was I to know?"

One of Mr. Johnson's hands rose up and clutched at Mr. Reemer's silk necktie. Absently, Mr. Reemer pushed it away. For a few minutes they just squatted on their haunches, watching the old man.

"Is he still breathing?" said Mr. Payne finally.

"Ye—no, no he's not."

"Were we *supposed* to make him stop breathing?"

"De La Cerda said it would be best to just scare him, but if anything happened because of his heart condition, we shouldn't feel responsible."

"Good," said Mr. Payne. "I hate feeling responsible. Let's move him over by the phone and get out of here. This place stinks. It's bad for my health."

"Hey, Payne, look at this." Mr. Reemer picked up a business card that had fallen off the telephone table and handed it to Mr. Payne.

"'Michael Mouton,'" Mr. Payne read. "'General Manager, Escargot's at the Hotel Bienvenu.' Isn't this the guy De La Cerda wanted us to ask him about?"

"It is, but we never got the chance. Nice of him to leave that where we could find it."

"You know what?" said Mr. Reemer as they were leaving.
"What?"

"Man should have held onto that dog. A good dog can protect you."

"Not if somebody's determined to get past it."

"I resent the implication," said Mr. Reemer. "I'd never hurt a dog."

The weather was sufficiently hot that one of Mr. Johnson's neighbors called the police to report an odor the very next day. People gathered on their stoops and watched the men from the coroner's office bumping the black-bagged body down the steps on a gurney. "It's a shame," a woman told the neighbor on the other side of her duplex. "He was a fine man."

"Ummm-ummm, you know you telling a lie. He was a nasty old thing."

"I ain't gonna speak ill of the dead. I was getting kinda tired of hearing him go on about that restaurant, though."

"Child, I know it. I don't care about that restaurant. I was gonna vote against it at the neighborhood meeting just to shut him up. Now I don't guess I will."

"Me neither. What we care anyway? They fixing it up nice. It's one less place for the vagrants to set on fire."

"Yeah, you right," said the second woman, glancing with ill-concealed relief at the slowly departing van.

° ° °

Rickey and G-man sat in the Apostle Bar staring at the pair of frosty green drinks that Anthony B had just set in front of them. The drinks were served in martini glasses and garnished with twists of lime peel impaled on cocktail umbrellas.

"You getting fancy on us, Anthony?" said G-man.

"What is it again?" asked Rickey.

"It's called Laura's Limeade. She makes it with New Orleans Rum, the local stuff, and fresh lime juice and a dash of gin. It's pretty good."

"Yeah, it is," said G-man, sipping it. "It's real good. This is what I always call a dangerous drink. The kind where you can't really taste the liquor."

Rickey drained off a third of his drink, then reminded himself to slow down. He didn't have time for another hangover. The drink was good, but it seemed vaguely girly to him; he'd been in the mood for a shot of Wild Turkey. He wasn't really listening to the conversation until he realized that Anthony had asked him a question. "Huh?" he said, looking up.

"G-man was just telling me about running the test kitchen. I asked about the other stuff. The licensing and all—it's going OK?"

"Oh," said Rickey. "Well, it's going kinda weird." He found himself telling Anthony about Rondo Johnson's complaint and their meeting with the old man. He wasn't sure he should talk about it, but he was curious to get Anthony's opinion. "I don't know," he concluded. "Lenny said he was gonna take care of it."

"Oh, Lord."

"What?"

"Nothing."

"I'm not in the mood for this, Anthony. *Oh Lord* what?"

"Well, nothing really. Only Lenny took care of somebody for me once, and the guy ended up in the hospital."

"I don't believe you. Lenny wouldn't get his hands dirty."

"Course not. He don't do it himself. He hires people. Lenny's my friend, but he knows some awful bad people."

"We might need some bad people on our side," Rickey mused. "There's enough of 'em on the other side, that's for damn sure. Who'd he take care of for you?"

"Aw, this guy was some kinda gang leader over by the St. Thomas project. Trying to shake me down for protection and everything."

"What happened to him?"

"He went to Charity with a broken arm and a couple teeth knocked out. Said he got jumped by two guys he didn't know. Him and his crew never bothered me again."

"How'd you feel?"

"What you mean?"

"I mean, did you have a problem with it? You're Catholic, right? Did you feel guilty that this guy got hurt because of you?" Rickey gave G-man a sidelong look. "Or did you figure, well, he wouldn't have gotten hurt if he hadn't started the shit himself?"

"Know what I like about you, Rickey?" said G-man, finishing his drink. "You're so subtle. I admire that."

Anthony wrinkled his forehead. "I don't remember that I ever felt guilty about it. You think I ought to?"

"No," said Rickey.

"Yes," said G-man.

Rickey smacked the bar, making the two martini glasses jump. "*Why?* Why should he feel guilty for protecting himself? Why should *we?*"

"Because that's not the way to solve a problem."

"What are we supposed to do, then? Buy a *Mass?* Say a *novena?*"

"Dude, will you get off this Catholic thing? It's not very attractive. I can't help how I was raised, but I'm not Catholic any more, you know that. I just can't believe you're trying to convince me that it's OK for Lenny's thugs to beat up an old man so we can open a restaurant."

"Well, when you put it *that* way . . ."

"What other way you want me to put it?"

"I don't know. Anthony, you got any more of that limeade?"

G-man put his hand on Rickey's arm. "I'm not gonna be involved in something like that, Rickey. I'm serious. If that old man ends up in the hospital or something—"

"What?"

G-man didn't answer.

"Well, what? C'mon, finish the sentence. If the old man ends up in the hospital, then what? You'd walk out on me? All because of some evil old bastard who's probably working for Mike Mouton?"

"I wouldn't walk out on you."

"But you wouldn't work with me any more?"

"I wouldn't work with Lenny any more. I *couldn't.*"

"Uh huh. Sounds like walking out to me."

G-man bowed his head. There were tears in his eyes. Through their blurred film, he saw the fresh drink Anthony had set in front of him, picked it up, and drained it in two swallows.

"Probably it'll all work out OK," said Anthony. The words hung thin and implausible in the dark, smoky air of the bar.

chapter 24

It was five o'clock in the morning and Rickey was sitting on the porch. He'd spent the past two nights sitting here staring at the houses across the street, the occasional car bumping along Marengo toward Tchoupitoulas, and the tree branches moving against the purple summer sky. He couldn't sleep and didn't feel like lying awake in bed. He wasn't drinking, didn't even want to.

They'd come home from the Apostle Bar, fallen into bed, barely spoken the next day. That had been bad enough. The day after that they'd started acting civil toward each other, which was worse. They had to be civil; nothing had changed with the restaurant, at least not yet, and there was still all kinds of work to do. They had to talk about who was going to the test kitchen, who'd call the flooring company about the mats that hadn't arrived, who needed the car when, all the usual day-to-day crap that had seemed easy enough before. Rickey decided there was nothing more terrible than being reduced to basic civility with the person you loved most. Even flat-out fighting would be better than this limbo.

He knew he was the only one keeping it going, too.

G-man wasn't mad at him, had in fact been giving him wordless, heartbroken, pleading looks that Rickey tried to ignore. But he couldn't ignore the fact that G-man had essentially threatened to desert him and the restaurant. It was unthinkable that G-man would leave. It was unthinkable that he had even said such a thing. But he had, and even though it was all still hypothetical, Rickey couldn't quite forgive him for it.

Lenny claimed that the problem had already been solved. "There was no need for unpleasantness," he'd said. "I just made sure the complaint will be disregarded. You'll get your license."

Lenny must have paid somebody off. Surely G-man could live with that; it was the way business was done here. Maybe things would be OK now. Rickey was tired of the war going on in his heart, half of him pissed off and unwilling to capitulate, half of him wanting things to be like they'd been before, even if it meant scuttling the whole damn restaurant.

The front door creaked open behind him, and G-man came out carrying two steaming mugs. "I couldn't sleep either," he said. "I thought you might want some coffee."

"Thanks," said Rickey, taking a mug. Their fingers touched briefly, their eyes met, and Rickey almost said something—he wasn't sure what. Then the moment passed and he looked away. That was how it had been since the night at the Apostle. Horrible.

G-man sat on the steps and picked up the newspaper that had landed there an hour ago. He paged through the sports section, found little of interest now that the NBA playoffs were over, glanced through the local news. Reading over his shoulder, Rickey saw that all the top stories seemed to deal with people who had died while fishing, swimming, or boating. Drinking and drowning was a major cause of death in summertime Louisiana. He was toying with the idea of making a tasteless joke about life jackets when G-man turned the page, sucked in his breath, and handed the section to Rickey. Rickey was pretty sure of what he would see before he finished scanning the page. It was the daily list of obituaries, and a blurry picture of Rondo Johnson glared out from halfway down the second column.

"Oh, fuck," said Rickey. He had reconciled himself to the idea of Johnson getting knocked around a little, but he'd never thought Lenny would have the man killed. He read further. "Wait a second, dude. It says he died of heart failure. He told us he had a heart condition, remember?"

"And he just happened to keel over right after Lenny promised to do something about him?"

"What you think Lenny's capable of, anyway? He ordered the guy's heart to stop?"

"I think the paper's not telling the whole story."

"And I'm starting to think you're looking for a reason to turn your back on me."

G-man started to get up, then sank back onto the steps as if Rickey's words were weighing him down. "How can you say that? I don't even know how to answer that. I'm looking for a way to *keep from* turning my back on you, and you're making it impossible."

"Impossible? You're the one who threatened to walk out—"

"And you're the one who wants to keep working with a murderer!"

"Then just go!" said Rickey. "There's no way I'm ever gonna live up to your goddamn altar-boy ethics. Just go on and forget everything we've ever done together. *Fuck* it!"

He threw his half-full coffee mug into the yard and heard it shatter on one of the paving stones that led up to the porch. A light came on in the house next door, a shutter swung open, and an old woman's voice yelled, "You people knock it off before I call the police!"

"I'm not going anywhere," said G-man. "I'm not forgetting anything. But I want to talk to Lenny."

"You gonna ask him how he killed that old man? Not even give him the benefit of the doubt? 'Hey, Lenny, I know it says he died of heart failure but c'mon, you took out a hit on the guy, right?' That'll go over real well."

"I don't care how it goes over. I want to hear what he has to say."

"What about the restaurant?"

"What about it?"

"If we piss Lenny off . . ."

"Rickey, what's *happened* to you? You used to say Lenny could go to hell if he didn't like the way we did things. Now it's like you're living out of his pocket. Yeah, tell me to fuck off if you want, but it's true."

Rickey put his head in his hands. It *was* true, he realized. He had grown dependent on the monthly stipend, on Lenny's vast knowledge of the restaurant world, on the ability of Lenny and the suits to handle any problem that cropped up. He'd become so impressed with this ability that he had stopped asking himself exactly how the problems were being handled. He guessed something had been bound to blow up in his face sooner or later, but this was uglier than anything he could have imagined.

"Let's just try to calm down," he said. "The sun's not even up yet. Why don't we fix some breakfast and call Lenny later?"

"I don't feel like fixing breakfast. Lenny's used to dealing with emergencies, and as far as I'm concerned, this is an emergency. I'm calling him right now."

G-man went back into the house. Rickey sat hunched on the steps clutching his temples. He could feel the first tectonic rumbles of a truly awesome headache. This was even more terrible than he'd thought. G-man had never refused to fix him breakfast before.

$\circ$ $\circ$ $\circ$

Ninety minutes later they were in Lenny's office at Crescent. Rumpled and unshaven, Lenny glowered behind his desk. For the first time since they'd met him, he looked well and truly angry. The obituary page lay before him. He picked it up with two fingers as if the feel of it disgusted him, considered it briefly, and let it fall back to the desktop. "I can't even believe I'm looking at this," he said. "Are you actually *accusing* me of something? Should I call De La Cerda?"

"I'm not planning to nark on you, if that's what you mean," said G-man. "I just want to know what happened."

"Evidently the man had a heart attack. I don't know how you think I made that happen."

"C'mon, Lenny. On Tuesday afternoon you tell Rickey you're taking care of the problem. The guy drops dead Tuesday night. We're not supposed to wonder about that?"

"Fine," said Lenny. "So G-man thinks I'm a murderer. Rickey, what do *you* think?"

Rickey, who had been staring at the floor, looked up. He knew exactly what Lenny was doing. Whatever had happened to Rondo Johnson, Lenny must have had a hand in it. But Lenny was using all kinds of misdirection, pretending his feelings were hurt, trying to intimidate them a little (not too much, though—Rickey had expected the lawyer to be here and had been surprised to find Lenny alone). Now he was feeling around the edges of their solidarity, checking to see if he still had an ally in Rickey, knowing he probably did. It was a loathsome, brilliant strategy, and Rickey was shocked to realize how much he admired it.

"I don't think you made Mr. Johnson drop dead," he said. Technically it was true—he doubted Lenny had ever laid eyes on Rondo Johnson. "I'm only here because G talked about leaving. I can't do the restaurant without him."

"*Oh yes you can,*" said Lenny.

"No way. We've always been in this together."

"Listen. G's a great cook—of course we don't want him to leave. But when you own a restaurant, you get ruthless. You don't *take* shit from people who want to mess you up. You don't *stop* just because something upsets you. And you don't *say* you can't get it done without some other person, *because you never know who's going to walk out on you.* So is he walking out? Looks to me like he's still here. G-man? You going anywhere in the next few minutes?"

G-man didn't answer.

"Well, then, Rickey, you assume he's still your partner and you proceed accordingly. It's a lot like being on the line.

You're slammed, right? It's the middle of dinner service, you have fifty tickets up—do you start crying about how many *more* you might get?"

"No. You just keep putting 'em out."

"OK. So that's what you do here. Any questions?"

"Yeah," said G-man. "What happened to Mr. Johnson? I'm not gonna do anything about it. What the hell could I do about it? I just want to know."

"I have no idea." The anger seemed to leave Lenny; his shoulders slumped; he looked terribly tired. For the first time, Rickey found himself wondering whether Mr. Johnson could have died a completely natural death. He didn't believe it, really, but Lenny was so damn convincing. "G-man, what do you want me to do? I don't know how to react when a friend suspects me of murder. Do you want me to *swear* I had nothing to do with it? Do you want a *deposition?*"

"I guess not," said G-man. He had begun to look slightly embarrassed. "But it's our restaurant. It should have been our *problem*. If you didn't do anything to the old man, how'd you make the problem go away?"

"What do you think I did? I paid somebody off."

"Who?"

"Lance Taliaferro on the City Council. Sammy Marx at the Finance Department."

"You got any proof of that?"

"Of course I don't have any *proof!* It was a *bribe!*"

This sounded so utterly New Orleanian that Rickey was certain he could see G-man being convinced—or deciding to be convinced; that was what it came down to, and Rickey had already realized that would be good enough. He knew G-man still wanted to be with him and work with him. Unlike Rickey, G-man needed to have at least a reasonable doubt about Lenny's culpability in the death of the old man, and Lenny was trying hard to give him room for that doubt.

"I understand where you're coming from," said Lenny. He leaned across the desk and steepled his fingers as if in prayer. "I can see how it looks, the guy keeling over right after I said I'd take care of him. But I'm not some kind of *thug,* and you're in over your head. You don't just go around accusing people of murder. We still have to work together. I won't hold this against you, but I'd really like to know whether I'll have to deal with this kind of thing in the future."

"I been in over my head for a long time. Rickey has too—he just won't admit it."

"That's not an answer."

"No," said G-man sullenly. "You won't have to deal with this kinda thing in the future. Not from me, anyway."

Rickey looked at G-man and saw the last of the fight go out of him. He felt ashamed, then quashed the feeling. This was best for both of them. They were already into Lenny for more money than they could imagine. They really had no choice but to go ahead. Besides, without Liquor, what did they have? They'd be back to working line jobs and worrying about the rent. And if they made an enemy out of Lenny Duveteaux, their viability on the New Orleans restaurant scene might be severely limited.

G-man was right: they were in way over their heads, and had been for a long time. But what the hell? When you were in over your head, you couldn't expect to get rescued. You could only swim for the surface and hope you ended up in

Waikiki, not on some godforsaken desert island populated by cannibals.

Rickey said all this to G-man in the car on the way home. He got excited about the cannibal metaphor and swerved into the other lane, but it was still very early and there was little traffic on Magazine Street. "I mean, how can we *not* do the restaurant?" he concluded. "I know you still want to. Anyway, didn't you believe Lenny?"

"I kinda believed him while we were sitting there. He's a real good actor. Now that he's not here, I don't believe him one damn bit. And you don't either—I can tell."

Pretending to watch a city bus in the rearview mirror, Rickey didn't say anything.

"You're right, though. I still want to do the restaurant. But I got a few conditions."

"Like what?"

"Like we stop letting Lenny handle every problem that comes up. I don't know what happened to Mr. Johnson, and maybe I don't want to know. But I *do* know we could have tried to handle it ourselves."

"We did try."

"I don't mean just going to his house. We knew that wasn't gonna work. C'mon—Lenny's not even *from* here. We're local boys. We know how to talk to local people. We can make ourselves welcome. We didn't have to go crying to Lenny just because some old man was *mean* to us."

"Yeah, but we had so much other stuff to deal with—"

"Rickey, we have to deal with *everything*. Otherwise we might as well be working in one of Lenny's kitchens."

Rickey parked in front of the house and killed the engine. As they got out, he saw his broken coffee mug on the front walk. Embarrassed, he kicked it into the tall grass at the side of the yard.

"I never liked that mug anyway," said G-man.

"G, listen . . ."

"Yeah?"

"I'm really sorry about all this. I wish it never happened."

"I'm sorry too." G-man turned to look at Rickey. "I never would've walked out on you."

"I know you wouldn't," said Rickey. He put his arms around G-man and kissed him square on the mouth, not giving a damn about who might be watching or what they'd think.

"You want some breakfast?" said G-man. "I was thinking about fixing some French toast. I mean, if you still feel like it."

"I'd love some."

"You got any cheese dough in the fridge I should know about?"

"No, I was too upset even to make cheese straws. I was too upset even to have a *drink*."

"I know what you mean. I wanted a drink last night, and then I just thought, why bother?"

"We can't let that happen again."

"We won't. You know it's a bad situation when you can't even be bothered to get drunk."

"We just gotta remember two rules: we're in this together no matter what, and there is always alcohol."

"It's a deal," said G-man as they let themselves into the house.

chapter 25

L enny opened the top drawer of his desk, dislodging the tiny directional microphone that peeked through the keyhole. He ran the tape back a few minutes, then pressed PLAY. "We still have to work together," his voice said from the speaker. "I won't hold this against you, but I'd really like to know whether I'll have to deal with this kind of thing in the future."

"I been in over my head for a long time. Rickey has too—"

He rewound it to the beginning, ejected the tape, and marked it in a way only he could understand. He'd been taping his phone calls for a decade, but only a couple of years ago had he begun to record the conversations that took place in his office. Once he'd started, he couldn't imagine why he had waited so long.

He wondered whether Rickey and G-man believed his wronged-innocent act. Probably they didn't; they were naïve but not stupid. But if he had managed to plant even a seed of doubt, that would be good enough. G-man wouldn't be a problem; maybe he'd had some momentary twinge of Catholic guilt, but Rickey was the alpha male of that pair, and Rickey didn't give a damn what Lenny had done to Rondo Johnson. Lenny suspected that Rickey would have cheerfully strangled the old man himself had he thought he could get away with it. Nothing was going to come between that kid and his dream restaurant. Lenny liked that. In time, he thought he and Rickey would truly come to understand each other.

He took out the business card De La Cerda had given him, the one De La Cerda's guys had found in Johnson's house, and dialed the number on it. "Escargot's kitchen, Terrance speaking," said the voice on the other end.

"Let me talk to Mike, please."

"He ain't here. Probably won't be in till ten or so. You like to leave a message?"

"No thanks. I'll give him a call later."

Lenny flipped through his Rolodex and dialed a number with a Metairie exchange. "Yeah?" said Mike Mouton's sleepy voice after four rings.

"Jesus Christ," said Lenny in the voice he used when one of his cooks had fucked something up really badly. "Don't tell me you're still in bed while your staff sets up the kitchen."

"Huh? Who is this?"

"This is Lenny Duveteaux. You there, Mike? Take that pillow off your head and listen good. I know what you're doing. I know you called me at Crescent that night. I know about the other trouble you stirred up. None of it's going to work."

"I don't know what you're—"

"Let's dispense with the bullshit, Mike. You haven't changed a bit since I worked with you at the Fontainebleu. Why do you have such a hard-on for Rickey anyway?"

"Why do I *what?*"

Lenny could hear the actual sound of Mike biting his tongue, torn between losing his threadbare temper and kissing Lenny's ass.

"Don't want to share, huh? Well, I don't really care. But understand this—it needs to stop, and not just for our sake. You're really going sideways, buddy."

"So you *are* bankrolling them!" Mike said. "I knew it!"

"They're my friends, you numb fuck. I look out for my friends. See you around town."

Lenny hung up, smiling with the satisfaction of a job well done. Liquor was completely back on track now; he could feel it. Time to pay some attention to his own restaurants. He opened the kitchen log his chef de cuisine had left on his desk last night. *Daunte never showed up for dinner service,* he read. Daunte was one of the PM dishwashers. *Ran short of plates thru-out service until Polynice got here. P. scraped and loaded plates all night, plus did his other work.*

Daunte was history, of course, like anyone who missed a shift without calling. Lenny decided to promote Polynice to the chief porter's job. He sort of hated to do it; a good night porter was hard to find. Most guys just didn't want to hump garbage, hose down floors, and empty grease traps for six-fifty an hour. Polynice had never complained. He deserved the promotion. Lenny thought he might even be able to put Polynice on the line eventually. He didn't know why; it was just a feeling he had. He'd always been proud of his ability to spot a good cook.

○   ○   ○

Mike let the receiver fall to the floor without even trying to find the cradle. He scrabbled through the clutter on his nightstand, located a small plastic bag, and sucked a blast of medium-grade cocaine up each nostril. These two hits left the bag almost empty. He pressed the disconnect button on the phone and dialed NuShawn's beeper. Only when fifteen minutes had crawled by and NuShawn still hadn't called back did Mike notice that it was eight in the morning.

Why had Lenny called him so early? And what was the terrible thing he'd said—*Why do you have such a hard-on for Rickey?* It was the disgrace, that Lenny could even think that. When Mike looked back on the past year, it seemed to him that things had been fine until he'd hired Rickey. All his problems dated from Rickey's tenure at Escargot's and, even worse, the time right after Rickey had quit. Now Terrance, Mike's only reliable dishwasher, was quitting to work at Rickey's restaurant; he'd put in his notice a week ago. Pinky Mouton had stepped up his usual insinuations about how Mike was never going to amount to anything, almost as if he were comparing his son with Rickey. Lenny Duveteaux, one of the richest and most powerful restaurateurs in New Orleans, was calling him up and threatening him.

When Mike had learned about Rickey's arrest warrant, he'd just tried to help Lenny out. It wasn't his fault if Lenny didn't want to be helped. But what had Lenny meant when he said *I know about the other trouble you stirred up*? He couldn't know about the old man on Lafitte Avenue. How could he? Rondo Johnson had worked as a security guard at one of Pinky's properties years ago and was ridiculously loyal to the Moutons. He wouldn't have told anybody that Mike was paying him to raise a stink about the new restaurant.

Mike got up and started a pot of coffee in his tiny modular kitchen. His mind was racing as he drank his first cup and flipped through the morning paper. The Saints wanted a new stadium. Another idiot had drowned in Bayou Segnette. The mayor was trying to award himself a third term. Mike turned the page and ran his eye down the column of obituaries. A swallow of black coffee stuck halfway down his throat, and he coughed convulsively, spraying it all over the paper.

Rondo Johnson was dead. Jesus Christ, was there anything these people wouldn't do to fuck with him? In some hazy part of his mind, Mike knew he was crossing the boundaries of real paranoia. Certainly Rickey had assaulted him and mocked him and turned people against him, but could Rickey really have had anything to do with Johnson's death? Mike shook his head. They wouldn't have killed a man just to spite him, would they? Then he remembered Uncle George, shot to death in the very property Rickey was now leasing for his restaurant. Obviously it tied in somehow.

Mike gnawed the inside of his cheek. All of this was aimed at him, a big gaudy slap in the face. If they would kill an innocent old man just to fuck with his head, mightn't they kill him too if he kept getting in their way?

He locked his apartment, got in his car, and pulled onto the service road that led to the I–10. Once on the highway, he didn't take the French Quarter exit but continued until he reached the exit that would deliver him to NuShawn's house. Early or not, he couldn't face this day without some help.

° ° °

For the second time this morning, Terrance answered the kitchen phone. "Escargot's, Terrance speaking."

"Yo, T, your boss sittin on my stoop!"

"Say what?"

"He crazy!" NuShawn sounded genuinely unnerved. "He woke me up ringin the bell. I looked out the front window and seen him sittin there. Momma ain't up yet, but she will be pretty soon if he keep on ringin and knockin."

"I guess you better let him in, then."

"You know I don't handle no business here! Shit! Momma'd kill me if she thought I done anything like that. He ain't even supposed to know where I live."

"Well, I didn't tell him."

"What I'm gonna do with this crazy white man? I leave him sittin out there lookin like a rich motherfucker, he probably get robbed or somethin."

"You wanna do me a favor? Sell him his shit," said Terrance. "He don't have it, he's gonna make my day miserable. Give him his bag and tell him to go to work."

"But Terrance—"

"You don't wanna do it, then don't do it. It ain't my problem. Look, I'm busy, I gotta go."

Terrance hung up, shaking his head. He was happy to be leaving Escargot's; he knew life would be better at Liquor. But he wasn't ever going to be able to leave his family.

Mike showed up an hour later. NuShawn must have worked something out with him, because he looked almost healthy and he didn't start yelling at people right away. In fact, everything was pretty much OK until late that night.

Service was over at Escargot's, and a bunch of employees were drinking in the bar. Kendall had been training a new bartender, a big Irishman named Duncan. Tonight Duncan had held down the place on his own, and now he appeared to be getting piss-drunk, perhaps to celebrate. "So you're leaving us soon?" he asked Terrance.

"Fraid so. I'm getting out of the dishwashing business. Got me a cooking job."

"Nice," said the Irishman ruminatively. "Very nice. Cooking beats the hell out of washing dishes, and you'll get away from that asshole Mike."

"That's true."

"I already hate that guy. If I had to put up with half of what you do, I would have left ages ago. How d'you ever stand it?"

"Just patient, I guess," said Terrance.

"There's a difference between patient and spineless," said Duncan. He was kind of an abrasive guy, really. Terrance decided to get off the subject of Mike.

"I look forward to cooking," he said. "I never done it professionally before."

"Where's the job?"

"New restaurant being opened by a couple friends of mine. Place called Liquor."

"Funny name for a restaurant."

"Well, there's a story there," said Terrance. He explained

about Rickey and G-man's ignominious exit from Tequila-town and Rickey's subsequent brainstorm in the park.

Duncan burst into deafening laughter. "Liquor! A whole restaurant based on liquor! I love it! That Rickey fellow must be a genius!"

Of course, Mike picked that very moment to walk into the bar. The edges of his nostrils were dusted with white powder and his eyes whirled like pinwheels. Puffed up with cocaine courage, he strode over to the bar and prodded Duncan's chest with his forefinger. "Don't *ever* mention that person or that restaurant in *my bar!*" he said.

For a split second Duncan just stared down at Mike's forefinger poking him in the shirt pocket. Then he let out a drunken roar of rage, seized Mike's wrist, and dragged him halfway over the bar. Terrance stepped back as bottles, glasses, and coasters went flying.

"Touch me, will you?" the Irishman hollered. "I'll touch *you,* all right, you prick!" He let go of Mike's wrist. Mike slid back across the bar and fell to the floor. Duncan was already coming around the bar. He grabbed Mike by the collar of his shirt and hoisted him. Mike tried to kick the Irishman in the shins, but Duncan held him at arm's length.

"I've been wanting to beat the piss out of you since the first day I worked here!" Duncan said. He looked at the Escargot's employees scattered around the bar. "Can anyone give me a single good reason not to beat the piss out of this prick?"

The employees glanced at each other. Some of them shrugged; some shook their heads. Finally a waitress said timidly, "You might go to jail."

"I've BEEN to jail!" roared Duncan. He shoved Mike

against the bar and got him in a headlock. One of the line cooks ran up behind them, hesitated, then kicked Mike in the ass.

"Call the police!" yelled Mike. "Somebody call the police! Terrance!"

Terrance went behind the bar and picked up the phone. This didn't seem like a real emergency, so he dialed the regular police number rather than 911. "Police," said a bored-sounding dispatcher.

"Hello," said Terrance. "Uh, there seems to be a melee in the bar at the Hotel Bienvenu."

"Melee!" cried Mike, seizing on the word. "Help! Melee!"

"Shut up," growled Duncan, tightening his brawny forearm around Mike's throat.

"A *what* in the bar?" said the dispatcher.

"A fight," Terrance told her. "A violent disagreement."

"Does anybody have a weapon?"

"Well, there's a couple knives for cutting lemons and things . . ."

"How about a firearm?"

"I don't think so," Terrance said.

"We'll send an officer as soon as we can."

Terrance hung up. Mike and the Irishman were halfway across the barroom now. One of Mike's shoes had fallen off. The line cook was still darting in and out like a small dog trying to play with a couple of bigger ones. He stomped on Mike's sock-clad foot with his heavy workboot, and Mike screamed. The scream wasn't very loud above the rising noise in the bar. This really *was* turning into a melee.

"You're WORTH going to jail for!" thundered Duncan.

He lifted Mike clear off his feet and grabbed the back of Mike's belt. A split second too late, Terrance saw what was going to happen.

"Don't do it!" he yelled, but it was too late. The bartender sent Mike crashing straight through the big stained-glass window that separated the bar from the lobby.

∘ ∘ ∘

Late that night, Rickey and G-man parked in Liquor's back lot and got out of the car carrying a duffel bag, a thermos, and an armload of pillows and blankets. They had been waiting for the perfect night to camp out at the restaurant, after it was all fixed up but before the opening. Once it had opened, it would belong to the dining public as much as it did to them.

It seemed strange letting themselves in like this, with no one else on the premises and no work to be done. "I know it's our place," said Rickey as he disarmed the security system and fitted the key into the front door, "but it still kinda feels like we're breaking in."

"That's why we're doing this, huh?"

"What do you mean?"

"Getting drunk here, sleeping here and stuff—it's like we're saying to the restaurant, 'OK, you're really ours now.'"

"Yeah, I guess so. Yeah. I like that."

They locked the door behind them and went through the dark foyer. When they reached the bar, Rickey turned on one small lamp near the cash register. Some of the liquor stock had already been delivered, and the full bottles gleamed mellowly in the soft light.

"At least we know we won't run out of stuff to drink tonight," said G-man.

"Dude, we gotta leave that stuff alone. It all needs to be new and perfect when we open."

"I know it. I'm just fucking with you. Let's have a drink, though."

"Let's go in the dining room and have it there."

A leaded glass window between the bar and the dining room allowed the lamplight to filter in. There was a little ambient streetlamp glow from outside, but not much. Wanting the interior to have a cozy, clubby atmosphere, Rickey had had the decorator cover the windows with translucent green-striped shades. The tables and chairs were stacked on one side of the dining room. Rickey and G-man spread the blankets in the very center of the room and sat down with the thermos between them, picnic-style. The carpet was so thick and lush that they might have been sitting on a huge green mattress.

"Want me to get some ice?" said G-man.

"No, let's have it warm and crappy, just like we did in the park that day."

G-man opened the thermos and poured large slugs of vodka and orange juice into two plastic go-cups.

"Here's to Liquor," said Rickey, touching his cup to G-man's, then waving it around to encompass the whole restaurant.

"Here's to Liquor," said G-man, drinking.

"Here's to us."

"Yeah, you right. Here's to us."

"And here's to Lenny."

G-man hesitated, then said, "What the hell. OK, here's to Lenny." He drank deeply. "I'm ready for another one."

After he finished his second drink, Rickey lay back on the blankets and gazed up at the tin ceiling. He wasn't drunk, just tipsy enough that its patterns seemed to swim a little in the half-light. "I feel perfect," he said.

"I can't even remember the last time I heard you say that."

"I do, though. I feel totally comfortable here. Like it's the best place in the world. Don't you?"

"I like it a lot. I don't know if I have the same feeling you do, though. It's your restaurant really."

"Don't say that. It's ours."

"It's ours because you say so," said G-man, draining his cup and stretching out next to Rickey. "And that's cool. I mean, I totally want to do it. I'm excited. But if you wouldn't have had the idea, I'd still be working on the line some-where."

"You're probably right," Rickey admitted. "You always did need me to drive you."

"See, you got ambition."

"You make that sound like a bad thing."

"It's not all bad," said G-man. "I gotta admit it's nice to have some money."

"What we need is a *lot* of money. I still want to buy Lenny out someday."

"That'd be great," G-man said dreamily.

"You're never gonna forgive him about the old man, are you?"

"No," said G-man. "I'm not gonna keep being mad at him, but I'm not just gonna pretend it never happened."

"Are you mad at me?"

"Why would I be mad at you?"

"Because I don't really care what happened to that old man. I could try to act like I did, but I'd be lying."

"No reason you should lie. If you don't have a problem with whatever Lenny did, what's the point in pretending you do? You're the one who has to live with it."

"There's some kinda commentary in there, but I don't really want to think about it right now." Rickey rolled over onto his stomach and poured another drink.

"Don't worry about it. I still love you—that's not gonna change. Hey, pour me one."

"We killed it," said Rickey, peering into the thermos. "I thought we came better prepared than this."

"We're as prepared as anybody can be. What's the point of owning a restaurant if you can't even have a drink from the bar?"

"Well . . ."

"I'm gonna get a bottle," said G-man, pushing himself up from the blankets. "If you don't want another drink, speak now or forever hold your penis." When Rickey didn't say anything, G-man set off on a slightly weaving path toward the bar.

Rickey watched him go, then turned his gaze back to the old tin ceiling. Now clean and free of cobwebs, it shone softly in the near-darkness. In two weeks, if all went well, people would be eating and drinking beneath it.

When he thought back to the day he'd had the idea for Liquor, sitting in Audubon Park swigging vodka and orange juice out of this same thermos, Rickey could hardly believe less than a year had passed since then. Twelve months ago he'd been a line cook in a crappy restaurant. Ten months ago he'd been unemployed, fired by the crappy restaurant. Then, in his unseasoned opinion, the manager who had fired him had been nothing but an asshole. Now he had a restaurant of his own, with a full staff of employees who would doubtless have their own reasons to think *he* was an asshole. He didn't intend to be one, but an unwritten law of restaurant work was that occasionally you were going to hate your boss. Now he would be the boss, and sometimes people would think of him the same way he had thought of Brian Danton at Tequilatown. It was overwhelming.

"Hey," he called to G-man, "hurry up with that bottle."

o   o   o

Mike sat on a hard blue chair in the Fast Track emergency room of Charity Hospital. Despite its name, Fast Track was the lowest-priority section of Charity's ER. None of the other people even looked like there was anything wrong with them. Probably they were just trying to get drugs or a free place to sleep.

Eyeing the spiderweb tracery of cuts on Mike's face and left arm, the other patients edged away from him as if he might be diseased. He couldn't remember hitting the window; there was just the image of the big bartender picking him up, then the memory of sprawling in a pile of colorful shards trying to assess his damages. The most terrible moment had been when Terrance came out and helped him up, brushed the glass off his shoulders, and went back into the bar without saying anything.

He'd gotten a nice-sized bag from NuShawn this morning and had been hitting it all day, so he wasn't hurting too much yet, though his shoulder was badly bruised and his scalp was bleeding. But that was part of the reason he'd come to Charity: he only had $1500 on his credit card and he knew he would have to buy more coke soon. He couldn't go to NuShawn. He couldn't return to Escargot's or associate with anybody who had anything to do with the place. Obviously Terrance was keeping an eye on him for Rickey. NuShawn might be in on it as well. At the thought of Terrance telling Rickey what had happened tonight, Mike's skin crawled and his sphincter contracted.

The big Irish bartender must know Rickey too. He and Terrance had been talking about Liquor when Mike walked into the bar. They were all probably involved in the murder of Rondo Johnson. Now they were after Mike.

Mike went to the nurse's desk and asked for a phone book. He flipped through the white pages to the R's, running his index finger down the columns of names. He had pulled Rickey's résumé and stared at it for a long time last week, but he couldn't recall the contact information now. That had been happening to him a lot lately; it was almost as if his mind were being controlled by outside forces. Maybe that old lady in the French Quarter wasn't so crazy after all, the one who wore a hubcap on her back and lined her hat with tinfoil ... There was the listing, RICKEY, JOHN R. on the ass-end of Marengo Street. As if the résumé lay before him, Mike suddenly remembered that Rickey's middle name was Randolph and that he had attended Frederick Douglass High School. When you got right down to it, there wasn't much he didn't know about Rickey.

He made a note of the address and returned to the hard blue chair. "Family Feud" was on TV, not even the classic version but some new thing. The host asked the family members to name something a chef would use, and they started shouting out answers: "A knife!" "A stove!" "Salt!" This couldn't be real. Everything was being manipulated to fuck with his head.

Mike had to wait ninety more minutes before his name was called. An unimpressed doctor rotated his shoulder and looked at his pupils. "I think I need stitches in my scalp," Mike said.

"Nah," said the doctor. "We'll just clean it out." He left the cubicle. A few minutes later, a nurse came in with a pink plastic disposable razor, shaved little patches of hair around the worst cuts on Mike's head, and rubbed them with some kind of burning disinfectant.

"Aren't you even going to put a bandage on it?" Mike whined.

"It'll heal faster if you let it dry and crust over. It's not very serious." The nurse's tone was neutral, but her eyes warned *Don't fuck with me.*

When he got back to his car, Mike couldn't even look in the rearview mirror at his crusting bald spots and swollen face. His shoulder was beginning to throb, so he removed his bag from his pocket and took another poke. Then he drove uptown, found the address on Marengo Street, and sat staring at the narrow little house where Rickey lived. The windows were dark. There was no car parked in front, but people in these old neighborhoods parked wherever they could, and he didn't know what kind of car Rickey drove.

Though Mike sat there for a long time, he saw nothing but two young black men walking silently down the middle of the street. At last he started his car again and drove across town to the Broad Street property where his uncle had died, the property people were now calling Liquor. There was one car in the parking lot, a black-and-gold Plymouth Satellite so decrepit that Mike assumed it had been abandoned. Rickey must not have gotten around to having it towed. Maybe he would run his whole operation like that, Mike thought hopefully, overlooking little details until the place crashed and burned.

He couldn't tell whether any lights were burning in the restaurant, but the longer he sat in the parking lot, the more certain he became that nothing was going on in there. Rickey wasn't at home and he wasn't here either. Probably he was out somewhere with Terrance and the big Irishman, celebrating a job well done.

Mike drove to his apartment in Metairie and began to pack a small suitcase.

chapter 26

Rickey stood by the big cutting board looking at his six cooks and three dishwashers, all of whom returned his gaze expectantly. For the first time since quitting the Apostle Bar, he and G-man were dressed in chef's whites. He wondered if this was pretentious, since they weren't going to do any cooking today, but right now the uniform and G-man's presence at his side were the only things allowing him to feel some modicum of confidence. Rickey had already worked with most of these cooks in the test kitchen, and a couple of them—Terrance, a guy called Shake from their Peychaud Grill days—he knew quite well. Today, though, he had a horror of coming off like the world's biggest shoemaker. He'd kept waking up all night, haunted by fantasies of the whole kitchen staff deciding *We can't work for this asshole* and walking out of their first meeting. Toward dawn he had gotten up, fixed coffee, and gone over the menu. He passed out copies of this menu now, a rough handwritten thing that would probably be revised several times before opening night.

Liquor

~ Opening Night Menu ~

Starters

Prosciutto-Wrapped Figs in Calvados + Blue Cheese-Cognac Cream

Pan-Fried Risotto Balls with Absolut Citron Vodka
+ Vermouth Tapenade

Aquavit-Cured Salmon Carpaccio with Roasted Capers

Fresh Marinated Sardines in a Galliano Sweet and Sour Sauce

Pork Terrine with Wild Mushrooms and Bushmills Irish Whiskey

Soups & Salads

Cold Sapphire Cucumber Soup (Bombay Sapphire Gin)

Salad of Mixed Greens, Macadamias, and Manchego Cheese
with Walnut Eau de Vie Vinaigrette

Creole Tomato Salad with New Orleans Rum-Pickled Red Onions
and Cranberry Beans

Main Courses

Pecan-Crusted Gulf Fish of the Day with Rum Beurre Blanc

Roasted Duck on the Bone + Sauce of Sun-dried Cherries,
Roasted Garlic, and Kirsch

Grand Marnier-Fennel Osso Buco + House-made Orecchiette

Garlic-Perfumed Beef Ribeye Flamed with Cognac

Roasted Pork Loin with White Beans, Fresh Fennel, and Grappa

Tequila-Stewed Gulf Shrimp and Avocados
+ Louisiana Popcorn Rice

Pan-Fried Rabbit with Mustard and Herbsaint

Cognac-Flavored Wild Mushroom and Arugula Lasagna

Only after everybody had had a chance to read the menu did Rickey speak again. "I'm sure we'll make a few changes before opening night, but we're basically pretty satisfied with this. We'll all be back in here the day before we open to see the final menu, check out Tanker's desserts, and go over composition and plating of the dishes. Anybody got any questions right now?"

Terrance wanted to know what orecchiette were, and Rickey explained about the little handmade ear-shaped pasta.

"Some of you already know us well enough to know how we work," said G-man. "The rest of you should be able to figure us out pretty soon. We're the laziest, most useless bastards in the world when we're off work, but when we're here, we're hardcore rollers. We expect you to work as hard as we do."

"In exchange," Rickey said, "we won't dog you with a bunch of moronic rules—just a few. Number one: We don't care what you do in your free time. We don't even really care what you do here as long as you do your job. I'm not gonna forbid you to have a couple beers during your shift. Just don't come in too fucked up to work.

"Number two: If you can stand up, don't call in sick.

"Number three: You work in your uniform at all times. I been seeing cooks in T-shirts, but I'm kinda conservative about this—just like you might have noticed the decor in the dining room is kinda conservative. I think your whites remind you to take yourself and what you're doing seriously. You can wear one of our paper toques or you can wear a bandanna like I do if you want. No baseball caps, because they don't really catch sweat, and none of those little square hippie caps, because with all due respect, they look like ass.

"Any questions?"

There were none, but the crew looked happy, as well they might; they were used to managerial harangues about Being Part of a Team, and Rising to the Challenge, and Communication. Rickey began to relax. These people weren't going to walk out on him or judge him to be a shoemaker. They were just kitchen people like all the others he'd known—even better, because he and G-man had hand-picked them. This was easy.

"We don't have an employee handbook," said G-man. "We're not gonna give out Xerox sheets about our vision and all that shit. We think the best way you can understand our vision is by cooking with us."

"We told you about our food and heard your ideas when we interviewed you," said Rickey. "I don't really see the point of standing here now and making giant sweeping statements about what great food we're gonna make. Of *course* we're gonna make great food—I think we all share that standard. We wouldn't have hired you if we thought you just cared about slamming it out."

"Of course, you gotta be able to slam it out," G-man said.

"Sure. But we all know we can do that. What we might not all know, but what we can keep learning, is that the food has to be perfect *every single time*. Yeah, I see some of you giving me that skeptical look. I been on the line for twelve years. I know it won't always be perfect. But that doesn't mean it's not *required* to be. Do you get it? Do you all know what I mean?"

The dishwashers looked blank, but the cooks nodded.

"OK," said Rickey. "So does everybody know what they're supposed to do on opening night? I'll be expediting. G's on sauté. We got Terrance on the grill, Shake doing cold apps, Tanker in the dessert ghetto back there, but he can help with salads if you need him . . ."

They got the positions sorted out, took a few more questions, then dismissed the kitchen staff and watched them clock out. Terrance stayed behind, and as soon as the others were gone, he said, "Mike's disappeared. You heard?"

"No," said Rickey, who hadn't been paying attention to anything but the restaurant. "What do you mean, disappeared?"

Terrance related the story of the melee at Escargot's. Rickey and G-man laughed at the part where the bartender threw Mike through the window, but Terrance scowled. "I didn't like it," he said. "It was like using an A-bomb to kill a rat. It was too much."

"So he's gone now?" said Rickey.

"After I brushed the glass off him, he just ran out the place. Never showed up the next day. Nobody seen him since."

"Not even NuShawn?"

"NuShawn says he ain't seen him in a week. That's what really makes me think something happened."

"Maybe somebody finally threw him in the river like he deserves," said Rickey.

"I don't know. It's crazy—the owner's son been coming in, and he's a hotel guy. Don't know a damn thing about restaurants. Kinda nice, though, compared to having Mike around. Still, I'm real glad to be out of there."

"You should be," said G-man. "You're gonna have a good time in this kitchen."

"Yeah," said Terrance on his way out, "except when I gotta cook them nasty-ass hunks of steak fat."

Then they were alone in the kitchen, in uniform with everything set up around them for the first time. Rickey leaned back against the counter and sighed. "I think they actually listened to us."

"Weird, huh?"

"No kidding. We're the assholes now."

"Well, we just gotta be the best assholes we can be."

They had decided to open "soft" for a week, notifying a few potential customers and letting word of mouth bring in the rest. Then they'd start running ads in the local papers. Rickey got the advertising material from the small office at the back of the kitchen, and they went into the dining room to go over it. The furniture had been moved into place since the night they'd camped out here. They sat at one of the tables in a diffuse pool of light, poring over the papers before them just as they had seen any number of chefs and managers doing in other restaurants. Acting like bosses still seemed a little strange, but they were beginning to get used to it.

chapter 27

No way, Tank," said Rickey. "I'm pretty open-minded, but there's just no such thing as Camembert ice cream."

"Try it," Tanker urged. "It's good."

The day before opening, and they were in the kitchen working out the last kinks. Tanker's dessert menu was mostly brilliant: he'd taken classic cocktails and reconstructed them into sweets. There was the "Mint Julep," a tuile cookie cup filled with chocolate-mint and chocolate-bourbon mousses; the "Amaretto Sour," lemon curd touched with di Saronno in an almond tart crust; the "Fuzzy Navel," two perfect poached peach halves in a Grand Marnier sabayon sauce; the "Margarita," orange and tequila-lime sorbets served in a sugar-edged martini glass garnished with a chocolate-dipped pretzel swizzle stick.

There were others, and Tanker was just trying to narrow them down to five that could be served on opening night. But his concept for a big, expensive signature dessert hurt Rickey's brain. Though he was calling it a Napoleon, it had nothing to do with puff pastry or cream. That would have made too much sense. Instead, he'd found an actual reproduction of Napoleon Bonaparte's death mask and coated the inside with chocolate to make a mold, which he proposed to fill with a frozen mousse of Napoleon brandy surrounding a scoop of the terrifying Camembert ice cream.

"C'mon, Rickey. It's no more extravagant than a whole baked Alaska. They do those at Antoine's and charge a fortune for them."

"Yeah, but people actually want to *eat* baked Alaska. Nobody wants to have some guy's face for dessert. And why the Camembert?"

"To follow through on the death mask theme. I want it to have a little bit of a corpsey flavor."

"You're nuts!"

"Just try it."

"I don't want to."

"Remember what you told me when you fixed those kidneys?" said G-man from his spot by the sauté station. "A good cook is a fearless cook."

"So I suppose you tried it already?"

"Sure."

"And?"

"It's pretty gross," G-man said cheerfully.

"There you go," Rickey told Tanker. "My sous chef is authorized to make decisions for me. I don't have to try it."

"Just a little taste," said Tanker, undiscouraged.

Sighing, Rickey took the spoon from Tanker's hand and sampled the ecru dollop. There was a sour edge to it, rather like Creole cream cheese but with a little more rankness. He let it sit on his tongue and melt, then said, "Give me one more taste."

"See?" said Tanker, hunting for another dessert spoon. "You like it."

"It's not bad," Rickey admitted. "It might be just weird enough to appeal to the freak contingent. But I don't know about having a death mask on the dessert menu."

"Aw, come on. You know how much New Orleanians love Napoleon. They even got a little apartment still fixed up for him on the top floor of the Napoleon House, down in the Quarter. It'll be a big hit."

"Why you gotta make something like that?" said G-man, coming over to the dessert nook. "Why can't you make something normal, like a chocolate Superdome?"

"Suck my ass, yat boy."

"Yeah, where *you* from? Rocky Mountain High?"

"I'm actually a Yankee," said Tanker. "I was born north of the lake, in Covington. C'mon, Rickey, let's just try this. I got an inspiration. People don't like it, we'll take it off the menu."

G-man shook his head and went off toward the walk-in. Rickey considered the Napoleon. It was insane, but it seemed to give Tanker a thrill, and the other desserts were winners. Between themselves, Rickey and G-man had already agreed to do pretty much whatever it took to keep Tanker happy. He was a rarity. And who knew? Maybe the death mask would be a big hit, kind of a morbid Mile High Pie. "How many would you prep?" he asked.

"Not a lot. This is, like, a fourteen-dollar dessert for the whole table to share. I could make a bunch of the masks—

molded chocolate keeps real nice. But prepped up with the fillings for a regular service, I might do five or six."

"I guess," said Rickey. "But I'm letting you do it because your other ideas are good, not because I think this one is."

Rickey knew he pretty much had to accept whatever Tanker wanted to do anyway, because he didn't have time to argue about desserts. He and G-man had been here since eight o'clock this morning, and they had a million things going. The white beans and cranberry beans were simmering; the pork terrine and the tapenade for the risotto balls, both made yesterday, were resting in the reach-in; the figs were steeping in Calvados. G-man was showing Matt and Shake how to prep cold-pantry stuff like the salad dressings and rum-pickled onions. Rickey was simultaneously making pasta dough and prepping sauces. They'd made their stocks the previous day, with Terrance and Shake looking on to learn how they wanted it done.

Leaving Tanker to deal with the weird ice cream, Rickey turned back to his project of the moment, a bordelaise sauce that would accompany the roasted duck. He browned some shallots and duck trimmings in clarified butter, added red wine and kirsch, and let the sauce reduce over medium heat. When the alcohol had evaporated, leaving only its flavors, he put in the stock—three parts chicken to one part veal. Leaving this to simmer, he took out his pasta dough and shaped half of it into orecchiette. The rest would be rolled out into thin sheets for the wild mushroom lasagna.

After twenty minutes he reseasoned the sauce and strained it. Tomorrow he would finish it with whole roasted garlic cloves and sun-dried cherries plumped in more kirsch.

For now, he put it in the lowboy by the sauté station and headed back to the walk-in to get some more veal stock.

Some of the meat had come in this morning, but the seafood and produce wouldn't arrive until tomorrow, and the cooler still seemed empty. Rickey stood just inside the heavy steel door for a moment, his breath making a little cloud in the refrigerated air. He knew this was the last time he'd see it this way, shiny and clean just like the rest of the kitchen. After tomorrow its shelves would be crammed with boxes, crates, Lexans and hotel pans, cases of beer for the kitchen crew, the occasional forgotten item developing into a new and moldy life-form. Somehow he felt that this was his last chance to sense the presence of the murdered man, if there was a presence to be sensed.

He stood there until the thin layer of kitchen sweat beneath his clothes grew chilly and a shiver ran down his spine, but the only departed presences in here were some nice fresh pieces of cow, pig, and bird. Maybe he just wasn't sensitive, or maybe the guy really was completely gone. It had been more than twenty years, after all. At any rate, Rickey couldn't let it creep him out any more. He had a kitchen to run now, and this walk-in was an integral part of it. Satisfied that he had gotten any residual creepiness out of his system, he fetched his veal stock and returned to his sauces.

° ° °

They spent the rest of the day taking care of details. They called purveyors to confirm tomorrow's orders. They had a last short meeting with their maître d', Karl—a tall, shaven-headed, ebony-skinned man who was also acting as the de facto dining room manager—to make sure everything would go smoothly in the front of the house tomorrow. They touched base with Mo about the drink specials and reminded her of their Drunkard's Agreement with Sid Schwanz. They printed up an optimistic fifty copies of the menu. After they dropped these off at the restaurant, they drove around for a little while, considered stopping by the Apostle Bar or some other place, eventually decided they didn't really want to talk to anybody else and just went home.

They sat at the kitchen table smoking a bomber packed with enough weed to make two or three normal joints. There was a sanguine air to the evening, for they knew now that whatever else went wrong, barring major catastrophe, they were at least set up for opening night. There was no further licensing problem, no nascent hurricane spinning in the Gulf, nothing on the horizon that looked likely to stop them. It was too late even to be scared. By the time they finished the bomber, there was only a pleasant, thrumming nervousness between them.

"How many you think we'll get?" said Rickey. "Ten?"

"We got more than that guaranteed. My folks, your mom and her boyfriend, Lenny and the suits . . ."

"I don't mean people we know. I mean walk-ins."

"Oh . . . well, we sent out those two-for-one entrée coupons to the neighborhood association. Some of them'll probably show up. Maybe Sid Schwanz, maybe Anthony B. But I figure we'll have a pretty slow start. I mean, that's how we want it, right?"

"I guess. It'll be better that way—let everybody get used to working together, get used to the menu. But you know what? I feel like I'm ready to roll."

"I know what you mean," said G-man. "We been think-ing about all this other stuff for so long. It'll be good to get back in the kitchen and just go."

Rickey nodded. "Exactly."

"You know, I thought you'd be more keyed up than this."

"So did I. Hell, I thought I'd be bouncing off the walls. But I guess I got it all out of my system. I feel great. I want to do this. I'm ready."

"That's good," said G-man. "This would be a real bad time to change your mind."

"Yeah, and spend the rest of my life working for Lenny."

"Dude, don't even say that."

"Not gonna happen," said Rickey. "Who knows? Maybe Lenny'll be working for *us* someday."

"I take back what I said about you being calm," said G-man, feeling Rickey's forehead as if checking for fever. "You need some rest."

"I need *sex,*" said Rickey. "I don't think anything short of a hard-on is gonna get my mind off the restaurant."

"I think I can take care of that for you."

One of Rickey's favorite things was to lie in bed with G-man and just kiss for a long time before they did anything else, but he didn't have the patience for that tonight. He left a suck mark on G-man's neck, licked the length of his spine, gnawed on his hipbones. They'd had their dry spells, but they were blessed with a talent for enjoying each other as easily and thoroughly as they had at sixteen, with the added intimacy of many years together. Sometimes, Rickey thought, the taste of G-man's skin was the only thing that calmed him.

chapter 28

They didn't really have to be at the restaurant until midmorning on opening day. The deliveries wouldn't start arriving until then, and if there was any kind of dinner crowd, they might stay open late tonight. But they woke with the sun and couldn't get back to sleep, so they decided to go on in.

Carrying their trusty thermos (full of chicory coffee and milk today, not liquor), they let themselves in the back door. Rickey drained the figs that had been steeping in Calvados and began wrapping them in thin strips of prosciutto. G-man started making the blue cheese–cognac cream to serve with them. Since this had been one of the most popular dishes at the Apostle Bar, they could make it on automatic pilot, and the familiar motions had a calming effect.

Their order from Old Country Seafood was lugged in by a man old enough to be their grandfather. It was kind of a lousy job for a guy in his twilight years, but Rickey was too busy examining the order to spare him any pity. As usual with Old Country, it was perfect: the shucked oysters were fat and smelled of clean seawater; the 16/20-count brown shrimp were so fresh they seemed to quiver; the redfish was translucent and glistening.

Rickey hauled the fish and oysters back to the walk-in while G-man started prepping the shrimp. A few minutes later the produce order arrived, and Rickey examined it as carefully as he had the seafood. "These tomatoes are hard," he said, holding up an unripe Creole.

"They nice," said the deliveryman.

"No they're not. C'mon, I got a Creole tomato salad on my menu. I can't serve these. Take 'em back."

"Ain't nothing wrong with them tomaters."

"Would you let your momma cook with them?" said Rickey, irritated. "I know we're a new restaurant, but I been through this a million times in other people's kitchens. You can bring me good tomatoes or I can start ordering from Favre Brothers, but either way, these fucking softballs are going back on your truck."

"Awright, awright," said the produce man. Unperturbed, he loaded the tomato boxes back onto his dolly and trundled them out. It was just a dance they had to go through, a kind of test to see what would fly with the new customer. Some restaurants would accept the inferior tomatoes without batting an eye, and Rickey supposed the purveyor wanted to see if Liquor was such a restaurant. He pulled out his cell phone and called them. "Look," he said, "I know you guys are gonna fuck me from time to time, but I wasn't expecting to get crappy tomatoes on my *very first day* doing business with you."

"Sorry about that. We'll send some ripe ones right over."

"How about a free case for my trouble?"

"Nope."

Rickey and G-man didn't talk much over the course of the morning, but fell into their usual kitchen routine, each doing his own work in a companionable semisilence, occasionally helping each other out without ever getting in each other's way. Tanker arrived around noon and ensconced himself in the dessert nook. Soon the other cooks began to trickle in. Since they weren't required to be here this early, Rickey figured they must be excited about opening night. He'd had jobs he loved and jobs he loathed, but there were very few times he'd voluntarily arrived early for a shift unless he knew he was going to be slammed and wanted to play catch-up. These guys didn't need to play catch-up yet, so he and G-man must have done something right.

Gradually the elements of the night fell into place. G-man had his sauté station ready to go and was helping Shake set up the cold pantry. Terrance was prepping his grill station. The new tomatoes arrived, ripe and fragrant. At four-thirty, Rickey went out to the dining room for a last-minute meeting with the rest of the front-of-the-house staff. "Tonight shouldn't be too rough even if it gets busy," he told them. "Most of the customers will probably be people we know, people who are already pulling for us. By the same token, these are gonna be the people spreading our word-of-mouth publicity, so let's give 'em something good to talk about." He went over the menu one more time, his heart sinking only a little when he realized one of the waiters still didn't understand what tapenade was. All in all, though, they looked good: Karl in a green silk suit that matched the dining room, Mo in cigarette pants and a cream-colored blouse, the rest in white shirts, black pants, and spotless white aprons, everyone with an electric edge of first-night jitters.

Rickey was too nervous to eat the staff meal G-man had prepared, so he went into the foyer to see the flowers that had arrived throughout the day. There were mixed bouquets full of dyed daisies and baby's breath from his mother and various members of G-man's family, a bunch of irises from Anthony B, a flashy spray of exotics from the Duvet Corporation, a dozen pink roses from "H"—guessing that must be Helmut, Rickey pulled off the card and threw it away. There were various smaller assortments from other friends and colleagues. Strangely, there was also a cross made of white carnations like something you'd see at a funeral.

Frowning, Rickey looked more closely at this last item. It was definitely a cross, and it hadn't been delivered by mistake: the card said "John R. Rickey," nothing more. Maybe it was somebody's idea of a twisted joke. Opening a restaurant? In sympathy; R.I.P. if you can. He could imagine that coming from some of his old colleagues. It would look weird to customers, though. Rickey carried the cross back to the kitchen and threw it in one of the big trash cans.

"What's that?" said G-man.

"Aw, we got some kinda funeral flowers. Somebody's a comedian."

"Mike?"

"Huh?" said Rickey, who hadn't even thought of that.

"You think they're from Mike?"

"I don't know. I just figured . . . Shit."

"Well, don't worry about it. Probably nothing."

"I don't got time to worry about it. Did Terrance cook the pasta yet? We need to get rolling."

°   °   °

G-man could have kicked himself for mentioning Mike. He'd expected Rickey to think of that possibility at once, but apparently he hadn't. Rickey was already keyed up and didn't need anything throwing him off his game.

Rickey didn't seem distracted, though; he just turned away and started talking to Terrance. Reminding himself not to say anything else that had the potential to alarm, inflame, or agitate, G-man went back to his station. He had a six-burner stove, a small oven, a lowboy, a cutting board, and a bain-marie that held his sauces and the hot soup. One of his burners was occupied by a pot of water that would be kept at a boil for dunking the pasta. With the other five burners at his disposal, he was responsible for the risotto balls, the pecan-crusted redfish, the tequila shrimp, the rabbit, and the pork. He had the veg lasagna too, but that was moronically easy.

After taking care of everything possible on his station, G-man went around checking the others. "How's those tomatoes?" he asked Shake.

"Succulent as a young girl's pudendum," said Shake, who had always prided himself on the erudition of his foul mouth.

It was just after six now. Technically they were open for business. G-man went to the front of the kitchen where Rickey had set up his expediting station. The ticket machine here would spit out orders as the waiters typed them into the computer. Rickey would see them first and call them out to the various stations. He also had a long table upon which he would finish the plates with the herbs, oils, and other items in his mise-en-place. On the shelf above his station were a boombox (silent; Rickey liked to have the option of music in the kitchen but rarely played it), a water bottle, a flask of Wild Turkey, an empty pastry bag, and a big stack of clean side towels for wiping the edges of plates.

"Whatcha think—" G-man started, then forgot what he was going to say as the ticket machine came to life and began chattering out their first order. For a long moment they just stared at it as if they'd never seen a ticket before. Finally Rickey pulled it out of the machine, scanned it, and said, "Shake, ordering two tomato salads, one sardine, one terrine, two figs."

"Two tomato salads, one sardine, one terrine, two figs," Shake called back to him.

"Terrance, ordering one ribeye medium-rare, one duck . . . G, get back to your station, you slack bastard . . . ordering two redfish, one shrimp, one pork."

"One ribeye medium-rare, one duck," Terrance repeated.

Instead of returning to the sauté station, G-man went to peek into the dining room. The entrées wouldn't need to be fired for at least fifteen minutes, and he wanted a look at their first customers. He saw Lenny, Bert Flanagan, and Oscar De La Cerda sitting at a six-top with two women— G-man thought one of them was Flanagan's wife—and a man he didn't know. Beyond them, Karl was leading another couple to a table.

G-man returned to the kitchen. "It's Lenny and the suits

with three other people," he told Rickey. "And a deuce just sat down."

"We're in business," said Rickey, looking as if he might faint.

While the salads and appetizers were being prepared, Rickey sent the runner out with *amuses-bouches* of a poached oyster, a morel, and an asparagus tip arranged on a crouton with a touch of the sauce Robert. The second ticket came in just as Lenny's first courses were going out. The deuce had ordered risotto balls, the oyster soup, and two redfish. Rickey called out these orders, then told Terrance and G-man to fire the entrées for Lenny's party. G-man started the risotto balls and arranged his redfish, shrimp, and pork in various sauté pans. He now had only one burner free.

"How's that ribeye coming?" he called over to Terrance.

"Just fine. Way you taught me this, I could do it in my sleep."

"Don't fall asleep. You'll burn yourself."

The runner came back with the plates that had held Lenny's party's first courses. "Chef, table ten," he said, and G-man saw Rickey glance at the plates to make sure they were empty. Rickey had read about this practice somewhere and decided to implement it; if anybody had left more than a bite or two of food, the runner would have said, "Chef, *this is* table ten," and Rickey would have checked the leftovers to see if there was some problem. It was a good system for a control freak. In this case the plates were shiny-clean, and were soon followed by Lenny himself coming in to congratulate them. "There's three more tables sitting down right now," he said. "Two deuces and a four-top. I knew this would go well."

"Jeez," said Rickey. "Where are they coming from? How'd they hear about it?"

G-man suspected that Lenny had bent a few ears, but he wasn't going to say anything if Lenny wanted to keep quiet. Instead he said, "Who are those people at your table?"

"Oh, that's Jasper Ducoing and his wife. He writes the restaurant reviews for the paper."

G-man winced as Rickey dropped a ladle.

"You brought in *Chase Haricot?*" said Rickey. "The *Times-Picayune* critic? On our *first night?*"

"Don't worry, he's not gonna write his review based on tonight's meal. He loved your Calvados-marinated figs at the Apostle, and he said he simply couldn't wait any longer to have them again. That's a direct quote—'I simply can't wait any longer.'"

"Great. Thanks for telling us. Now get out of here."

"OK, guys. Good luck. Call me."

"Dude!" said Rickey when Lenny had gone. "The restaurant critic's here! On our first night!"

"Just forget it," said G-man, lifting a corner of his redfish with an offset spatula. "Don't even think about it."

"I gotta sneak out there real fast and see what he looks like. C'mon, it'll help if we can recognize him when he comes in to do the review. I'll go now, before the next tickets come in."

"Stay where you are!" said G-man in a tone that, for him, was quite sharp. "I got a good look at the guy. I can recognize him just fine. Get your mind off it. Concentrate, Rickey. Concentrate."

Rickey sighed. "You're right. I just can't believe he brought the guy in on our first night."

"*It doesn't matter.* Are you bored? I got hot shit needs to go on plates over here, if you don't have anything to do."

"I got stuff to do," said Rickey, shaking off the distraction. "You're right, it doesn't matter. Fuck 'em." He pulled another ticket from the machine. "Ordering two green salads, one tomato . . ."

Rickey did go out to the dining room when his mother came in with her gentleman friend, Claude. By then they were busy enough that he didn't have much time to circulate, but he took the chance to point out Chase Haricot to Karl. Karl squinted at the man, then nodded and said, "I got him memorized."

"I said hi to Haricot," Rickey told G-man upon returning to the kitchen. "Didn't let on that I knew who he was."

"Any of my folks here yet?" G-man asked. He didn't want to talk about Chase Haricot. Rickey could get fixated on a thing like that and have his whole night thrown off.

"I didn't see any of 'em. I'm sure they'll all come barging in the kitchen."

"Yeah, probably so."

When the dessert orders began coming in, it quickly became apparent that Tanker was screwed. Within an hour, four tables had ordered the Napoleon death mask. "'I'll just prep five or six for a regular service,'" Rickey mocked. "'That's all we'll need.'"

"Fuck you!" said Tanker, losing his cool a little. "You didn't even *like* the idea. What do we do? You wanna 86 it when we run out, or you want me to prep some more?"

"Do a few more," said Rickey. "Looks like it's gonna be more popular than we thought."

"Yeah, go on. Say *I was wrong, Tanker, and you were right.*"

"Sure," said G-man from the sauté station. "Ask him for a pony while you're at it."

G-man's parents, five siblings, and assorted in-laws showed up around eight, talking and laughing until Rickey had to herd them out of the kitchen under the guise of making sure their table was ready. G-man would have dealt with them himself, but he was so busy he'd barely been able to give his mother a kiss. His speed wasn't a problem, but he wished he had about four more burners.

For a first-time cook, Terrance was brilliant. "How you doing over there?" Rickey or G-man would ask him periodically, and Terrance always replied, "Maintaining." He was going to be solid, just as Rickey had predicted.

The worst thing that could happen in a restaurant kitchen was meltdown, where no one knew what he was supposed to be doing and everybody was left to flail in the weeds. This crew was almost at the opposite extreme, working in near-perfect sync. When they all knew each other a little better, G-man thought, they would be unstoppable. They'd learn each other's rhythms, habits, and foibles, just as he and Rickey had done long ago, and they'd be able to handle anything the starving hordes could throw at them.

They would begin their late-night schedule next week. This week, in order to feel out the capabilities of the crew and the demands of the clientele, they were only serving until eleven. The orders started tapering off around ten-thirty, and Tanker sent out his last desserts at twelve-fifteen. Rickey came over to the sauté station, clamped an arm around G-man's neck, and said, "Our kitchen! Our menu! Our goddamn restaurant! You believe this shit? We actually did it!"

"Course we did," said G-man, laughing. "I always told you we would. You wanna quit strangling me to death?"

"Sorry about that," said Rickey, and went over to put the same chokehold on Terrance, who bent slightly at the waist and lifted him clear off the ground.

"So how many you think we did?" said Karl, coming in.

"I was trying to keep track," said Rickey. "I think it was about eighty."

"Eighty-eight. Not too shabby for a soft opening."

As they finished breaking down the stations, G-man kept glancing over at Rickey. He looked as happy as G-man had ever seen him; there was a kind of radiance about him. They'd had a nice time these past few months, living off Lenny's stipend while they got ready to open the restaurant, having lots of sex, checking out restaurants they'd never had the time or money to try before. It was the closest thing to a vacation they'd had in their adult lives. But a restlessness had started to come over them, and over Rickey in particular. It was good to be back in the kitchen.

In the bar, Mo had a Dave Brubeck CD cranked up on the stereo system. Everybody sat on barstools or stood leaning on the long zinc slab, and from a distance they appeared as a solid line of white, black, and houndstooth, punctuated by the tall green column of Karl. The sense of giddy camaraderie was helped along by Mo's industrial-strength tequila sunrises.

"You were jamming on that grill," Shake said to Terrance. "You sure you never done any cooking before?"

"I never cooked in a restaurant. I spent plenty time watching other people do it. And I like to barbecue when I get a chance. Now *that's* stressful, my whole family crying for ribs and chicken."

"You got kids?"

"No, I just cook for my relatives. Some of 'em kinda act like kids, though."

"So did Sid Schwanz ever show up?" G-man asked Mo.

"Unfortunately, he did. Waving his Drunkard's Agreement in my face and hitting on me all night. I think you guys made a bad deal there. Why'd you do it anyway?"

"Aw, he wanted to write an article about some shit that happened here like twenty years ago—"

"Shut up!" said Rickey. "Tell her some other time. I don't want to hear about that tonight. It's a jinx."

Mo raised her eyebrows at Tanker, who shrugged; he hadn't yet heard the story of the Red Gravy Murder.

Eventually people began drifting homeward. Rickey and G-man stayed at the restaurant until everyone but the night porter had left: writing tomorrow's prep lists, figuring out what they needed, calling in orders. When they finally got home, they realized they'd been at the restaurant for twenty hours, and pretty soon they would have to go back and do it all over again.

chapter 29

After a week in business, Rickey had almost stopped experiencing a reflexive rush of panic every time a ticket came in. He read the latest one, then called it out: "Matt, ordering one tomato salad."

"One tomato, Chef."

"Shake, ordering one sardines."

"One sardines."

"G, ordering one pork, one bunny."

"One pork, one bunny . . . you mean there's a table that doesn't want redfish? I can't believe it," said G-man. "Whenever a ticket comes in, I just automatically reach for that redfish."

One of the runners, a Tulane exchange student named Hedo, came in with a load of salad plates. "Chef, this is table three."

Alerted by the two extra words, Rickey stopped what he was doing and turned to examine the plates. Three were clean or nearly so. The fourth, which had held a green salad, was still half full of lettuce. Rickey used a tasting spoon to poke through it until he found a large, untorn, partly wilted segment of radicchio. "Matt!" he said.

"Yes, Chef!"

Rickey walked over to the salad station and dropped the oily radicchio segment in the center of his youngest cook's workspace. "When you order a salad, do you want to eat something that looks like that?"

Matt nudged the offending segment to the far edge of his cutting board and used a side towel to wipe the spot where it had landed. "I guess not," he said.

"You *guess* not? You wanna try it and tell me how it tastes?"

"No thanks," said Matt, plating tomatoes even as Rickey dogged him.

"Well, if you don't want to eat it, then don't *serve* it, OK? Please? Is that reasonable?"

"Yes, Chef. Sorry about that."

"Don't tell me *sorry,*" said Rickey, returning to the expediting station. "Just sort the goddamn greens before you put 'em on the plate."

"Jeez," said Matt under his breath.

"Hey, he's right," said Shake, who was working next to him. "Nobody wants to eat brown lettuce."

"I know, I know."

"You doing OK, kid?"

"Yeah. I just feel kinda out of my depth."

"You are," said Shake, not unkindly. "But you'll learn. Besides, everybody hates doing salads."

Matt finished arranging the layer of tomato slices, made a ring of pickled onions on top of them, and topped that with a spoonful of cranberry beans. He garnished this vivid red plate with a small bunch of bright green pea shoots. Shake reached over to Matt's station for a handful of baby greens, sauced his plate, and laid three marinated sardines on the yellow pool of sauce.

Rickey made six *amuses* of cured salmon, crème fraîche, and asparagus tips. "Yo, Hedo," he said as the runner came back in, "take four of these to table three and tell them we're sorry about the problem with their salad. Take the others to five."

"Yes, Chef."

On his next trip to the kitchen, Hedo said, "Chef, the couple at table five keep talking about their meal. Like—" He made a scissoring gesture at his belly. Hedo was from Turkey, and his English was almost perfect, but sometimes a word escaped him. "What do you call it when you cut up a dead person?"

"Dissecting?"

"Yes. They are dissecting their meal. I think they must be food writers."

"Oh my God," said Rickey. "I hope not. We're doing good, but we're not at the top of our game yet." Over at the cold-pantry station, Matt winced, certain that these words were meant for him.

°   °   °

The people at table five were lying back in their chairs groaning over how much they'd eaten when Rickey came to their table. He'd always been slightly scornful of chefs who left their stations to go swanning around the dining room, but now he could see the point of this behavior. People loved it when the chef came to their table. It made them feel coddled, and some of them acted like they'd just met a rock star.

"Hope you folks are enjoying yourselves," he said. He'd settled on this phrase as a way of expressing interest without seeming to fish for compliments.

"It was *excellent,*" said the lady. "*Thank* you for serving fresh sardines. I wish we saw them more often."

"Very fine rabbit dish," said the man. "The best I've ever had, I think."

"Thanks. I really appreciate hearing that." What the hell, Rickey decided; he'd ask them the question that had brought him out here. "So y'all are writers?"

The man snorted with laughter. The lady smiled as if she rather liked the idea. "Not at all," she said. "Whatever made you think so?"

"I'm not sure," said Rickey, reluctant to blame Hedo for gossiping about them. "Somebody said something about writers coming in tonight. I thought it might be you."

"Sorry, no. We'll be regular customers, definitely, but I'm afraid we can't write you up. I don't think you'd want our endorsement anyway."

"How come? What do you do?"

"He's a poet," said the lady, "and I'm the coroner of New Orleans."

o   o   o

Rickey was a little pissed off when he returned to the kitchen. He was certain the lady had been pulling his leg, and though he couldn't see the point of it, it seemed vaguely condescending. Some people just assumed that cooks were stupid; they thought cooking was menial, uneducated labor. But why would you want to make fun of somebody who'd just cooked you a nice meal? It didn't make sense.

"What's the matter?" asked G-man.

"Aw, some lady out there was fucking with me. I asked her and her husband what they did for a living, and she said she was the coroner of New Orleans."

"What'd she look like?" asked Tanker, who had come up to the cold-pantry station to help Matt with the salads. "Kinda small, kinda cute, red hair?"

"Yeah."

"That *is* the coroner of New Orleans. You wouldn't think it by looking at her, but I seen her on TV."

"No shit?"

"No shit."

"Damn," said Rickey. "Gross." He hadn't liked it when he thought the lady was making fun of him, but he wasn't sure he preferred having the actual coroner at his restaurant. How could she eat a piece of pork after cutting up dead bodies all day?

"It's a job," said G-man. "Somebody's gotta do it."

"I guess," said Rickey dubiously.

"Whatcha gonna do otherwise?" said Shake. "Just let the bodies pile up?"

"I hope she orders the Napoleon death mask for dessert," said Tanker.

"What's she want to do that for?" said Shake. "She's already gotta look at stuff like that all day. She doesn't want to *eat* it."

"She ate pork, didn't she? I heard human flesh tastes just like pork."

"You guys are a bunch of morbid fucks," said Rickey. "Shit. I wish they would've been food writers."

"You said we weren't ready for food writers yet," G-man reminded him.

"I don't know if we are. But at least then I wouldn't have to listen to all this crap about dead bodies."

"Don't be so squeamish," said Tanker. "We're just like her. We work with dead bodies every day." He leaned over to Shake's station and picked up a slice of terrine on a plate. "Look, Rickey, this pig died for you, and you cooked him and ground him up—"

"Leave me alone, you sick bastard. Get back to your station. I think I hear their dessert order coming in."

Tanker walked back to his nook and pulled the ticket off his machine. Disappointment spread over his face.

"A Margarita and a Fuzzy Navel," he said. "What a waste. She would've loved my Napoleon head."

o o o

For the fifth or sixth time tonight, Sid Schwanz picked up a drink menu, folded it lengthwise, ran his thumbnail along the resulting crease, and put it back on the bar. The tic was driving Mo crazy.

"So what's this Irish Channel Cocktail?" he asked.

As she had done when Schwanz asked her about the Broad Street Julep, the Ninth Ward Iced Tea, and the Rising Sun, Mo restrained herself from pointing out that the drink's ingredients were listed on the menu. "Whiskey, crème de menthe, and green Chartreuse," she said.

"Whoo! You manage to drink one a'them, you ought to get one for free!"

In the week Liquor had been open, Schwanz had already visited the bar four times, twice with obnoxious friends from the racetrack. As far as Mo knew, he hadn't eaten anything except bar snacks. They were high-end bar snacks—spicy mixed nuts, crab and bacon toasts, homemade cheese straws—and he could put away a lot of them as he stood there soaking up his Maker's Mark and ginger ale. And he was constantly, clumsily flirting with her. She'd been bartending for years, so this was nothing new, but her heart sank a little every time she remembered that this man was entitled to drink here free for a whole year.

"Hey," she said, hoping to distract Schwanz from the drink list, "what's the deal with this Red Gravy Murder you're not supposed to write about?"

"Aw, I don't know if I oughta tell you that."

"Sure you can. I'm the bartender. No one's allowed to keep a secret from me."

"Well, it's funny you should ask, cause I just happened to look it up in the morgue recently."

"The *morgue*?" Jesus, maybe this guy was weirder than she'd thought.

"That's what they call the archives at the newspaper. I looked up the story on microfilm. Not that I'm gonna write anything about it, a'course, but I been hanging out here a lot and I got to thinking about it. Place used to be here was called Giambucca's, one of these old-style red-gravy joints. You're too young to remember it—you can't be more than, what? Twenty-two?"

"I'm twenty-nine."

"Damn! I wouldn't believe you if you didn't have an honest face. Well, Giambucca's was owned by a couple guys who worked for the Marcello family—not real Marcellos, just small-time hoods. The victim was a manager, name of George Mouton. I feel kinda sorry for the guy—he loved the ponies, like me. Except he loved them a little bit too much, thought he could pick a sure thing, started skimming money out the till and blowing it at the Fair Grounds."

"That was stupid."

"Yeah, but the ponies'll get their hooks in you if you're not careful. Say, did I ever tell you how I got this limp?"

"Yes," said Mo hastily. She had already heard the story twice, complete with Schwanz's toenails turning black and falling off. "What happened to the manager? Mouton, was that his name?"

"George Mouton. Owners found out he was stealing from them, took him in the cooler one night, shot him in the knees—blam! blam! and he's writhing around bleeding and hollering for mercy—and then shot him in the head. Twice. The Mob always puts two bullets in your brain, just to make sure."

"Jesus." Mo pictured the immaculate walk-in with its neat rows of crates and Lexans. "Are you sure that's where it happened?"

"That's what the stories said. Makes sense to me. It's soundproof."

"I suppose it is," said Mo. She felt a little sick.

"Hey, darling, all this talk's making me real thirsty. How's about another Horse's Neck?"

"Coming right up," Mo said wearily.

∘ ∘ ∘

It was an uneventful night. Schwanz stayed until just after eleven; Karl seated about a hundred and twenty-five people. Mo closed out the bar at midnight. In the process of restocking for the next day, she went to refill her caddies with cocktail napkins and Liquor's signature swizzle sticks, which were topped with little martini glasses. They came from a Texas novelty company in smaller batches than any other swizzles she'd ever used, but she was still surprised to see that she had already gone through a box. That was a lot of drinks.

She went in the back to get more, but first she wanted to tell Rickey she'd used up a whole box. "He was getting ready to write up tomorrow's orders," said G-man. "He's probably in the walk-in."

Sure enough, she found him back there with his clipboard. "Cool," he said when she told him about the sticks.

Mo glanced around the inside of the refrigerator. "So this is where they killed George Mouton?"

Rickey's reaction was not overtly startling. He just straightened up from reading the number on a box and looked at her. But she'd always found his eyes a little unnerving anyway—they were the bluest she'd ever seen, turquoise really, and not just intense but slightly mad. The expression in them now made Mo take a couple of steps back.

"*What* did you say?"

"C'mon, Rickey, everybody knows about the murder—"

"Not that. What did you say his *name* was?"

"Sid Schwanz told me it was George Mouton."

"Mouton? Are you sure?"

"Yeah, I'm sure."

Rickey appeared to zone out for a few seconds. "That's

right," he said, apparently talking to himself, "he told me he couldn't remember the guy's name. He must have looked it up since then. Mouton. But it doesn't mean—no. It couldn't be. My luck's not *that* shitty." He shook his head as if to collect himself, then looked back at Mo. "Is Schwanz still here?"

"No. We're *closed,* Rickey."

"I guess I can call him at the paper tomorrow," said Rickey, not listening. "Or ask Anthony B. He might remember."

"What's this about, anyway? It happened more than twenty years ago. You didn't know the guy, did you?"

"No . . . no, I didn't know him." Some of the blaze went out of Rickey's eyes. "It doesn't matter. I'll tell you some other time, OK?"

"Absolutely," said Mo, and beat a hasty retreat. She had no desire to stay back here in the cold with the ghost and the crazy man.

° ° °

"There's lots of people named Mouton," said G-man. "And even if he was related to Mike, what difference does it make?"

"I don't want to be *tied* to him. I don't want that connection."

"What connection? It doesn't tie us to Mike. It doesn't mean anything."

"In his mind it would," said Rickey. "I bet he already knows."

They were on their way to the Apostle Bar to see if Anthony B knew anything about the identity of the murdered man. G-man considered this a useless quest, but he knew Rickey would obsess about it until he found out one way or the other.

"Maybe Mo heard wrong anyway," he said. "Maybe Schwanz said something else."

"She was sure it was Mouton. I asked her."

"I bet you did. You probably scared her half to death—she probably agreed with you so you'd leave her alone."

"Let's just ask Anthony."

Anthony was tending bar when they walked in. A pair of men with their names stitched on their shirt pockets were playing darts in the back, but otherwise they had the place to themselves.

"Awright, y'all!" said Anthony. "Hey, I'm sorry I ain't been in to eat yet, but I gave Laura a week off while we're slow. I'm gonna try to make it Sunday."

"What was the name of the guy that got killed in our restaurant?" said Rickey without preamble.

"You know, I was trying to remember that awhile back, but I—"

"Was it Mouton?"

"Yeah! Yeah, that's it. His people are still in town. In fact, I thought you worked with one of 'em . . . his nephew, maybe?"

Rickey walked over to one of the tables and sat down. For a moment, hoping against hope, G-man thought he might take it calmly. Then he said, "Why can't I ever do any goddamn thing without some *fucked-up shit* happening?" With that, he slumped across the table and folded his arms over his head.

G-man turned to Anthony, who looked stricken. "I didn't mean to *do* nothing," Anthony said. "He *asked* me."

° ° °

Fifty years ago, New Orleans East was a swamp. Thirty years ago it was a prosperous family neighborhood. With the Louisiana oil bust it had begun to crumble. Now it was scented with the synthetic slime of the shipyards, plants, and waste disposal facilities that had sprung up near the Industrial Canal.

Mike had a forty-dollar room at the Paradise Motor Court on Chef Menteur Highway. He had bounced around other, similar places since he left his apartment two weeks ago, but he intended to keep the room at the Paradise as long as he could. Short of setting fire to the rooms, no one cared what you did there.

Right now he was sitting on a stinking sofa in what once must have functioned as someone's living room. Several mattresses on the floor were occupied by people who ignored each other. The coffee table was strewn with plastic bags, loose currency, an automatic pistol, and a silver tray heaped with white powder. A baby wailed somewhere in the house, low and monotonous, as if used to crying unattended.

Mike couldn't have said exactly what the sofa smelled of. There was a piss element; there were ghosts of the chemical-smelling smoke produced by burning cocaine; there was old food and beer. But there were other things too, things he could not identify and didn't really want to.

"How many you want?" asked the skinny white man sitting on the other side of the coffee table. His head was badly shaved, with little nicks and gouges all over the scalp, and one of his front teeth was missing.

"How much can I get for five hundred?"

"I can give you seven for five hundred."

"The other guy gave me eight last week," Mike whined.

"The other guy ain't here no more. You want 'em or not?"

Mike gave the man the $500 cash advance he'd drawn from his credit card, stashed his purchase, and drove back to the Paradise. There he took out a cheap hand mirror and dumped a generous amount of cocaine onto its surface. The powder was yellowish-white and smelled faintly of petroleum—these people out East never had the really good stuff—but to Mike's eyes it sparkled like precious jewels.

He snorted it greedily and felt the prickling rush spread through him, starting between his shoulder blades, working its way up the back of his neck and down through his bowels. He looked over at the little pile of as-yet untouched glassine bags on the dresser and bestowed a tender smile upon them. It was the only sight he still found beautiful: a bag of cocaine that belonged solely to him, that he didn't have to share with anybody.

○   ○   ○

It was eleven o'clock Friday morning and Rickey was making a batch of mirepoix. Matt usually did the mirepoix later in the day, but there was something weirdly soothing about cutting carrots, celery, and onions into millions of infinitesimal pieces. At least, there was until he had almost finished. Then he used the back of his knife to clear a pile of minced onions from his workspace, and the blade scraped against the steel countertop. It made a sound like a razor being dragged across a mirror, which reminded him of Mike, not that he needed reminding.

Forget it, he told himself. *And if you can't forget it, be philosophical about it. You got no choice, really.*

Last night, even as he laid his head on the Apostle Bar's table, Rickey realized that he'd been here too many times already. He was tired of letting crises overwhelm him. He needed to be able to handle other people's crises now, not to be floored by his own. The glamour of the emotional, screeching chef was just a cliché; it didn't do anybody any good in real life.

He went over to the sauté station, where G-man was prepping tonight's rabbit dish. "What's up?" said G-man as he finished wrapping a sheet of pork fat around a rabbit saddle and secured it with a long piece of kitchen string. "How you doing?"

"I'm doing great," said Rickey. "You know what?"

"What?"

"Fuck Mike. I'm not gonna waste any more time on him. So what if his stupid uncle got his stupid self killed in our walk-in? Fuck 'em both. I'm done with it."

"That's the spirit."

"I mean it."

"I believe you." G-man stopped what he was doing and gave Rickey his full attention. "I know you can do anything you decide to do. I just been waiting for you to decide Mike wasn't worth worrying about."

"Well, I decided."

Rickey turned away from the sauté station to go finish his mirepoix. "Hey," said G-man.

"Yeah?"

"Good call. I'm proud of you."

chapter 30

Three days ago, when Mike put his credit card into the ATM and asked for another cash advance, a message had popped up on the display screen informing him that he was over the limit. That phrase had been bouncing around in his head ever since. It seemed to sum up his life perfectly.

The people out East wouldn't front him anything, even when he promised that he would get money from his father. He was afraid to go back to NuShawn; after all, NuShawn was Terrance's cousin, and Terrance worked for Rickey now. Mike had driven as far as the corner of NuShawn's block before turning around, certain that people would be there looking for him, just as they must have looked at his apartment. He tried not to imagine how bad the pain would be when they kneecapped him and shot him in the head like Uncle George.

Mike hadn't had any cocaine for forty hours. He'd demolished his last bag over the course of a day, telling himself he was going to make it last, then breaking down and doing just one more line, and one more, and one more.

When it was gone, he'd forced the tip of his tongue into the empty glassine bag, questing for stray crumbs of coke even though he knew they would produce no discernible effect.

An hour after that he had a full-blown panic attack. He pulled the covers off the bed, threw his toiletries across the bathroom, kicked at the walls until somebody in the next room yelled at him to shut up. He tried to smash the mirror over the sink, but only succeeded in bruising his hand. At last he took out his pistol, the one thing he'd never considered pawning, and sat on the edge of the bed with the barrel pressed to his forehead. Surely the time had come to go through with it. He had no home, no job, no more way to snowblind himself to his own wretchedness. He really thought he was ready to do it. His finger actually tightened on the trigger before he realized what had kept him from finishing it long ago: he hadn't been alone in getting to this point, and it wasn't fair that he should go out alone.

He laid the gun on the nightstand, stretched out on the bed, and thought about this for a long time. He was so absorbed in his thoughts that he almost forgot his clogged sinuses, his itching scalp, his sour stomach, and the longing for cocaine that lay behind it all.

After an hour, he got up, slid the gun into a vinyl portfolio, went to his car, and pulled out of the parking lot. That was the last he saw of the Paradise Motor Court.

He got on the I-10 and drove to Metairie. The hour was well past midnight, and when he parked in front of the house, all its elegant windows were dark. Mike kept his finger on the bell until he heard footsteps approaching the front door. Then it swung open, and Pinky Mouton was standing there in a pair of Jockey shorts and a hastily belted bathrobe that didn't quite close around his ample gut. His face creased in surprise, then flushed with disgust. "What the hell are you doing here?" he said. Mike pulled the Luger out of the vinyl portfolio and shot him twice in the mouth.

The noise surprised him, as did the relatively small amount of blood. He'd rather hoped his father's head would explode. But if it had, Mike would have missed one important fact: the expression in his eyes never changed. Even as he fell, even as he died, the contempt never left Pinky's face.

"Rot in hell, you old bastard," Mike said.

Glancing around, he saw lights coming on in the surrounding houses. People in this neighborhood weren't accustomed to late-night gunshots. Mike ran to his car and headed back toward the city. He felt better than he had in days. It was almost like being high again.

He exited the highway at Claiborne Avenue, cut over to Broad, and pulled up behind Liquor. The restaurant looked closed, but there were still a few cars in the lot. Mike approached the back door. Just as he was about to ring the bell, he heard somebody whack the pressure bar on the other side of the door. A young black man came out carrying two bags of garbage: the night porter. Perfect. Mike stepped forward and pointed the gun at the man's head.

The porter froze, his face expressionless. "I ain't got nothin," he said through lips that barely moved.

"I don't want money," said Mike. "I want information."

The porter didn't say anything. Tears sparkled at the corners of his eyes.

"You're closed, right? Who all's still in there?"

"Terrance," said the porter. "Big motherfucker. You don't wanna mess with him."

"I don't care about Terrance. Who else? Where are they?"

"Terrance . . . G-man . . . Tanker. The bartender . . . I forgot her name. Tanker's lady. They up in the bar. And Rickey . . ."

"Rickey," Mike breathed. "Where's Rickey?"

"Last I seen, he in the kitchen somewhere."

"Good. Now get the fuck out of here."

Mike gestured with the gun's barrel. The porter dropped the two bags of garbage and took off running across the parking lot. Mike tracked him with the gun for a few seconds, then lost interest as the young man disappeared down Toulouse.

He went through the back door into the restaurant.

° ° °

Three in the morning and Rickey was sitting in the walk-in on an empty tomato box, enjoying the refrigerated air after hours of kitchen heat. He rested his clipboard on his knees, checking off items on the order sheet according to whether he needed them or not. Until recently he would have done this standing up, but as the weeks accumulated, he was learning to rest his feet whenever he got the chance. Eventually he hoped to be able to leave Tanker or Shake in charge of the kitchen sometimes, but he didn't feel comfortable with that yet, so he and G-man were still working sixteen to twenty hours a day. When they did get home, Rickey fell into bed and spent a few hours dreaming about the restaurant.

He stretched his legs and took stock of his condition. His feet felt sledgehammered; his leg muscles were watery with exhaustion; his lower back felt like someone had driven a couple of nails into it. He'd been working sauté this week, letting G-man expedite, and a fresh burn on his wrist was just beginning to scab over. For all that, he felt pretty good. He was pleased with the way things were going. They'd set a record last Saturday, serving a hundred and thirty-eight diners. The food was getting better and better as the crew learned what Rickey wanted from them. Because the stakes were so high, Rickey was willing himself to become a better cook too, and he thought it was working; tonight's marrow-mushroom sauce was one of the best things he'd ever made. Chase Haricot would certainly review them in another month or two, and Rickey had no fear. He wanted at least four beans and he was pretty sure he would get them.

Fifteen minutes ago, G-man had finished his own closing duties and gone up to the bar where the others were drinking. Rickey intended to join them as soon as he left his orders on the purveyors' answering machines. As he reached for the cell phone in the side pocket of his checks, the walk-in door swung open. Rickey looked up, figuring G-man had come back to see what was keeping him.

But it wasn't G-man at the door. It was Mike Mouton, sweaty, pasty-skinned, and sick-looking. His eyes were like pinholes in a dirty sheet of paper. His hair looked as if it hadn't been washed in weeks. His clothes gave off an aroma of stale sweat. The front of his shirt was flecked with something that looked very much like blood. Rickey noticed all this in the couple of seconds it took him to realize that Mike was holding a gun. The hole at the end of the barrel appeared impossibly huge, but Rickey supposed that was because he was looking straight into it. Instinctively, he dropped the cell phone and put his hands where Mike could see them.

"I know about everything you've done to me," Mike said. "Your friends can't help you now. Get on your knees, Rickey."

° ° °

Wardell, the night porter, finally stopped running six blocks away from the restaurant. He didn't want to stop, but a stitch in his side forced him to. He sank down on the stoop of a gutted house and tried to catch his breath.

He wished he hadn't run off like that. Rickey and G-man were the best bosses he'd ever had. He hated to think of that crazy-looking man with the gun doing anything to them, or to Terrance or Tanker, or especially to the pretty bartender. But in his eighteen years, Wardell had seen his uncle, his big brother, and two friends shot to death. He knew heroics were useless when somebody pointed a gun at you. It wasn't even the thought of dying that bothered him so much as the knowledge of what it would do to his mother.

Wardell knew he should try to find a pay phone and call the police. He could report the incident at Liquor without giving his name. But then he started thinking he might get blamed for whatever the gunman was going to do. He'd let the man into the restaurant, hadn't he? The cops would fig-ure he had something to do with it. His ass would end up in Orleans Parish Prison, maybe for murder.

His feet sore and his heart heavy, Wardell pushed him-self up from the stoop to begin the long walk home.

° ° °

"The fuck I will," said Rickey. "You want to do something, let's see you do it."

He felt as if he'd been expecting something like this to happen, but perhaps that was just a side effect of sudden terror. He'd seen a few guns before, but nobody had ever actually pointed one at him. There was a weird high buzzing sound in his skull. Though he knew he should try to tear his eyes away from the gun's barrel, try to look at Mike's face and read his intentions, Rickey couldn't make himself do it.

"You better listen to me," said Mike. "I saw those people up in the bar. Your buddy and Terrance and the others. They didn't see me, but I saw them. I'll go back up there. If you won't deal with me, I'll deal with them."

"Don't do that," Rickey said quickly. "Come in here. Let's talk about it."

Mike stepped all the way into the walk-in and pulled the door shut behind him. As it closed, Rickey caught a glimpse of the kitchen over Mike's shoulder. The line was deserted, the sinks empty, the surfaces clean. Rickey wondered if he had just seen his kitchen for the last time, and he felt a sudden crushing loneliness.

"So, uh, have a seat, Mike." Rickey nodded at a box that had held artichokes. Mike's eyes never left Rickey: his gun hand never wavered. But as he settled himself on the box, Rickey saw that Mike's knees were trembling. Mike was in bad shape, no doubt, but Rickey didn't know how he could use that to his advantage.

"What is it you think I did to you?" he asked. He thought it might be harder for Mike to shoot him if they were talking.

"You know what you did."

"Well, I'm just trying to narrow it down."

"You cost me my job," Mike said. "You turned people against me. You murdered Rondo Johnson. You opened your stupid restaurant right here where my uncle died. You made me kill my father."

The first glimpse of the gun hadn't scared Rickey as much as those last six words did. He looked more closely at Mike. Yes, those were tiny spots of blood on his shirtfront, the kind he might have received if he'd shot somebody at close range. They weren't even dry yet.

Rickey thought longingly of his knife bag, but it was in the office. The only tools he had on him were a little plastic-handled vegetable peeler and the pen he'd been using to mark off his order sheet, both clipped into the front of his jacket. The peeler had a sharp tip for gouging out potato eyes, but it wouldn't be any good against a gun. Maybe there was something else.

He almost glanced at the cell phone on the floor beside him where he'd dropped it, half hidden by the box he was sitting on, then forced himself not to. Instead he said as casually as he could, "Why'd you want to kill your father? I thought he looked out for you."

"He never fucking looked out for me," Mike said. "He was the meanest, crookedest bastard I ever knew. He hated me. He thought I was a loser. He thought more of you than he did of me, and you never even met him. Or did you?"

As Mike spoke, Rickey let his arm slide off his lap and

dangle at the side of the tomato box. His fingertips con-
nected with the phone. He could feel that he'd managed to
open the plastic cover before dropping it, and he began to
think there might be a way out of here. Carefully, his eyes
still fixed on Mike, his head nodding slightly in feigned
agreement, Rickey ran his finger along the line of speed-dial
buttons and pressed the top one.

° ° °

G-man was telling Tanker the story of his aunt Charmaine,
the one who wasn't going to smoke pot any more, when he
heard his cell phone ringing in his knife bag. He almost let
it go, but it was 3:30 in the morning and his folks had this
number; maybe it was something important. He pulled it
out of the bag, flipped it open, and said, "Hello?"

At first it didn't sound as if anybody was there. He was
about to hang up when he thought he heard Rickey's voice.
He put a finger in his other ear and turned away from the
others, trying to listen.

"I'M SORRY YOU SHOT YOUR DAD, MIKE,"
Rickey said, enunciating each word very clearly. "BUT
WHAT ARE WE DOING IN THE WALK-IN?"

"You know what the fuck we're doing here," said
another muffled voice, and G-man's heart went cold.

° ° °

"What? He's where?" said Lenny. The phone had awakened
him from a sound sleep.

"Some crazy guy!" said Tanker, sounding as agitated as
Lenny had ever heard him. "He, like, kidnapped Rickey!
G-man says they're in the walk-in! With a gun, maybe!"

The words *crazy guy, kidnapped,* and *gun* made Lenny's brain snap into focus. "Mike Mouton?" he said.

"I don't know, man! I think you better get down here!"

"Did you call the cops?"

"Yes! They're on their way!"

"Where's G-man?"

"He and Terrance went running back there . . ." Tanker paused for breath and came back sounding marginally calmer. "Terrance was trying to catch him, but G just took off for the kitchen."

"Who else is there?"

"Just me and Mo."

"OK. Get out of there. Go outside and wait for the cops. I'll be there in ten minutes."

"But—"

Lenny hung up the phone and started getting dressed.

"What's wrong?" said the big-haired young woman on the other side of the bed.

"Bad news, baby," said Lenny. "Maybe the worst I ever heard."

°   °   °

Terrance had already grabbed G-man once at the pass and once by the sauté station, but G-man had gotten away from him both times. The second time, he'd jammed his knee sharply into Terrance's thigh, and the muscle cramped up when Terrance tried to run. He never would have thought such a skinny guy could be so strong.

"Leave it!" he yelled as he saw G-man sprinting toward the walk-in. "You want him to kill you both?"

He threw himself forward and managed to snag a handful of G-man's jacket. G-man tried to pull away again, but Terrance wrapped a meaty arm around his chest. "Police gonna be here soon," he said.

"I don't give a fuck! I'm going in there!" Terrance felt G-man straining against his arm with a trapped, terrified strength.

"What if you scare Mike?" Terrance said into G-man's ear. "What if he's just talking to Rickey, and you make him shoot?"

G-man hesitated, then lunged against Terrance's arm again. Terrance almost lost him, hung on, overbalanced. They both stumbled backward and crashed into the steel countertop. Terrance smacked his head on one of the heavy pots that hung above the line. His grip on G-man loosened. G-man tore himself away and made for the walk-in.

○ ○ ○

"So I just shot him," Mike said. "Right in the face. He can't talk any more shit to me. He can't ever *look* at me again."

Rickey, who had been staring at Mike, looked away. Then he looked back, because he was scared not to.

"You got any blow?" said Mike, suddenly hopeful.

"No, man. Sorry."

"I haven't had any for . . . I can't remember how long. Did you talk to those people out East? Did you tell them not to sell to me?"

"No. I think they should've sold you whatever you wanted." And wasn't that the truth, Rickey thought.

"You say that," Mike whispered, "but you lie. You

always did lie. You and Pinky both. Did he hire you? Did he send you to Escargot's? I know he had Uncle George killed. Did he want it to happen to me too?" Mike's voice broke. "Did he have little *cameras* there? Was he watching when you told me other people had lives, but I didn't? Did he see you knee me in the nuts and slam me against the walk-in? He did, didn't he?"

The walk-in, Rickey thought. *Oh, fuck.* He had almost forgotten the dustup on his last day at Escargot's, but now it came back to him in vivid detail. How had Mike blown it to such ungodly proportions? It didn't matter. Mike was fried, toasted, over the edge, and Rickey had no idea what to say to him. "I never even met your father," he tried.

"You lie," Mike said again. He half-rose from the artichoke box, leaned across the space that separated them, and almost tenderly placed the muzzle of the gun against Rickey's forehead. Three thoughts ran simultaneously through Rickey's mind, erasing all else: that he hoped G-man wouldn't be the one to find his body, that he was glad his mother had lived to see him open his own restaurant, and that this was a goddamn gyp of a way to die.

Something thumped against the outside of the walk-in door. Mike's head turned a fraction of an inch, and Rickey saw his chance. It wasn't much of a chance, but it would have to do. He brought his left hand up sharply and pushed Mike's arm aside. With his right hand he grabbed the vegetable peeler out of his jacket and jammed it into Mike's throat.

The gun went off in his face. The muzzle flash blinded him, and he felt a searing pain.

o   o   o

G-man yanked the door open and saw Mike reel to one side, his right hand clutching a pistol. He kicked Mike in the back as hard as he could. He was still wearing his heavy work-boots, and Mike sprawled forward onto the walk-in floor. The gun went spinning away. Terrance, right behind G-man, leaned over and grabbed it.

"Rickey?" G-man hauled Rickey off the floor, touched the blood that covered the side of his head. *"Rickey!"*

"I'm OK," Rickey said. "I think it just grazed my ear. Stings like a bastard."

G-man looked closely at Rickey's ear. There was a defi-nite notch in the top of it, but no other damage. For a long moment he just stared at Rickey, as if assuring himself that Rickey really was alive. Then he let go of Rickey's shoulders, turned, and kicked Mike in the ribs. Mike groaned and rolled halfway over. Some black plastic object was sticking out of his throat. He tried to crawl away, but there was nowhere to go. G-man pounced on him, knelt on his chest, and punched him in the face.

"Leave it, G!" said Terrance. "You gonna kill him!"

"I don't care!"

G-man grabbed the black plastic thing and yanked it out of Mike's throat. He didn't register that it was a vegetable peeler; he saw only sharp metal, which was just what he wanted. He was about to jam it into the underside of Mike's jaw when somebody caught his wrist. He turned on the per-son, ready to attack them too, but it was Rickey.

"Come on, dude," said Rickey. "I'm fine. I need you over here. Forget about him."

o   o   o

Lenny made it halfway to the restaurant before he got pulled over for speeding. "There's some kind of hostage situation," he implored. "Check it out on your radio." The cop just kept examining his driver's license as if translating the Rosetta Stone. Lenny pulled out his trump card: "Come eat at my restaurant. Either of them. Any time you want."

"I'm from California," said the cop. "I hate all that rich stuff. You people are going to kill yourselves."

Lenny accepted his ticket and drove a little more slowly the rest of the way. Liquor's parking lot was a riot of whirling blue and red lights. Lenny saw paramedics loading a stretcher into an ambulance. He pulled up, got out, and was relieved to see a detective he knew. "What's going on, Frank?"

"It's all over," said the detective. "You know these people, right? You can go on in."

"Is anybody dead?"

"Everybody's OK except that one guy they just put in the ambulance. I don't know who he is."

The restaurant's interior was a solid wall of uniforms. Lenny pushed his way through to the kitchen. The crowd was thickest around the open door of the walk-in. He saw Terrance, Tanker, and Mo talking to cops. Despite what the detective had told him, he was almost afraid to look into the fridge.

Terrance caught sight of him. "Hey, Lenny," he said. "Everything's cool. They're fine." He stepped out of the doorway, and Lenny saw Rickey and G-man sitting on a tomato box, their arms around each other, their foreheads pressed together. Their whites were bloodstained and one side of Rickey's bleached hair was stiff with gore, but they appeared reasonably intact. An invisible bubble seemed to envelop them, as if they had simply shut out all the surrounding people and events. Lenny was about to turn away when Rickey looked up and saw him.

"Hey, Lenny," he said. "I guess you weren't such a dickhead for giving me that cell phone. Thanks a million."

chapter 31

(From Sid Schwanz's column, one year later)

> This just in from my erstwhile Fair Grounds corre-
> spondent, the Sheik of Arabi and Chalmette:
>
> Q. If a little boy wears his daddy's trousers, what
> New Orleans street corner is he standing on?
> A. Toulouse and Broad.
>
> OK, so the Sheik ain't much when it comes to
> jokes. But it's a good way to remember the location
> of Liquor, the local restaurant that just snagged a
> James Beard Foundation nomination for Best New-
> comer. That is, one of the best new restaurants in the
> USA. The winner will be announced in May at a
> gala gathering of restaurant professionals in New
> York City. (Bet they don't serve rubber chicken at
> that banquet.)
>
> Used to be when you thought of Broad Street in
> Mid-City, you thought of the jail if you're an opti-
> mist and the morgue if you're a pessimist. Now you
> might find yourself wondering where you should

eat. The stretch of Broad between Tulane and Esplanade looks to be our new Restaurant Row, with at least five chowhouses opening their doors during the past year. At the head of the trend and still the hottest ticket of them all is Liquor. The few readers who don't know it for the eclectic French-influenced menu (hey, that's how they told me to describe it) may recognize it as the scene of the 1980 Red Gravy Murder and last year's Chef Stalker case. I tried to do an investigative follow-up on these cases, but had little luck. The Red Gravy folks all seem to have gone to that big pasta buffet in the sky, and Chefs John Rickey and Gary Stubbs of Liquor said "No comment" (actually that's a polite version of what they really said). Michael Mouton, nastily but not fatally injured in the events of the case, hasn't answered my letter. Sources tell me the Angola Prison P.O. is pretty slow—I'll let you know if I hear from him.

Fortunately you don't have to rely on my journalistic prowess, since Stiletto Press has published *Dark Kitchen*, the new book by my colleague Chase Haricot. A riveting account of the two cases and the strange connections between them, *Dark Kitchen* has already topped local bestseller lists and could end up being the *Midnight in the Garden of Good and Evil* of the restaurant world. You heard it here first . . .

"God, I hope not," said Rickey. He'd already seen customers carrying copies of *Dark Kitchen,* though so far nobody had asked him to sign one. He wasn't sure what he would say if they did. He hated the book, but between it, the four beans

Haricot had given them, and the Beard nomination, they had as much business as they could handle.

"Well," said G-man, "you didn't have to let Haricot interview you for the damn thing."

"I thought it would turn out even worse if I didn't."

"Yeah. So why'd you cut your hair so short? It wasn't to show off that notch in your ear, was it?"

"No!" Rickey ran his hand over his close-cropped hair. "I just got sick of all that bleach."

"Uh huh."

It was inventory day, the first Monday of the month, and they were sitting in the bar after having counted, weighed, and made a note of every last item in the place. They had decided to drink some Irish whiskey with an eye toward featuring it in tomorrow's dinner special. Highball glasses of Old Bushmills, Jameson's, and Power's were lined up on the bar. They'd been sipping these whiskies for about an hour, batting around ideas for the special but in no hurry to decide on anything, before Rickey picked up the newspaper. He had already read Schwanz's column early this morning, but he felt compelled to glance at it again and again throughout the day, just as he had done with the four-bean review, the *Big Easy* magazine profile, and the two-page *Gourmet* article entitled "Stalker in the Fridge."

Haricot's book freaked him out, though. A newspaper story was gone after a day, a magazine article after a month. That book would be in the stores for God knew how long, might even be some kind of big hit if you believed Schwanz. What if people started coming in just because of that, crowding out diners who actually cared about the food?

They'd have to find ways to keep that from happening, Rickey thought. The book, the Beard nomination, the endorsement offer he'd recently gotten from a cell phone company ("Cell phones save lives," they wanted him to say, smiling earnestly into the camera)—he couldn't let himself start thinking any of it was too important. If he got distracted, the restaurant would find some way to smack the shit out of him, reminding him that it demanded his sole, undivided attention at all times. This happened on a regular basis, and Rickey was almost used to it by now.

"I was looking at the books last night," said G-man. He had rediscovered a talent for math forgotten since high school and was now doing all Liquor's accounts. "You know what?"

"What?"

"The profit we turned since last September is more than we made in our entire previous careers."

"That's kinda sick."

"Yeah, I thought so."

"Probably we ought to hand out some more raises," Rickey said.

"Hell, we ought to do that just for loyalty." They were amazed to still have the same kitchen crew they'd started out with. No one had been fired; no one had quit. There had been plenty of turnover in the front of the house, but the kitchen was solid. Not even a dishwasher had left. Rickey and G-man had gained major points with those guys when they tracked down Wardell, the young night porter Mike Mouton had chased off, and told him his job was waiting for him if he still wanted it.

"Let's do it, then," said Rickey. He took a long sip of Bushmills. "You know what this would be really good with?"

G-man pushed his shades up on his nose and waited for Rickey to tell him.

"Lobster *flambé au whiskey* . . . we could roll it out to the table on a gueridon."

"What's a gueridon?"

"Remember those carts they use to do the bananas Foster tableside at Commander's? Those are gueridons."

"Oh my God." G-man rolled his eyes. "Here we go with the fossil foods again."

"It's not a *fossil*—it's a *classic*. There's a difference, you know."

"And what's that?"

"The classic stuff still tastes good."

"OK, but why you gotta put shit on a gueridon?"

"They do it at Commander's."

"And it's cheesy there, too."

"Bite your tongue," said Rickey. "It's great. It's drama. It's fucking rock and roll."

They were still debating the merits of a gueridon fleet when Lenny and Anthony B came into the bar laughing like a couple of loons at something Karl had said to them. "Looks like we're not the only ones getting drunk on a Monday," said G-man.

"Aw, we just had a few beers," Anthony said.

"You had more'n a few," said Lenny. "I thought the bar owner was supposed to be a model of sobriety."

"You thought wrong."

Lenny slung an arm around Rickey's shoulders. "I heard some news," he said.

"Yeah? What?"

"It's just a rumor at this point."

"Well, then don't tell me," said Rickey. "I hate rumors."

"But it's a *well-substantiated* rumor."

"It's about the Beard Awards," Anthony said, and Lenny shot him a dirty look.

"What?" said Rickey. "What is it?" The usual ambient sounds of the restaurant—the hum of the air conditioning system, the traffic outside—suddenly seemed very far away. He could feel the warm buzz of the whiskey creeping up on him.

"Can't tell you," said Lenny. "Let's just say you might have to reconcile yourselves to going to New York at least once in your lives."

Rickey drew himself up straight on his barstool. G-man was grinning at him, but Rickey felt very serious. Seriousness seemed to befit the occasion. He picked up the glass of Bushmills, tipped a solemn toast to the three cooks who had brought him to this moment, and knocked back the remainder of his shot.

"Gentlemen," he said, "what are you drinking? The next round's on me."

about the author

Poppy Z. Brite is the author of six novels, three short story collections, and a fair bit of miscellanea. She began her career in the horror genre, but gradually became more interested in writing about the unique culinary subculture she knew from working in several restaurants and being married to a chef for more than a decade. Her other works about Rickey, G-Man, and the Stubbs family include the novel *The Value of X,* several stories in the collection *The Devil You Know,* and the forthcoming novel *The Big D.* Brite lives in New Orleans with her husband, Chef Chris DeBarr. Find out more about her at www.poppyzbrite.com.